THE GUNS OF
RIDGEWOOD

A Western of Modern America

Aaron Cooley

MELNORE PRESS

© 2017 Aaron Cooley

First published as separate ebooks
The Guns of Ridgewood and *The Young & the Dead*
by Melnore Press, January 2017
First Paperback Edition, February 2017

ISBN 978-0-9985946-2-0

Cover Photos by Whitney Cooley
Cover Design by June Cooley

Melnore Press logo by Rick Thompson

CONTENTS

This book is supposed to be at its heart a novel about three daughters; and so I dedicate it to my own,
Beatrix Hope.

THE GUNS OF
RIDGEWOOD

"Put your sword away," Jesus said to him, *"for all who draw the sword shall die by the sword."*

Matthew 26:52

They rode in silence, their mission heavy on their souls.
And on their minds, the horrific events for which this was to
be their response.
They knew vengeance could never be achieved like in the
stories they once told their children,
but believed this was the only quest that might bring quiet
to their pain.

Only a soul as tortured as their own would have any prayer
of stopping them...

THE GENTLEMAN FROM OHIO

When Jamal saw the three silhouettes appear on the fiery sunset horizon, he couldn't help but think that such a sight might have been one of the last ones his Great-Great-Grandfather Buck had laid eyes upon before the slave catchers caught up to him and shot him dead on that dirt road outside Charleston. Indeed, Jamal thought, from this vantage those silhouettes could've been riders on horseback – if not for the fact this was not nineteenth century South Carolina, but twenty-first century Ohio. These were bikers, some sort of Hell's Angels on their Harleys or weekend warriors on their Kawasakis, coming down the hill into the Westlake housing development dominated by the Payne estate.

Jamal had been the personal security detail to Congressman Stephen Payne (D-OH) for almost half a dozen years now, so it wasn't new for him to be sitting in his Escalade outside on the curb. But it was unusual that he was still sitting out there past dark, past 7 PM on a random Tuesday night in October. Jamal had been hired over five years ago to keep away glad-handers, bill beggars and special-interest stalkers when the Congressman was walking a rope line or in a hurry to get through an airport terminal, not for twenty-four hour care during another sleepy holiday recess in the Eleventh District.

But of course, Jamal was hired long before the brutal murders of Congresswoman Barbara Carpinello (D-ME) and her family in their home.

There were no motives nor suspects in the Carpinello murders, at least none mentioned in the briefing given to all Congressional security teams by Parker Poughkeepsie of the FBI's High Value Targets team. George Aug, Homeland Security's Under Secretary of Intelligence &

Analysis, had added that their own full investigation was under way into whether foreign actors had played any role in the murders, while also being careful to specify that no evidence to support such a theory had thus far been recovered.

With the magic hour sun at just the brightness that made visibility its worst, Jamal didn't even realize what these bikers were wearing when they pulled up in front of the empty lot across the cul-de-sac; he didn't see their body armor, didn't notice the modular lightweight load-carrying equipment rigs hanging from each of their chests, filled with ammunition magazines and explosives; couldn't see the communication buds they were each plugging into their ears. It was only when the silhouettes of long guns, military-style rifles, appeared in each rider's hands, only when each started locking and loading and lugging these machine guns across the street, up and over the grassy center island, and marching towards the Payne driveway, that Jamal realized something serious was about to go down.

"Hey!" he was already calling out as he opened the driver's door of his Escalade and stepped down off the running board and onto the concrete of Charles Court. "Stay where you--"

One of the rifles spit back at him before he completed his sentence, the glass between his chest and theirs tinkling, intense pain shooting through three different spots on his torso. He tried to look down at the damage he knew the furthest biker's gun had inflicted, but it was too late, his fingers already too weak to keep ahold of the door. He was falling backwards. He had to concentrate just to put his hands down, to catch his fall. He thought he got his palms down, but the back of his skull still slammed hard on the asphalt, bouncing like the rock he used to dribble through his Atlanta neighborhood every afternoon growing up, its impact jarring his last few moments of consciousness into strange fragments:

One of the bikers standing over him, staring down into his eyes -- *Cocky sonsuvbitches don't even bother to wear masks,* Jamal's last coherent thought -- The gaping maw of the biker's gun replacing his face in Jamal's eyeline -- The flare in the muzzle silent, seeming to go on forever in dramatic '80s movie slo-mo, until its slug descended right between his eyes -- and all went black.

Chase looked up from the red stamp on the nose-bridge of Payne's security guard. His *only* security guard, they knew from their weeks of surveillance and recon. He nodded back to Bowser and Tats that the guard wouldn't be of any concern to them, and with their guns all raised, they spread out, mounting Payne's lawn at a jog, approaching the front door. Their rifles swiveled in all directions like they were invading some insurgent fortress in Fallujah, despite their firm belief there would be no other security measures. That didn't matter. These guys were all former Boy Scouts; they were always prepared, prepared for any eventuality in this world.

They had so thoroughly rehearsed this, they didn't need to make a sound or even exchange eye contact to know that Tatsumi would first breach the house, slinging his rifle and bringing his H&K M320 forward. An explosives artist, Tats had always preferred his grenade launchers standalone, rather than mounted under his rifle, so he could get more precise aim. (They all went by nicknames that had stuck from way back, usually all the way back in basic: Tatsumi was Tats, even though he didn't have a single one inked into his skin; Brenden, Bowser; Chase, Chaser.) Tats slammed a 40MM shell into the side of the weapon while Chaser and Bowser took positions just north- and southeast of him, eyes and guns on the street for approaching reinforcements.

The sound had always been gratifying for Brenden, that thwok of a grenade thrusting out of a gun that signaled go time. He looked over just in time to see the grenade blow the door in, the wood plank flying out of its hinges and smashing back against an inside wall, splintering horizontally at its midriff. A house alarm sang out, as did a few cars behind them, jostled by the sonic thunderclap.

"Three minutes," Chaser called out as he set the countdown into his watch, and the others synchronized. The response time of the neighborhood patrol had been 4:46 when they triggered a false alarm a week earlier, and the police a full seven minutes after that, but any phone calls from neighbors swearing they just heard gunshots or screams could very well push this night onto a tighter schedule.

The gunmen sliced into the smoke crowding the foyer, and kept moving without signals or commands. They had done so many Real Urban Trainings in real homes and neighborhoods, they had cleared so many houses and buildings in Iraq and Syria, a Direct Action like this one was performed all on instinct. They moved into their room clearances without a word, Tatsumi charging up the stairs, Brenden around the corner to the kitchen – all this, they had decided while studying the house plans plucked from public records. This was how they had practiced it around a taped-out mock up on a warehouse floor, like Broadway performers preparing a new production. But, as with any live show, they had to stay alert, had to stay ready for the hiccups in their precise choreography.

Brenden crossed into the western wing of the house, eyes performing a whip-survey of the casual dining and TV area just off the kitchen. His boots padded back onto the tiles of the kitchen itself, and around the center island, his barrel dancing high and low for any potential hiding places. Finding none, he turned to return to the staircase. "Kitchen clear," he joined the chorus of his Teammates confirming the same from other rooms of the house.

But before he was back around the corner, Brenden heard the little burst of saliva and breath behind him. He wouldn't have heard it just thirty seconds earlier, but the alarm was starting to wane in volume ever so slightly, a common feature put in home systems these days so false alarms wouldn't drive neighbors to insanity. It was just one little sound, a break in breath-holding that whomever was behind the pantry door had to take to keep conscious. *The pantry door* – the sound had come from just behind the pantry door. He couldn't step forward and open it, in case the occupant was in a crouch with his or her own firearm primed to fire.

So instead, he pumped a burst of fire into the door itself, his armor-piercers shredding through the wood like a needle puncturing a cross-stitch pattern. Brenden released the trigger, then his own breath.

The door shoved open, a body slumping through it, smacking face-first down into the tile. The brutal impact came with no reaction, no attempt to shield the nose from damage; whoever had been hiding in the pantry was already too dead for such concerns. Her long hair spread out from the back of her skull like an oriental folding fan, soaking through with the red flowing underneath it. Brenden kneeled to find her carotid, or at least, confirm it was no longer pumping with life.

"One," he said into his headset as he rose, turning for the stairs again-

A giant boom sounded just an instant before Brenden took a buckshot sledgehammer to the chest. It lifted him up and off his feet, sending him flying backwards, landing with his own smack on the tiles. He heard his rifle skittering away from him like a scared little scorpion. His first thought was to thank Sarah Beth for buying him new body armor when she saw that story on *The View* about how woefully insufficient the military issue was, but that was for just a split second, before he was back in the moment:

Whoever just got the jump on him was going to fire again. And maybe this time at his head, the head they had all agreed they would leave unhelmeted in an effort to go in lean and mean and weighted down with as few ounces as possible. *I have to be next,* his mind screamed at him, *I have to get the next shot off.* He yanked his Glock 19 from its chest holster and levelled it right at:

Danny Payne. That was the worst part of this, that in researching their targets they had learned about everyone in the family, learned everything there was to know about Payne's son, 17-year-old Daniel Weston Payne. Brenden knew he had to stay after school every Tuesday and Thursday for extra math tutoring, that he didn't have a girlfriend, that he smoked a Camel Light in the alley behind his school's auditorium every time his free third period came around. He was the one who had ambushed Brenden, he was the one holding a smoking Remington Pump in his hands like it was a live snake that might whip back and sink its fangs into his own forearm at any moment. "You k-k-killed my mom," the kid stuttered out. Brenden knew this boy didn't have a regular speech impediment, knew it was fear, shock and rage that gripped his tongue. "You fucking killed my mom." As if to accentuate this last sentence, he yanked back on the gullet of his gun, charging it for a kill shot.

The kill shot should have been Brenden's. The boy had made what should have been a fatal error: not having another shot ready, giving Brenden the split second he needed to squeeze off a Glock round first.

But Brenden didn't take advantage. He was too tired, too terrified of where this path they had embarked upon was leading. He pulled his finger out of his Glock's trigger guard. He closed his eyes, surrendering his fate into this boy's hands.

But instead of another Remington blast, it was the staccato drum fill of an AR burst that filled Brenden's ears next. He opened his eyes in time to see spurts of red splashing up from Danny Payne's back, to see the life draining from his eyes, before he plummeted face first onto the tiles like his mother had before him.

Danny's flimsy curtain of a corpse revealed Chase behind him, rifle maw smoking. "Two," Brenden heard both from his mouth and through the speakers on his ears. He could swear there was an extra bite behind that word, a disgust with Brenden for nearly allowing a high schooler to take him out. But Chase said nothing else, just spun on a heel and headed for the stairs.

For only a second Brenden wondered if Chase had noticed his surrender, if he had seen his closed eyes or the placement of his forefinger. Brenden shook it off, collecting his own AR, and following him up to the second story.

"Child Bedroom 2 clear."

Tats was just backing out of the bedroom on their right as Chaser and Brenden mounted the top of the stairs. Brenden could see the traces of pink just inside that door and fought to put his most horrific thoughts out of his brain. He exhaled relief when Tats shook his head: there had been no one in that pink room.

Tatsumi nodded down the hall to the final set of double doors. He had completed searches of all the other rooms on this second floor. Only the master remained. Chaser charged forward into point position – *I'm the OIC, I should take point,* Brenden asked himself in paranoia. *Is he doing it now because he saw how I froze up downstairs?* – reaching the double doors, placing a hand on the left handle. Chase met the eyes of his platoonmates, getting their nods of ready, then threw open the door, letting his rifle lead him inside.

Brenden could already hear the sobs, the mumbling, as he crossed the threshold last. He turned to his right, stepping up behind Chaser and Tats as they aimed their guns on the male figure on his knees before the Crucifix on the east wall.

"Congressman Payne," Chase called out, a statement of fact, not a question. They all recognized Payne's build, his blonde-and-silver spackled hair, even with his back turned to them.

But none of them could see the Beretta he had pressed between praying hands until he pushed up to his feet and turned around. They tightened up on their rifle grips in response, barrels getting a little more erect-- but Payne was already pressing his gun into his own sweaty temple. Personal safety instincts were replaced by worries that they wouldn't complete their objective, that they wouldn't be the ones to kill this man.

"You're not gonna take me!" Payne spit out like an asp. "Only the Lord can take me!"

A smile curled onto the side of Chaser's mouth. One slight squeeze of his trigger – and Payne's gun hand exploded in blood and bone, Beretta flying from his grasp as he dropped to his knees again, hand around that wrist, this time blubbering with the purest pain he would ever know in his life. "'The righteous cry,'" he recited from memory, "'and the Lord heareth, and delivereth from--'"

Tatsumi was the first to fire, eviscerating the Congressman's chest. And why wait? They weren't here to explain their quest to a dead man; Payne didn't need to hear any speeches from them; he just needed to die, so the world could begin to realize why they were on this hunt. Chaser joined in on the volley.

Finally, Brenden did too. He grit his teeth as he unleashed his rage into this man's body. This killing, he had to admit, like Barbara Carpinello's, this did feel good. Important. Deserved.

So Brenden was the last to lay off his trigger and let Payne's body fall from its imitation of one of those car dealership Airdancers flopping in the wind. What was left of his flesh melted into a pathetic Wicked Witch puddle in the rug. "Three," Chaser's voice rang into his ear. "One more."

As if on cue, a door opened behind them, footfalls padding from the bathroom in a sprint for the hallway and the staircase to freedom. The gunmen whipped around, raising their rifles on this last occupant of the house. "WAIT!" Brenden screamed out – as he reached over for Chase's barrel, shoving its aim down into the floor.

Emily Payne froze, a mere three or four footsteps from escape, eyes locked into Brenden's. An eternity seemed to pass as she stood there staring back at them.

They all stood motionless as Emily stared back. And as she sprinted out of the room. None of them fired as they had planned and intended.

None of them stopped Stephen Payne's nine-year-old daughter from sprinting out of the room.

"Fuck!" Chase screamed at the ceiling.

"We got Payne," Brenden assured him. "The op was Payne. It's done."

Chase turned on Brenden, drilling into his eyes with a look Brenden thought guaranteed he had indeed witnessed his inaction in the kitchen. "Oh, I know exactly what the op was."

"Quiet!" Tatsumi raised a hand between them.

And in the ensuing silence, they could hear the whine building from over the hill from whence they had come. Sirens, coming closer.

Brenden's face filled with business, draining of any emotion, transforming back into his natural role as the Officer-in-Charge. "Out," he commanded.

All three men threw down their rifles in the carpet, splatting in Payne's blood. Then went the pistols, and every extra mag they were carrying.

Tatsumi was the first one out the door. Chase couldn't leave without giving Brenden one more scowl, a look that not only expressed his detestation, but his deep concern about Brenden's suitability for the mission going forward. He was next out the door, Brenden right on his heels.

No more words passed between the three men as they descended the stairs, exited through the front door, crossed the cul-de-sac to their waiting motorcycles, and rode off into the night, their silhouettes disappearing under the full moon before anyone arrived to see them go.

A SOUR DISPOSITION

Jill had never even heard the name Sour Manco before the Congressman suggested it. (*Suggested* was a kind way of putting it; he had *ordered* Jill to find and bring him Sour Manco, overruling her vehement protestations.) What little she could learn about this ghost of a man (and that only after she sussed out his actual first name) did nothing to change her belief that bringing in an outside guy, someone she had never before met, was exactly the wrong move right now. She had just come from DC, where the Capitol Police had held an emergency advisory meeting with any independent security staff employed by a Congressional office; they had been strongly urged to circle the wagons, quarantine their Reps and Senators in their home districts, limiting access to their most trusted inner circles. Sure, this Clayton Manco had been a member of the FBI's High Value Targets team, but his was also a law enforcement career ended unceremoniously with a suspension for an unnamed faux pas, a suspension from which he mysteriously chose to never return. Bringing him into their team now was pure lunacy.

Mr. Manco had left the Bureau over a year ago, and from all indications, he hadn't left his hometown of Bryan, Texas in all that time. "Bryan don't look so bad," Randy commented from the rented SUV's driver's seat as they entered the College Station suburb. "Little towns like this remind me of home." Jill silently agreed as they glided down a cozy main street, then passed the openings to several neighborhoods, welcoming with that warmth of middle class Americana.

"Why they call this dude Sour anyway?" Randy tried to make conversation as they passed through Steep Hollow into Reliance, suburbia giving way to rurality, pieces of property getting bigger and lusher, littered with farm equipment well-loved and -worn. This was the first time he had been alone with Jill since she hired him nine months ago, and Randy felt like he still didn't have even the most rudimentary grip on her personality basics.

"The agent I spoke with about him," Jill explained, "he said in all his years at the Bureau, Manco always refused to carry a service Glock. No matter how many times they reprimanded him, he refused to pack anything but a Sig Sauer."

"That why he's no longer at the Bureau?"

Jill sighed. Her contact couldn't answer that, and neither did Sour's dossier. There was nothing in the files she could procure that even hinted at the reasons for his suspension, nor his decision to voluntarily make it permanent. She had hoped for more time to vet this guy, to maybe bring in a PI to do some digging, but the Congressman wasn't willing to wait a day longer. "Had to have been for more than that, right?" she guessed.

"*Your destination is ahead,*" the Waze app on Randy's iPhone purred from the cup holder, "*on the left.*" After setting the turn signal and waiting for the giant oncoming H-E-B grocery truck to pass, he rolled their wheels onto a long driveway, pebbly gravel darting up into the underbelly of their car as they bounced their way to the house a hundred yards in the distance. Jill took mental notes: of all the ranches they had seen on their drive out here, this one had by far the most overgrown grass, its wisps browned and crispy. Pulling up to the house, she couldn't help but notice the fissures of chipped paint, the door of the enclosed porch hanging off its hinges.

Jill got out and mounted the two steps up to that screen door, grimacing when her boot almost plunged through a soft, rotted spot in the bottom stair. She lifted the porch door up and open, and entered the screened enclosure, suppressing her first inclination to wince at the smell. She approached the front door with a purpose, only pausing to bat away a cobweb dangling in her way. She pulled open the front screen door and knocked on the wood border of the oval glass pane embedded in the main entry.

A minute or two of waiting brought not only no answer, but not even the sound of movement from within. Jill knocked again.

"I don't think he's in there," said Randy.

Jill checked her watch – it was still early. They had taken off from Reagan before 6, and gained another hour crossing into Central time. "It's not even 8. He's in there." She knocked a third time, then leaned into the glass, cupping her hands around her eyes to try to see into the darkness beyond--

The door pushed forward under her weight, whistling as it opened more than half-way. Jill didn't enter, but could see enough to get a thumbnail portrait of her quarry: the phantom shadows of bottles everywhere, on the mantle, covering the Hungry Man-sized kick-tray stationed between TV and couch, and in little group sculptures around the hardwood floor, usually pushed out of the way into corners.

"He's not in there," an unfamiliar voice confirmed. Jill jerked around and stepped forward, the screen door slapping shut behind her. She noticed Randy looking to her left, and followed his gaze to the pruned, emaciated face that had just popped up above the far fence line. "Usually in church 'round this time." The neighbor moved on with her hoe, while Jill exited the porch and stepped carefully down the steps to Randy's side.

"Okay then," she whispered to him. "Church." She headed for the fence herself, hoping the neighbor could tell them exactly which church, and where.

"Isn't it Tuesday?" Randy asked as he followed.

Though San Rafael Mission Church may have lacked the funding and support of many of the mega-parishes around Texas (including the 94-year-old St. Anthony's in the middle of Bryan), it more than made up for it in atmosphere and spirit. All three Sunday masses were standing-room only at San Rafael, pews and doorways all packed with the underappreciated migrant and domestic workers that kept Texas moving. Mass wasn't a high society mixer at San Rafael, it wasn't a status tournament, it was a celebration of the faith of people who perhaps needed it most. The belief was real, the spirit potent. These were the reasons that Abigail Manco had insisted that, if her father was going to force her to go to Mass every Sunday, she wanted to go to San Rafael.

But it was not Sunday when Jill entered San Rafael, it was a Tuesday in late November. There was just one man to be found in its pews, three rows from the back, staring up at its predominant cross, displayed against the green and red tapestries of the season.

Jill was surprised when she examined the back of the man's head – the hair a swirl of light brown, gray and silver, extending down onto his jowls with the lushness of a full beard, his ears and neck a sun-cracked Caucasian. She had figured the name Manco to be of some sort of Latin American origin, but this man sitting in the pews looked decidedly white. She stepped into the pew directly behind him, reaching down for the kneel stand. Finding there wasn't one attached to the bases of these simple benches, she instead kept her behind on the wood of her own, leaning forward to whisper respectfully into his ear, "Mr. Manco?"

The man's head slowly rotated on its axis like an amusement park automaton, until just one piercing blue eye was far enough around to take her in. He didn't answer her, didn't deny he was Manco, just stared right back into her soul.

"Mr. Manco." She repeated it in an attempt to gauge in that eye if he was indeed the man she sought. "My name is Jill Creete. I'm head of security for Congressman Homer Blunt."

As Sour's head swiveled back to the cross, Jill could almost swear she heard its oil-starved gears creaking. He waited until his neck was all the way untwisted before answering, "That's a new low."

"I'm sorry?"

"Accosting a man at church."

"I know. And I'm sorry about this. But it's important to the Congressman that he see you *today*. I'm sure you know why I'm here. This is about the murders--"

Without a word of response or acknowledgement, Sour stood. "Mr. Manco?" Jill pleaded. He shuffled to the end of his pew to give the sign of the Cross. Then he took the center aisle to the exit in back, and disappeared into the morning sun.

Sour was already opening the door of his late '80s Ford F-series when Jill emerged from the church behind him. "Mr. Manco! Congressman Blunt is inviting you to his home. He is really very desperate to--"

"His home?" Well aware how many miles away Homer Blunt's Second District happened to lie, Sour finally looked at her full face forward. Jill nodded with a cocky grin. "We brought a plane."

Jill considered his appearance without missing a beat – handsome, strong and intense, if more cracked and grayed than you might expect for his mid-1970s birthdate; however he had spent this overlong suspension, it had brought darker bags under his eyes and lighter streaks through his hair. His records might have indicated he was only 45, but he looked possibly ten years past that. He was tall and might once have been strong, but his clothes now hung loosely on his frame; he might have once been a thoroughbred, but had long ago been let out to pasture.

He turned back to his truck, starting the engine before even slamming the door. Jill crossed to his window, trying to project through the glass. "Please, Mr. Manco. He said to remind you of his promise. He said he promised not to ask for your help unless it was life and death for his family."

Sour just stared back through the glass, those eyes even more stabbing when used in unison. His lips moved, and though Jill had to strain to hear, she could just make out his saying, "I need to drop off my truck."

He whipped the vehicle in reverse. Jill had to bunny-hop backwards just to avoid getting her toe tips crushed. He wrestled the wheel-mounted gear stick into drive, then turned the beast onto the main road.

Jill rushed back to their SUV. As Randy joined her inside, he scoffed, "Yeah, I think I know how he got his nickname."

It took just over four more hours for Jill to deliver Sour Manco to her employer: about forty minutes for Sour to deposit his truck, get in the back of their rented SUV, and ride back through Bryan and College Station to Easterwood Field; just another twenty before they could board Blunt's Cessna Citation and take off; another two hours in the air across Texas and southern New Mexico and into Arizona, finally descending to Bisbee Douglas Airport; then another half hour drive until they were finally approaching the impressive castle nestled among amber crags, staring down upon the depressed Warren neighborhood like a castle from the clouds. Sour knew why Blunt had bought this house, knew that he enjoyed looking down upon his serfs like some medieval baron.

Sour didn't say a word as they passed through the security booth and ascended the long driveway up to the palatial turn-of-the-century adobe abode. But his eyes took note of all the different security guards, six at least he could eyeball, walking the property with assault rifles, one even stationed atop the red clay tiles of the mansion's roof.

A wound-tight young man in his 20s greeted them at the open front door and escorted them into the great room, before panting over a shoulder, "I'll let the Congressman know you've arrived," and rushing out. Sour was for a moment drawn back to the memory of his last night in DC, and the only previous time he had spoken with Blunt. *Was this kid working for him a year ago?* he wondered for a hair of a moment. *Working for him when--* But he stopped himself. It didn't matter now, didn't matter anymore, he just needed to grit his teeth through the next ten or twenty minutes. He crossed to the wall of windows, staring out upon the Mule Mountains.

"Randall Cunningham!" he heard a familiar boom behind him, then the slapping of flesh on fabric as Rep. Homer Blunt (R-AZ) slammed his palms down on the tops of Randy's Men's Warehoused shoulders. Blunt had nicknamed Randy after his favorite African-American athlete, the famous Eagles quarterback, and Randy went along with it because he generally liked Blunt – and because he was the one signing his checks, so, let's be honest, he could call him whatever the fuck he wanted. "Thought your kid was pitching tonight?"

"Um, that's right, he is, Congressman--"

"Then what the holy hell you doing here?"

"Well, I mean, you got a guest, and Ms. Creete, she requested I--"

"*Get outta here.* I'm sure Jill and I can handle ol' Sour. Isn't that right, Jilly?"

"Ye-yes, Sir," Jill stuttered back.

"You sure?"

"That's an order!" Blunt barked at Randy. "Go on! Git!"

Sour hadn't turned from the window, but he could almost hear the shocked grin crossing the young man's face, and definitely couldn't miss Randy's feet as they danced into a quick about-face and sprinted out of the great room. Sour didn't need to turn to know the command Blunt had instantly exerted over this room; men like Homer Blunt instantly took over any room they entered, just by walking in. Sour didn't need to *see* him; he could feel his very presence permeating through the skin on the back of his neck. Blunt was one of those men who could make you do something, do *anything,* could make you feel privileged just to be asked, and lucky to even know him. Sour had fallen victim to many powerful men like that in his years in Washington. He promised himself that past was just that, passed. He was a different man now, not swayed by charisma and compliments.

"Nothing more important than family," Blunt said as he crossed from behind Sour's right shoulder to beyond his left. "Isn't that right, Sour?" Sour heard the scrunch of a pair of tongs picking up ice, the tinkle of the cubes falling into a glass. The splash of liquid onto the frozen cubes. The impact of another thick glass tumbler being set beside that one. This one didn't get ice, just a dabbling of liquid; this one was meant for Sour.

He felt Blunt stepping closer to him, heard the cubes shifting in his tumbler as he held out the other one for Sour. He could already smell the sweet nectar within. "Mezcal, right?"

Sour had known Blunt was going to offer him a drink, that that's how he would attempt to ply him, weaken him. Four hours after church – he was normally down below the label line of his first bottle of the day by now. But he had promised himself he wasn't going to drink here.

Sour took the drink.

Blunt let loose a laugh from his belly. "You know the key to always getting re-elected? Remember everyone's favorite drink." He stepped away, and Sour heard leather twist as he lowered himself into the couch. "Sit and drink with me, Sour."

"I sat the whole flight," he replied without looking back.

Blunt just smiled, leaning forward to launch into his spiel. "I've already spoken to Gene Horvitz about Abigail. He's the general manager of the best care facility in Tucson. I know it's not next door, but I figure, you work out of here into the early afternoon, I can get you up there on the plane in time for dinner every--"

"I wouldn't be here if I knew we were going to be talking about my daughter."

Keenly skilled at picking up when he was being stonewalled, Blunt deftly pivoted to a different tack, standing and stepping up next to the window where he could eyeball Sour's profile at least. "You don't know how many times I almost called. But I kept my promise, didn't I?"

Sour just stared out at those mountains. He was barely listening to Blunt, just fighting with all his strength to keep that glass down at his waist, and not up at his lips.

"My wife and kids haven't been allowed to leave the house either," Blunt continued after his own heavy pull. "Since Stephen-- since Congressman Payne. Since we realized we were dealing with some sort of, of serial killers." He glanced over, searching for some indicator that Sour was listening to him. "Do you-- Stephen Payne? Barbara Carpinello? You do know that's why I brought you here, don't you?"

Sour raised his glass to his navel, then brought his other hand around it too, as if his two paws would battle for supremacy over the drink, his right wanting him to suck it all down, his left pushing it away. "I haven't been catching the news lately. You're going to have catch me up."

For the first time, Blunt had doubts about his plan. If Sour was such a hermit, so off the grid that he hadn't even heard about the Congressional Killers, would he really be the most effective hound in tracking these guys? And what about the way his hands were shaking around that glass? His ghostly pallor, his drained weight – the man didn't look well.

But this was still the man who had saved Leader Dudley's bacon long before he was party Leader, the man who made sure it would someday be possible to even consider Clyde Dudley for Senate Majority Leader. He may be an anorexic lush, but this was still the Sour Manco who made sure no one in the LDS church found out about the distinguished Senator from Utah's second family, who made sure it never got out that the husband of the Senate's most famed defender of traditional marriage had his own taste for young, blonde male hustlers. This man was the only hope Homer Blunt had.

"Barbara and I were freshmen together. Sworn in the exact same day. January 10, 1989. And Stephen. I helped him get the youngest committee chairmanship in…" Blunt looked down, bringing his fist to his lips as he choked back the moisture from his eyes. "They were both murdered. Right in their homes. Killed in cold blood. Execution style. They and their families. Stephen's daughter somehow escaped, miraculous little girl, but the others-- eight dead all told when you count security."

For the first time since he entered the great room, Sour's neck had moved, his face had turned, his eyes had found Blunt's. "I'm in no shape for a body job," he responded.

"I'm not bringing you back to protect me, Sour. I'm bringing you back to do what you do best."

Sour turned full around, walking back to the couch to set that drink down on the table just over the armrest. "The FBI will find these guys."

"And then what?" Blunt's voice raised into that octave usually reserved for C-SPAN soliloquies. "Huh? They get to be world famous? They get to spend the rest of their lives tucked away in cozy little solitary cells because it's too risky to put them in general pop? They get to have every meal and night of shelter and shirt on their backs provided for them the rest of their lives? They get to just live off of the American people for ten, twenty, twenty-five years, before finally drifting off to a nice, delirious, drug-induced death?" Sour hadn't moved from that side table, so Blunt crossed closer to him, stabbing a finger at the floor to punctuate his words. "Whoever these killers are, they declared war on the United States Congress; they deserve far worse than all that."

Sour looked up into Blunt's eyes once more. The Congressman smiled, bringing his drink to his lips to suck its ice cubes dry. "They deserve you, Sour."

"Goodnight, Congressman," Sour replied, then walked out on his host.

"I will pay you triple your old fee!" Blunt called after him. "No expense spared! You'll have the entire pool house here to yourself! And Abby will be..." He trailed off when he heard the shutting of the front door echo around the columns marking the entrance to this room.

He put his hands on his hips, looking down into the creamy rug for a chuckle. It wasn't an admission of defeat, of course not, just the realization that he was going to have to roll up his sleeves and try a little harder.

"Well," Jill sighed behind him. "That was worth a shot, and now we can move on to more--"

"We're not moving on, Jill. There won't be any moving on."

"Congressman, he's just not right--"

"He's the only one who's right. The only one who can end this the right way. Silently. He's the only one who's right on this planet."

THE YOUNG AND THE DEAD

He didn't dream every night, but when he did, it was the same dream.

He wasn't in the mall that day, he was still in Washington. He still had his career; that was the day his career ended. So the dream wasn't a memory, just a recreation of how it had occurred, down to every last detail. A visualization, like his mind's eye used to create when he was staring through a twenty-five power sniper's scope from a mile away, or walking a crime scene after he had joined the Bureau.

He couldn't bear to go to the Post Oak Mall for months afterward (he couldn't even tell you how many). When he did muster the strength for a visit, he walked right to the exact escalator the kid was descending when he did it, didn't stop to look at a directory, peruse a shop window or chew down a Cinnabon. He just stared up at that escalator, falling into a deep enough meditative trance that the shitty teenagers who passed couldn't help but point and giggle as they walked by.

He knew what the kid looked like – he had seen the autopsy photos. He knew what the barrel of a Glock looked like when it was staring down into a soul it had targeted, how it screamed as it fired, even the searing burn you felt when its shells ripped into you. He had read all the witnesses' reports; he knew what stores they were walking out of, what stores surrounded that escalator that day, even the ones that had closed in the months since Post Oak became known as a 'dangerous mall.' The Forever 21 was still there, and the Zara across from it, but as he stood under the escalator, in his mind's eye he returned the trinket stand that used to sit smack in-between them on the concourse, and transformed the Claire's back into the Apple Store that used to be there. The entire incident replayed in his mind's eye, from the sound of the Glock's report, to the answering percussion from below, to the craters on the boy's chest splashing blood as he met instant justice for what he had done.

The dream added nothing, it subtracted nothing. It played out just as it had played out on the day it had happened, and just as it played out in his mind's eye on the day he could finally bring himself to stand below that escalator. The boy fired once-twice-thrice-- before he himself was torn into. The guard who had taken him out was an Iraq veteran who had let himself 'go,' let his waist and his 40 time go too much for any serious PSD or law enforcement job, but he still had the shot Uncle Sam had helped him refine.

The last bullet broke off one side of the boy's jaw, a hit so horrific that later, two of the local reporters on the scene wouldn't be able to help but paint this murderous waste of flesh with a splash of sympathy. Seeing the boy's mandible detach in the dream, reliving it splatter blood all over the lower half of his face, didn't bother Sour at all. He savored every last second as the boy fell forward, smashing face down into the sharp edge of a metal stair, then rolling like an abandoned wet suit in the tide, the fabric of his hoody getting sucked into the throat at the bottom as it swallowed its steps, jamming the whole apparatus with a horrific buzz that only subsided when the same rotund security guard who had taken off his mandible sprinted over to the stop-box, holstering the heroic weapon as he waddled, tearing open the plastic covering and slamming an open palm down on the red kill switch.

On the day he visited Post Oak, Sour himself crossed to that plastic box, tore it open and froze those metal stairs. The wind-down of the escalator's motors, the gnashing grind as its gears ground their last gasps, these were the only sounds he had never heard, the only details he was missing in making his visualization complete. This pausing of the escalator was always the sound that signaled the end of the dream. Sour would sit up, looking first not at the clock (because he hadn't bothered to keep the batteries up-to-date in any of them), but at the sky through the window across from his headboard. *"That's so not feng shui, Dad!"* Abby had warned him when the family first moved in here, but he just chuckled back; he was a man living alone now, his bed was for utility, not some oriental spirituality. If that not-feng-shui window was filled with any light, he would get up and dress for church. Still dark, and he would grab from his bedside table the bottle he had brought to bed with him just hours before, and suck on that until he felt sick enough that he had to lay his head back down and fall into slumber for another restless sleep cycle.

The morning after his visit to the Blunt estate, it was still dark when Sour woke. Dark, but his head was clearer than it had been in days, and filled with damn horrible thoughts: maybe Blunt had offered him just what he needed, an opportunity, a chance to get back in with the DC types, to get working again. To get out of this house and away from his doldrums and his depression and *that dream.*

Sour grabbed last night's mezcal, not allowing himself to have those damn horrible thoughts again.

Sour had been standing in the hall outside Abby's room for four or five minutes, watching the therapist hold up different flashcards before her perpetually drooped eyes, trying to coach a response that would never come. It was after he moved the seventh or eighth card to the back of the pile, revealing the one with the remedial drawing of a car on it, that his eyes happened to pass by the window, lighting up with excitement as they caught Sour peering in.

Sour was late, sure – he had gobbled so much mezcal at around 3 AM that he didn't wake until past 8 – and maybe the therapist had another appointment to get to. *It says a lot that he would even stick around for that extra ten minutes after you were supposed to have shown up,* he could hear Diane's voice scolding him. It was always Diane's voice he heard when he needed, *deserved,* a scolding.

And Sour knew his daughter wasn't easy, but that didn't mean that he liked what he saw in that therapist's eyes: *relief,* that the session was over, that Abby's father had arrived to take her off his hands. Sour thought he should probably have another talk with Dr. O'Laughlin, requesting that a new therapist be assigned to Abby. But he had already done that three or four times, and the doctor had warned him they had run out of therapists she hadn't already seen.

"There he is!" the therapist exclaimed as Sour opened the door and took a step inside. "YOUR FATHER'S HERE TO TAKE YOU TO LUNCH," he bent over to say to Abby, raising his voice into that register people seemed to reserve for the foreign or mentally retarded. "ARE YOU HUNGRY, ABBY?" Abby didn't respond verbally, or with a movement, not even a batting of the eyes. She just kept staring straight ahead, like she always did.

What do you know, Sour scowled to himself as he looked away, *your yelling doesn't cause a magical breakthrough*. The therapist stood and crossed over to him, mentioning under his breath at a volume he didn't think Abby would be able to make out, "Only one seizure today."

Sour wouldn't get any acknowledgement from Abby until they had arrived in the Big Red's parking lot. Big Red's had always been her favorite, not because the food was particularly good, but because she loved that they served their virgin strawberry daiquiris in glass cowboy boots. Those boots had made her fall in love with the joint as a five or six year old, and she stayed in love as she grew – even after she finally noticed how dry the bison burger was (Sour guessed it was really just hamburger meat with too much extra pepper). Big Red's was her and her Dad's place, and that was more important than any side of beef.

But it wasn't the glorious sight of arriving at her favorite restaurant that made her react in the parking lot. She had no reaction as Sour pulled into a spot and pointed out, "Look, it's our place." It was only after he had pulled down her electric wheelchair (the one he had to ask Diane's father to pay for), unfolded it before her passenger seat, then unbuckled her seatbelt and lifted her out of the truck and down to the chair that she had any reaction: yelling and kicking, one of those sudden attacks of uncontrollable guttural grunts that seemed to come on whenever Sour was alone with her. When the Waterford orderlies moved her, when they transferred her from her bed to her chair, or her chair to Sour's truck, she never seemed to have that reaction; only under his rough-handed touch did she hyperventilate so horribly.

"I'm sorry, I'm sorry," Sour pleaded as he got her waist buckled down, taking her wrist to place her hand on the joystick she never used on her own anyway. With his hands removed from her body, her moans started to dissipate, her breath started to normalize. "Shh, shh, there you go. You're okay now," Sour purred as he got behind the chair and started to push her toward the entrance. He had a theory: she had always loved his old truck, loved sitting on the torn leather with the stuffing popping out. She had nicknamed the vehicle 'Beast,' and had always said that when it was time for her to learn to drive, she wanted Sour to teach her on Beast. These days, whenever he put her in Beast, she seemed to calm, like somewhere deep in the recesses of that addled brain it brought her back to rides of the distant past.

Sour used to love that Bryan was basically a suburb of College Station; when he had first moved here with Diane almost two decades ago, he quickly fell in with a group of drinking buddies that met to tailgate every A&M game. The Aggies were in the Big 12 then, and even if not all the guys in Sour's new group of friends were A&M fans, there was always another Texas or Oklahoma school coming through to satisfy one of their obsessions. Diane excused their worst misbehaviors – Sour stumbling in drunk hours after a game, his car parked haphazardly up on the lawn – because she was just happy to see him fitting in so well in her hometown. And once she got pregnant the first time (they would miscarry three months in; Abby would be their second attempt), she never even had to drop hints about Sour toning it down; he stopped going to the games all on his own.

That's when Bryan's proximity to A&M started to wear on him; he would grumble at the sight of any young person in Aggie maroon in their grocer, or when he would find a local business closed on a football Saturday. Sour had always been a nomad, and it wasn't long before he was gripped with that familiar feeling that he had let himself get too comfortable somewhere. The timing of this feeling coincided with his meteoric rise up the Bureau's ranks, and with the Director himself requesting his transfer to Washington. But Diane couldn't move, wouldn't move, not with her political aspirations. If there was one thing that the locals – the types who believed in Texas so much they supported secession – wouldn't stomach, it was a carpetbagging politician.

Sour regretted that he didn't stay for Diane, so now he was going to stay for Abby.

But Sour often found himself having to look the other way when the entitled reminders of Bryan's role as suburb-to-collegetown-USA reared their ugly heads. In Big Red's, it was the sound of a young man who couldn't be older than 19 slapping the side of his hand into his overbuilt chest, into the familiar "TA&M" logo emblazoned in bright, new white in the middle of his crispy maroon tee. His bulky arms, one labelling him **Lover Boy** in newish tat ink, seemed a testament to why he was matriculating in central Texas and not a northeastern Ivy League town – he had spent more of his teen-odd years in the gym than in the library. "Duuuuh, I'm retarded," he added to his pantomime, and his two friends, their heads of hangover hair even more mussed than his own, burst into laughter as if they didn't understand it before, spitting up their 10 AM hairs of the dog.

Sour looked away from them, returning his gaze back into the booth he was sharing with Abby, back onto his dry bison burger. A splash made his eyes whip up again – to Abby's soup. But she still hadn't touched it, or even lifted a hand to her utensils. No, it was the A&M meathead, this time bringing his own spoon to his face, splashing chili all over his cheek. "Look, I'm too retarded to eat!" The laughter of the peanut gallery crescendoed to an even more earsplitting extreme, one of the buddies even so overcome that he just fell into the booth and rolled around on the pleather.

Sour didn't respond. He put down his bison burger, scooted out of his side of his booth, moving around to Abby's side next to her so he at least wouldn't have to look at the idiots any longer. He ladled some soup into her spoon and brought it to her lips, pouring it onto her tongue. Ever so slightly, her lips closed around the spoon, trapping in the hot liquid. For

Sour, it was a breakthrough, and one that almost made up for the indignity Lover Boy had heaped upon his daughter.

Almost.

It wasn't until Sour was back in the parking lot, Abby lifted back into Beast's passenger seat, that the 'TA&M,' this time in its trademark maroon with white border, taunted him again, this time from his passenger door's sideview mirror as he belted Abby down. He stepped down off the running board and shut her door, bending to fold up her chair. He could do it blind by now, and his gaze stayed raised above the apparatus, hunting the parking lot for the origin of the logo's reflection.

There it was – on the back window of an immaculate Grand Cherokee behind them, posted just above the rear wiper and the silver letters spelling 'Jeep.' He deposited Abby's steed in the truck bed, then surveyed the rest of the parking lot with his eyes: at this early hour of a weekday, there were only two or three other cars in the lot, all more modest than the Jeep, none with any A&M labelling whatsoever. Though that window decal covered only a fraction of the vehicle, the SUV had frat boys written all over it.

Indeed, ten minutes later, the three young men emerged, demeaning some young co-ed in conversation as they returned to the Cherokee, the Popeye-armed pantomimer getting in behind the wheel. The one in shotgun swiveled his head to check his hairstyle in the reflection of his door's sideview mirror when he noticed only frayed wires hanging in its place. "Oh shit! Side-swiped, bitch!" he giggled as the car's owner shot out of the driver's side. He slammed his door behind him, enraged not that he might have to pay for this damage himself, or even that he might have to ask his father to open his checkbook, but that someone had dared impugn his honor with this act of vandalism. He circled around the back of the vehicle to inspect the damage himself--

And took a mouthful of mirror. The shock more than the force of the impact dropped him right to his knees. He brought his hand to his lips, already sure his central and lateral incisors were tearing away from their housings in his gums, pushing straight back into his tongue. He looked down into his palm as he felt the frightening flow of blood guttering into it.

Suddenly, all the hairs in the back of his skull were tearing him backwards, forcing his eyes up, into the sun – and into Sour's face. "What the f--" he opened his mouth to protest, but Sour cut him off, bringing the missing sideview mirror down into those teeth again. And again, and again, too many times for Lover Boy to keep count through the pain. He could feel teeth breaking in half or dislodging off the gum and onto his tongue, though there they mixed with so many shards of mirror, it was hard to differentiate pieces of dentin from those of reflexive plastic.

Sour released the boy's hair after seven or eight of the blows, letting him fall forward onto his palms, gushing red and white from his mouth. "Look at that," Sour said as the young man searched for teeth, "you *are* retarded."

Sour tossed the mirror, sending it skipping across the asphalt like a plastic stone. As he rose up to his own full walking height, he noticed the other two frat dogs had gotten out of the Jeep, staring open-mouthed not at their fallen friend, but the man who had just performed his horrific dental surgery. "Who's next?" Sour invited.

The boys hustled back into the car, shutting their doors and putting on their seat belts without a word as if their driver was even capable of transporting them somewhere now.

Sour returned to Beast, climbing up next to his daughter and growling his engine to life. "Okay, kiddo, let's get you home," he said to Abby as he pulled the gear stick into Reverse.

"Mr. Manco!" Sour was easing Abby's door shut, having left her in the opening throes of an early afternoon nap, when he heard the Waterford's

'Life Enrichment Director' approaching from down the hall. "There's something we need to speak about."

Kelsey O'Laughlin led Sour onto the elevator and down to his office on the first floor. Sour remembered an old joke he used to share with Diane, that 'Decorating with Diplomas' was a med school elective. O'Laughlin had displayed his family photos much more prominently than his academic achievements, but they were still there. *"You know doctors and lawyers,"* Sour remembered Diane saying the first time he visited her law office, *"the only professions that seem to need to display their academic careers for every visitor to see."*

"It's the new owners," O'Laughlin continued his explanation. Sour shook off his reverie, a frequent necessity with the sleep and alcohol withdrawal he was often combatting. "I didn't even know we were for sale. Then I wake up this morning and we're no longer a Waterford. As of the closing yesterday, Mr. Manco, we're now 'Comfort Hill.' A completely independent facility. Which means several changes--"

"You're jacking the price." Sour drilled his eyes back into the administrative bureaucrat.

"Look," O'Laughlin leaned onto his elbows, trying to widen his smile. He knew about the challenges Sour had faced since he left the Bureau, he knew he had *no choice* but to leave the Bureau, and O'Laughlin had worked with him when the price had increased just modestly six months before. But there was nothing modest about what the new chairman had planned, and no help O'Laughlin could offer Sour this time. "I want you to know this isn't any easier for me than it is for you--"

"You're not the one with a daughter here."

No, but O'Laughlin had always prided himself on his complete and total empathy for his patients; he didn't believe he needed to have a family member with mental or occupational challenges to be motivated to help them. He had realized right away, he had *thought* of Abby Manco just as the price increase was being mentioned on the conference call. He had known that the new costs would be an impossibility for Sour, and had tried to take steps in advance to assist in any way he could. "There is Sweet Home, of course, right off Highway 6. I've already spoken to--"

"You ever seen Sweet Home?"

"I used to work there, actually," O'Laughlin whimpered back, betraying the truth of the matter.

Of course Sour had seen Sweet Home himself; it was the far cheaper option to the Waterford, and it had been the first place he visited when choosing a new home for Abby. O'Laughlin knew the smell was different there, the screams in its corridors more cacophonous, the bedsheets stiffer and more yellowed with old piss. "Would you put *your* daughter in Sweet Home, Doctor?"

O'Laughlin tried to force a smile. "Obviously, it has some areas that could use improvement, for sure, and perhaps more than we here at the Waterf-- *Comfort Hill* may have. But I am confident, with the right level of family involvement, which I know you are prepared to provide--"

Sour stood and, not uttering another word, walked out.

It wasn't very often that Sour returned to San Rafael a second time in one day. Those A&M frat boys had made it a necessity. He may have hurt Lover Boy, sure, kept him from speaking up in class for the rest of the semester (as if he went to class), prevented him from scoring the hottest date for his frat's winter formal, or saddled his father with a new stack of dental bills, but judging by his crisp tee and crisper Jeep, his father could afford those dental bills. Sour couldn't afford to despise himself more than he already did.

Yet every time he let his true self out of the bottle, every time from boyhood to Bureau that he let that creature who had hurt that boy come out, the more he realized that *that* was the real him, the more he was convinced that savage was the true Sour. Every time he had one of his 'incidents' – and make no mistake, some incidents were more serious and violent and felonious than others, but ne'er a month would go by without at least one – he despised himself a little bit more.

The morning visits to San Rafael were supposed to stop those incidents, supposed to help him find some way to quell the creature. He knew therapy wasn't going to work for him; no yoga or some other bullshit would do the trick. But Jesus had worked for his mother, or at least so she always claimed; He had worked for Sour's father after he saw 'the light.' Sour was hoping he would someday soon see that light himself and Christ would cure him of his worst ills. Yes, he came to San Rafael to ask for mercy for Abby. He came to ask God or Jesus or the Holy Ghost or whomever he was supposed to for forgiveness for all the wrongs he had committed in his depraved life. But more than anything, he came to beg for control, for these wrongs to never again occur, for a magical twinkle of fairy dust to descend from the heavens and eradicate his inner monster, ensuring it could never again fight its way out of his soul.

But no matter how often he visited the church and kneeled and prayed, nothing could stop that monster.

"Señor Manco?" Father Tito's kind tone hummed from behind him. Sour kept staring up at Christ as the parish priest, dressed down in short sleeves (still with white collar) and stonewashed jeans that must have been set aside from the church's last secondhand sale, side-shuffled into his pew. "Are you here to confess?" he asked Sour in his Spanish sprinkled with its unique Filipino tinge.

Sour didn't look over to him, but he knew Tito Caluag's kind eyes well, knew every crater of his pockmarked cheeks that somehow imbued his face with even deeper compassion and understanding. "I changed my life, Padre," he answered back in the same language, and an even more regionally accurate dialect. "I come here every day. And still, He won't help me stop."

"We all sin each and every day of our lives, Clayton."

"No." Sour realized he was squeezing his praying fingers so tight, bringing so much red to the skin, they looked like they might even burst. "Not like me."

He stood and shuffled out of his pew.

Monday night was still Jazz night.

When Abby was only an infant, Clayton and Diane had decided they wanted to introduce their daughter to only the most refined musical options – no Barney, no skidamarink a dink a dink, but classical composers and bebop virtuosos. Diane's parents had claimed those were the only types of music they played for her growing up, and that was all Sour needed to hear. He wanted to raise another Diane; the world couldn't take a female Sour, and he wouldn't wish that on his daughter. So during mealtimes or bathtimes they would put on a symphonic or jazz record, and sure enough, as she became big enough to make her own extracurricular choices, Abby gravitated to dance and band, showing an aptitude for several different instruments. But she also, as young girls are wont to do, developed her own musical tastes, and was soon demanding that her stodgy old parents put on something more contemporary as they did chores or read. Though Sour wanted to at first outright refuse – she was the child, for one thing, and for a second, more important thing, contemporary music was god awful – Diane had a fairer solution: Abby could pick the music on Saturday nights. (Their ulterior motive of course was that this would also hopefully delay any desire to fill her Saturday evenings with her own plans outside of the home.) They created a calendar of what genres of music would be played each evening: Friday was classical, for example, Saturday Abby's choice, Sunday country-western (Sour had to lobby for six months for that one), and Monday jazz.

Sour continued to follow the schedule even now that he was eating alone. The last thing he remembered in most evening's drunken stupors, in fact, was that welty bounce at the end of a record. He would pull himself up off the couch or floor, remove the needle and shuffle to his bedroom to face plant into his mattress.

The Monday after he had been Blunt's guest in Bisbee, he had the 'trane blaring, the TV on silent as it displayed Fox News, as he ate a half-heated frozen pizza on that stand between television and his favorite chair. It wasn't the chyron about the 'Congressional Killers,' or the images of armed retinues surrounding the homes of various Senators and Congresspersons that drove Sour to cross to the phonograph and rip the needle off – it was the story right after it. He already had the remote in hand to switch to the Cowboys on *Monday Night Football*, in fact, when a familiar African-American face filled his screen.

The name on the chyron was even more eerie: **POSSIBLE NEW REVELATIONS IN MURDER OF JEROME YOUNG, JR.**

Sour pumped the volume to full blasting before he even turned for the stereo, and caught just snippets of the first words battling with Coltrane's sax: "*...Fox News has been contacted... unnamed Congressional sources... would be devastating for the FBI...*"

The jazz scratched to silence, and the tail of the report took over the room: "YOU THINK IT'S A VIDEO YOU'RE GOING TO BE RECEIVING?" Bill O'Reilly screamed to his DOJ correspondent over video link. Sour was too stunned to adjust the volume, and the screaming went on:

"THAT'S RIGHT, BILL. A VERY WELL PLACED SOURCE IN CONGRESS SAYS THEY WILL BE PROVIDING US WITH VIDEO THAT SHOWS THAT LAW ENFORCEMENT MAY HAVE BEEN COMPLICIT IN THE MURDER OF JEROME YOUNG, JR. YOU'LL REMEMBER HE WAS THE YOUNG CAPITOL POLICEMAN FOUND MURDERED IN THE PARKING GARAGE OF DC'S UNION STATION, APPARENTLY BY A SENATE INTERN NAMED CHERI LEVINSON. IT WAS ALWAYS ASSUMED THIS WAS SOME SORT OF LOVER'S SPAT BETWEEN YOUNG AND LEVINSON, BUT OUR SOURCE TELLS FOX NEWS THEY HAVE OBTAINED NEW VIDEO THAT WILL THROW ALL THOSE ASSUMPTIONS ON THEIR HEADS."

"AND WHEN DO YOU EXPECT TO GET THIS VIDEO?"

"BY THE END OF THE WEEK, IS ALL OUR SOURCE WOULD TELL US."

"THANKS, CATHERINE. WE'LL LOOK FORWARD TO THAT. NEXT UP, THE *FACTOR* TIP OF THE DAY--"

Sour dropped the volume, just in time to hear the buzz from across the room. His eyes shot to the kitchen, where his flip phone was crawling across the counter. He crossed the house in three steps and brought it to his ear. Blunt's voice was already glowing through the speaker, not even waiting for Sour to offer a greeting. "You still watch Fox News every night, Sour?"

"What did you do?" Sour growled back from the pit of his soul.

"Nothing yet. But you had to know, *someday* I'd use the video. Didn't you, Sour?"

Sour seethed. He wasn't out of options. He had three of them. (1) Go on the run and off the grid. (2) Spend the rest of his life in federal prison. (3) --

Well, Blunt made sure he understood he was the only one on the planet who could offer Sour a third option.

"You'd gotten comfortable, hadn't you?" the Congressman purred from Bisbee. "I think you'd forgotten… that I *allowed* you to have this life. You'd forgotten, that there are no statute of limitations on the sins you've committed. You'd forgotten who you really are, Sour Manco."

He hadn't.

"But who you really are, that can remain our secret. I have no problem leaving some officious Fox reporter high and dry with egg on her face. But you know what you're going to have to do.

"You're going to have to come to Bisbee… and ask me nicely."

THE RADIANCE OF PUERTO PALOMAS

When Sour woke to sky still dark outside the not-feng-shui window, he didn't lay his head back on his sweat-stinking pillow (funny, the smell had never bothered him while shit-canned). And he had brought no bottle to the bedside table to drown himself back to sleep this time. He knew he needed to get up and get to work.

The bottles were first. He couldn't even prepare for his journey with the history of all his lost nights looking down upon him like a judgmental tribunal. He grabbed a Hefty and swept through the house, depositing all the bottles into the bag in a chorus of clangs. Even his freshest provisions, the unopened tequilas and mezcales purchased within the last three days, met the bag. That yeasty pungency of a mid-semester frat basement still remained after he had deposited the sack out in the bin, but Sour took comfort in knowing he wouldn't be here to suffer the stench much longer. He could cover the fetor in the meantime with the scummy months-old lonesome Dove bar in his shower, with the shaving cream he would clear away with his trusted and rusted old straight razor. (The cream would refuse to spew from its canister, so he ended up using the shower brick to lather his face, too.) With his cheeks now baby-butt smooth, he threw his old Ranger-issue rucksack on the bed and filled it with clothes cobwebbed in his closet, plus some pieces he found in his dresser that weren't dotted with moth holes. He clasped on his Breitling for the first time in months (it was dead for now, but the movement of his arm would recharge it), and pulled on his old cowhide boots.

His leather shoulder holster went on with the least thought and effort, slipping on like an old pair of suspenders. Sour was surprised when he had to pull it back off and not loosen, but tighten, its screws, fitting it more securely on a frame malnourished by a year of liquid diets.

He caught himself. For a moment, he had forgotten his pledge, forgotten he had promised himself never to wear this holster ever again. But with the mission Blunt had set before him, he really had no choice, did he?

Sour went to his garage and rolled the combination into the dial of the expansive titanium box which dominated one corner. Its heavy door slid open in one attempt and Sour stared in at the arsenal he had spent years amassing. There weren't just the rifles for hunting that liberals would tell him was all he deserved to own, but rifles very much meant for war. When Sour was living with the two greatest women he had ever known, why wouldn't he want to protect them to the fullest extent allowed under his rights as an American? It was something he never for even a moment felt irresponsible about – he had been trained in the use of these weapons, and kept them locked up at all times.

He wouldn't need those rifles now, at least not yet, not until he got a bead on these killers Blunt wanted to sic him on. He just needed something to fill that holster. He knew the one he wanted, the words **Sig Sauer** staring back at him from their embossment on a pistol grip like an old flame eyeing you from the other end of the bar when the first measures of your favorite tune emanate from the jukebox.

Sour pulled out two magazines and slid them in the sleeves under the armpit opposite the holster itself. He reached back into the safe and closed his paw around the grip of the P220, pulling it just an inch from its pouch on the inside of the door. It was the weight more than anything that Sour loved about the Sig, a physical weight that seemed to match the weight of the finality of its purpose.

But Sour wasn't one to take pledges lightly, even ones he had made only to himself. Blunt wouldn't necessarily ever have to know about this pledge; only if Sour was successful in tracking the Congressional Killers would it become an issue. And Sour couldn't yet say for sure if they would ever show themselves again, or what trail they may have left behind. Maybe he would never find them, never come face-to-face with these men, and never be forced to reveal – or break – his secret pledge.

He opened his hand, letting the Sig drop back into its hibernation bed. He returned the clips and pushed the safe's heavy door closed until it clicked locked. Sour walked to his bedroom and pulled a jacket on over his shoulder holster. Without any weight added to it, he had already forgotten it was even there.

"Hey," Sour whispered to his daughter, angling his chair around the foot of her bed to try to get in her line of sight. "I need to talk to you." He grabbed the remote from her bedside table and turned off the blaring Nickelodeon. She didn't even flinch; Sour guessed it was the morning orderly who had turned it on and chosen that channel for her in the first place, one she would have despised even when it was age appropriate. (Abby was reading Camus by 10, not watching cartoons.)

"I'm going away for a while," he continued. "They know how to find me if you need me."

She didn't respond, of course, didn't even look up into his eyes, just kept them locked on the waves of fabric covering her torso.

"Abbs. They know how to find me if you need me."

Sour stood and went to her window. He reached around the old faded photos of happier times, of him and Diane with their arms around Abby, and lifted the frame of her at around that Camus age, holding frail Tippy in her arms during one of her last days, when the Siamese was already sick as a dog. Under the wood of the frame was a necklace, its thick pendant hanging off one end, a sweet cat's visage carved in silver smiling up at him. Abby called the necklace Tippy, too, as it had been a gift from Sour to remember her by. *"Wear this always,"* he remembered saying, *"and Tippy will always be by your heart."*

But Abby wasn't allowed to wear Tippy anymore, for fear she might strangle herself with it. Abby didn't need Tippy, probably didn't even remember Tippy was there. Sour needed Tippy more now.

He crossed back to his daughter, kissed the top of her head, and left.

A pugilist wasn't just at his best when he had done his hardest training, and rounded his body into its prime; even more important was that his mind be in fighting shape. It was Tyson's mind, more than his opponent Buster Douglas, that brought him down at his physical peak in 1990. And while Blunt was surely expecting Sour to call him soon after their conversation and ask him to send the Cessna, it was a journey he needed to do with Beast to get his mind right.

It was when Beast entered Hudspeth County, settling into a fine trot parallel to the Mexican border, that Sour first felt the old juice starting to course through his veins, as if just the proximity to the land of his birth could recharge his batteries. He rode the smaller roadways, the 85 rather than the 10, because he wanted to ride along the Rio Grande like an old cattle driver, and eventually, cross over it, as he did when the sun started to disappear over the flat, distant New Mexican horizon. He had forgotten any cassettes for his tape deck, but he was fine with that, instead busying his right fingers with the tuning dial of the radio finding only distant, hazy narcocorridos.

Sour didn't want to arrive at Blunt's in the middle of the night, but also knew he needed some distraction if he was going to stop. The pain of evening could only be clotted with one of two things, and Sour wasn't about to pick up a new bottle after throwing out several unopened ones. As the clock passed 9 PM, Beast had come to rest in the parking lot of the Pancho Villa Lounge just outside tiny Columbus, New Mexico. But the music and lights emanating from inside only made his skin crawl, as did the hollers and unison boot-clops of group line dancing. Sour found himself continuing on, hanging left on the 11, heading south for Columbus's sister city.

Unlike the most popular border crossings into Tijuana or Juarez, only two lanes, one each direction, led into the small tunnel of the Puerto Palomas station, and Sour had only to wait through two other cars before being waved into his father's native land, into the state of Chihuahua, and the city from which Villa had launched his attack on the States a century before. Now hanging from his rearview, Tippy sashayed back and forth as their tires searched for tread in the gravel of the bumpier Mexican road.

The border crossing was also like a portal for Sour's emotions, hurtling them back in time. The pastel-painted buildings, the men, young and old in their cowboy hats, the vaqueros trotting horseback among the cars on Avenida de Cinco de Mayo, all brought back the craggy, sun-raisined faces of his father's old friends on the reservation, the ones who always called little Clayton, 'Blancocito.' (No, he had never been just 'Clayton.')

Sour smiled as he remembered that black powder six-shooter he had bought off an old man, teaching himself to blast old cans off a splintered, uneven fence. *"You think you're some kinda gunfighter, don't you?"* his father chided in Spanish the first time he found him shooting, somehow spinning his ubiquitous toothpick between his teeth without puncturing the side of his cheek. *"Through and through,"* his booze breath choked out hot laughter.

Sour's face darkened as his thoughts slipped to the moment he left home, and his search for his missionary mother he never found.

The bustle of Puerto Palomas snapped him back to the present. The Pink Store & Restaurant seemed to be the commercial center of town, but Sour kept driving until he passed a pack of hungry young roamers. He rolled down his window to ask them if there was a joint in this town in which one could find a sporting woman. With knowing grins, they pointed him a few blocks further south down Cinco de Mayo, in the direction of the Terraza San Vicente.

The Terraza was a long, perfect white rectangle that looked like it must have been delivered on the back of a truck. Puerto Palomas was a family town, but if this establishment was ever filled with families, it was long past that hour by the time Sour walked in. He sat at the bar for a plate of food, and controlled himself enough to order two glass bottles of Coke rather than anything harder. He was savoring that sweet tinge of real sugar lining the bottom of his second bottle when he smelled the perfume approach behind him. A sweet mix of flowers and Aqua-Net took the stool next to his. A manicured finger, an orchid painted onto the nail, skimmed the air in the order of a tequila.

"Most Americans want to eat in the Pink Store," the English slid off her tongue as if she had known the language as long as her native one.

"Yo no soy la mayoría de los Americanos," Sour responded.

She dropped her head back for a belly laugh uncommon in someone her age, the laugh of someone comfortable in her surroundings and her own skin. Her hair was jet black, skin perfect, and she wore an old feather boa around her neck like she was portraying some old Spaghetti version of her profession. She was young, but not too young. "Me llamo Resplanda," she offered a hand of those flowered nails.

"Radiance," Sour translated as he took it. "Muy bonita."

"It could also mean 'Blaze.' That was the meaning my mother intended."

Sour grinned as he thought of Earl Long, and an old Paul Newman movie he once enjoyed. "She must have been a sporting woman like you."

"You are a strange man. What about your name, strange man?"

"Agrio."

She laughed again. "I can see that."

"Can you recommend a place to stay tonight?"

"Pay for your dinner. I'll take you there."

He followed her instructions to the letter, walking her out to Beast, but Resplanda laid her hand over his before he could put his key in the door. "We can walk," she explained. She started to turn, but he grabbed her and shoved her against his door, then gave her the first kiss he had given away in years.

"We can do that where we're going," she smiled when he pulled away.

"There's a lot-- inside me," he searched for the Spanish words. "I haven't been with a woman in so long. I don't know if I will be... soft. Pleasant."

She took his hand and led him deeper into Puerto Palomas, soon pausing ever so slightly at an intersection. If Sour weren't a trained observer of human behavior, if his senses were as dulled by drink as they usually were, he might not have caught it: she was, for just a moment, debating which street to lead him down.

And then she moved again, dragging him not left but right, to a modest two-story building, then up the outdoor stairs to the door to her apartment. She stopped short of putting the key in the lock. "I never bring men here. I don't know why I did tonight. Something in your voice. Your eyes."

He grabbed her arms and spun her around, gripping the back of her neck in a rough hand as he pulled her into another kiss. She broke away from it with a hard gasp. His hand was up her skirt, pushing away the fabric to caress her in that most tender spot. Feeling how wet with anticipation she already was, Sour opened his pants. As sloppy on him as the rest of his clothes, they plummeted, his big rancher's buckle ringing out from the top step.

Resplanda gripped him and guided him in. Sour's breath spewed out of his nostrils like a hellsteed, that monster, the one that had bashed in the A&M boy's teeth, coming out again. Each of his pumps grew in speed and intensity. He felt her orgasmic vise tighten around him as he released inside her.

They collapsed against each other, a puddle of sweat and giggles. She pushed his head off her shoulder to ask, "Do you want to see the inside?" He did, for one more sugary Coke at least.

All they did was sit and talk, her across her bed, he on the other side of the studio at the small kitchen table. All through the night they talked, about her life, her mother and the father she never met, the dreams she still harbored, until a rooster signaled the coming of the sun.

Sour stood, pulling his wallet from his pants. "I should go."

She crawled to the edge of the bed, and put a hand on his leather billfold, just as she had on his truck keys six hours before. "I don't want your money."

"What do you want then?"

"I want to keep talking."

Sour dropped his hands. There was something about his time with this woman. Her smooth mix of Spanish, English and plenty of giggles reminded him of his mother, while the calmness she brought to his soul was one he hadn't felt since his happiest days with Diane. "That's fine," he hummed, bringing his coarse palm to her cheek, "but there's something you have to let me do first."

She stared up into his eyes, her own orbs drenched not with fear or revulsion, but anticipation, and a willingness to ride anywhere with this man.

"You got any eggs in your fridge?"

Sour hadn't felt free of responsibility, of duty, in so long, and he swam in this freedom like he had found a hot spring on a cold mountain trek. He made love to Resplanda; he fed her; he heard her stories. He kept his own to a minimum, despite her insistent prodding. He fixed her leaky kitchen sink, and installed a heavy security screen on her front door.

If her goal was to keep him as her guest forever, her mistake was letting any little bit of America inside her home. Puerto Palomas was just close enough to the border that a pair of rabbit ears could pick up two or three US TV stations as long as it wasn't raining. On their second night together, when Resplanda snoozed deeply but Sour couldn't find sleep, he picked up her remote and turned on the little tube seated on top of her dresser.

The sound was off, but he didn't need it with the red breaking news bar filling the bottom horizontal of the screen, the loop of shots of flashing emergency lights, of shards of glass filling a street, of bodies covered with blankets. It was the type of story that had become all-too-commonplace on American news these days. A man had walked into a sports bar in Maryland and opened fire on the patrons.

Though this had nothing to do Sour, with anything he was avoiding, it still wrenched his mind back to the world, back to the Waterford, back to the cell phone he had left inert inside Beast for forty-plus hours, waiting to be turned back on and filled with dozens of messages both vocal and textual from Blunt pressing for his decision.

He slinked out of bed, pulling the wad from his wallet without counting it and leaving it all on her bedside table. He slipped into his shirt and pants and headed for that security screen he had himself installed just a few hours before.

"Haven't you felt it too?" he heard her voice behind him. He turned to find her sitting up, propped against her headboard, so gorgeous and innocent with one hand holding the covers over her breasts, as if he hadn't become intimately familiar with them over the last two days. "Between us?"

"Of course I have."

"Then don't leave. Not until you really have to."

"That was two days ago. Before I even got here."

Resplanda scoffed. "Americans should be more willing to blow off obligations."

He stepped back to the bed, and cupped her cheek in his palm. It was the same way he had caressed her when he had decided to stay, but she knew this time he wasn't going to waver.

"At least promise me," she demanded, "when it is done, you'll come back and finally tell me about you."

He kissed her forehead and walked out to reunite with his Beast.

JUST A REGULAR
ANNIE OAKLEY

"**I** see you've met my Daddy," Blunt's voice beamed from behind Sour. Clayton stood at the base of a giant floor-to-ceiling oil painting, its subject a dour man in copper mining helmet and soot-stained coveralls, a long-handled sledgehammer perched over one shoulder, a sharp wedge hanging from the fingers of his other hand. But most true-to-life were his darkened, tired eyes, exhausted from a lifetime of work or maybe already pained with the knowledge of the ravages of that life's work on his health.

"You'd look that serious too if you had as many headaches as him." Blunt stepped up next to Sour and admired the painting as if he hadn't noticed it in years, even as it dominated one whole wall of his home office. "The headaches are what I remember most from when I was a boy. He might have had every weekend off, but those weekends were all wasted. He was always in a terrible mood or laid up in bed with one of those headaches. I remember three, four times a year, the man Phelps-Dodge had sent down here to run the Lavender Pit Mine, he'd invite every miner and his family to spend a Saturday afternoon barbecuing, swimming, playing stick ball out behind the house on his gargantuan property. Those were the only times my Daddy faked a good head on the weekend, because he had to. That Phelps-Dodge man thought he was so generous, but those Saturdays were an expectation of every man, they were work.

"The mine shut down and Phelps-Dodge cleared out when I was away at U of A. Year or two later, Daddy's doctor sent him up to Tucson for confirmation he had stage four brain cancer."

He stepped away, moving to his massive desk, still shaking his head decades after he first heard the news from his mother. "But those headaches, they made it possible that I go to college, then to law school, then open my own firm, then run for Congress. No Blunt had ever won elected office before. And yet I, son of an Arizona copper miner, I became a member of the House of Representatives and the Republican nominee for Vice President of these United States!" Blunt smiled with another nod to the painting. "My Daddy, he died for us. That's why, when I bought this house up on the hill, this house that Phelps-Dodge man always made everyone come visit on the weekends, I promised him he would always share this office with me."

Sour turned to take one of the two chairs angled before the desk, and Blunt swallowed his self-congratulatory laughter to take his own seat. Sour just wanted to get everything having to do with this man done as quickly as possible. He had driven straight from Resplanda's apartment without even a piss stop, three hours straight, veering off Route 80 down into the suburb of Warren without even seeing main street Bisbee yet. "I want to start with some ground rules," he began.

"Shoot."

"I've got three. Break any of them, and I turn around and drive back to Texas. You think you can manage that?"

"Well, I better hear 'em first."

"You don't leave this house until I tell you my work's done."

"Of course."

"Congressman!" Blunt's aide-de-camp rushed from a corner, poking away at his iPad. Sour hadn't even been aware the boy was there. His senses obviously still had some drying out to do. "Congressman, your calendar is very full for the next--"

"Nothing we can't move or cancel, Thomas," Blunt replied with a mollifying hand.

"Recess was supposed to end next week, and all Congressional offices got a memo from Capitol Police yesterday that they will be ready for--"

"Then I guess Sour has a week to find these assholes." Blunt turned his big vote-grubbing grin back on his guest. "Number two?"

Sour reached into his right pants pocket, and when his hand emerged, a silver chain draped his closed fingers. He leaned over Blunt's desk, setting the pendant right in the center, its cat face smiling back up at the Congressman. Sour sat back, explaining, "I want that on your person at all times."

Blunt picked Tippy up between two fingers, back on his heels for the first time since Sour had met him. "Why, Sour, I'm sorry, but I don't--"

"She's my peace of mind. Long as you have that, I'll always know where you are."

Blunt looked to Jill in the other chair. Then, back to Sour, staring deep into his soul. His lips sputtered as he let out a laugh burst. Sour may have voodoo ways, but Homer couldn't argue with his record, not with the situation in which he now found himself. "Understood," Blunt added to the final guffaw, tucking the cat into his own front pocket. "And third?"

Sour let a beat settle in the room before he answered. "You're gonna tell me why."

"Why?"

"Why you're hiring me to do this."

Again, Blunt's eyes swept over Jill's first, leaving Sour to wonder if she knew the true answer to this line of inquiry, or subscribed to the line of horseshit he was sure he was about to be fed. "I don't want to get too political with you, Sour," Blunt said as he intertwined his fingers in his lap, "but the timing of your departure from the FBI was impeccable. You're the man who got off at the last port the *Titanic* ever saw. You talk about the shooting in that Iranian halfway house in Portland, how long it took them to make any arrests in the Supreme Court bombing – the FBI has lost the faith and trust of the American people, including many members of their Congress. Now you may know I'm on the House Oversight Committee, and that I chaired the special committee that investigated the Bureau's handling of these matters. Some commentators and many an internet user found it entertaining to pass the video of my grilling of the Director around for quite a few days. What do you call that, Thomas?"

"Trending, Congressman."

"That's right. I was *trending*. Hashtag Federal Bureau of Inadequacy, I believe. So I'll admit that hasn't done wonders for my confidence that they will be incentivized to get to the bottom of this particular matter."

"And you think you're next."

"I'm sorry?"

"You heard me."

Blunt laughed again, but this time it was uncomfortable laughter, the laughter of a man trapped. "I'm afraid I'm not following on this one. How would I even guess--"

"You're right, it doesn't seem to make sense, at least not yet. Payne and Carpinello were both Democrats. Carpinello is the daughter of Marcus Carpinello, for Chrissakes. There's no reason to think a Republican from Arizona would be next. So why do you?"

Jill reached over, putting a hand on the arm of Sour's chair. "Mr. Manco--"

"*Why am I here, Congressman?*"

Blunt swallowed. He cleared his throat. He took his time before looking up over Jill's shoulder. "Thomas, would you excuse us please?"

"Congressman," he huffed back. "I really don't think it's a good idea for me not to be present for any--"

"*Thomas.*"

Thomas relented, lowering his iPad to waist level before walking out, closing the door behind him.

Blunt brought his linked hands up onto the top of his desk, squeezing them tighter and tighter together, bulging a vein out of his temple. "I've never told anyone this before. Congresswoman Carpinello... *Barbara* and I had always been close. That first night we were sworn in, we had drinks together. It became a tradition, any night we were in Washington without our families. Eventually, we were having more than drinks." He covered his eyes with a quivering left hand--

Before balling it in a fist and slamming it down into the desk, and using that force to push him to his feet. "They're going to die. You're going to make sure they die. You're going to make sure they *suffer* as they die. You understand me, Sour?"

Sour stared at him, unwilling to commit to this sob story just yet.

Blunt pushed through, pointing through the double French doors behind them. "Jill will show you to the pool house. We've already got it set up with everything you will need--"

Sour stood. "The Copper Queen will be fine."

Blunt smiled. Every politician loved a power struggle, a cockfight; at least, every good one did. "You're not the only one with ground rules, Sour. You're going to keep everything centered here – in case I ever need to drop in on you for an update."

"Fine. But don't expect me to be here much."

"Then you'll take Jill with you," Blunt insisted with a quick swipe in her direction, "wherever you go."

"A chaperone?"

"An assistant. She's very capable, or I never would have hired her."

Sour turned and looked down at her, the slightest chuckle breaking through his pursed lips.

"Thanks," Jill popped back.

Sour's eyes were already back on his new employer. "And if this is a deal breaker for me?"

Blunt rolled his eyes as he opened the right-hand drawer of his desk. "In my business, we know deal breakers are like Santa Claus." He tossed a gator-skinned checkbook up on the desk, then unsheathed a fancy fountain pen. "They're a nice story to tell, but they don't really exist." Sitting and rolling his chair forward, he scribbled something into the check in that awkward scrawl of the lefthanded writer who had to levitate the side of his hand to keep it from smearing the ink. He tore the check off with a flourish, holding it up between thumbs and forefingers so Sour could read it plain as day:

Pay to the Order of: CLAYTON MANCO
One Million Dollars and NO/100

With Sour's appetite whetted, Blunt laid it down in the center drawer of the desk, then locked that shut with a set of keys from his pocket. "You get this when you do two things. You get to these bastards first, before the FBI."

He looked up at Sour with a grin, waiting for him to ask what the other thing might be. But receiving no such inquiry, he went right ahead on his own: "And second, you make sure they pay *properly* for what they've done. The kind of justice only you understand, Sour."

After giving his instructions to Jill and Thomas, Sour sacked out in the pool house's one bedroom. It was early for sleep, but he wanted to stock up some credit, and knew it would take them a few hours to do as he had asked.

He had of course made sure the blinds were drawn so he would wake to the sunrise. Stepping out into the main room, he found Jill and Thomas collapsed on opposite couches, still in yesterday's suits, binders of information stacked on the billiard table, every inch of wall covered with the headshots of every member of Congress.

"Good morning," he announced, and Jill stirred.

Thomas shot straight up like Sour imagined his carrot whenever subjected to even the tiniest bit of teasing. "I'm up, I'm awake!" he protested, getting to his feet to try to pace some blood flow back into his veins.

"This is everyone?" Sour confirmed as he performed a small circle, taking in all the fucking ignoramuses smiling back at him as if they were begging for votes through the camera's lens.

"That's everyone," Jill replied, now in the kitchenette, filling the top of the coffee maker with grounds. "Four hundred thirty-five members of the House, one hundred more in the Senate."

Sour went to the built-in drawers in the cabinet around the large flatscreen, opening and closing them until he came up with exactly what he needed: a red sharpie. He recognized Barbara Carpinello from his own years in DC, and crossed to her face to put a big red **X** through her nose. He stepped back for a moment and Thomas raised a finger at Stephen Payne. Sour did the same to his visage. "Four hundred thirty-three," he corrected Jill. "Plus the Senate. Five hundred thirty-three potential next victims."

With his back to them, Sour didn't catch Jill and Thomas's eye contact, a confirmation between colleagues that the newcomer had dropped his theories about Blunt being next. But Sour didn't need to catch that look to know it was there.

"So why these two first?" he pointed with the capped sharpie. "What links them?"

Jill moved to the pool table, digging for the largest of the binders. "These are profiles we put together on all the fringe groups that hate the Democrats. Militia groups, white supremacists, fetal rights activists…"

"The hatred of immigrants has been at a fever pitch with a Mexican-American in the White House," Thomas joined in.

But Sour didn't take Jill's binder, or pick up one of his own. He kept his gaze locked into all those faces, bringing thumb and forefinger to his chin, like he might find the answers somewhere in all those eyes staring back.

Thomas tried to keep the brainstorming going. "What about, could it be-- international? An ISIS cell, or that new group out of Iran, Qatil Kafii I think they're called? Or just local lone wolves who want to impress Raqqa or Tehran?"

Sour shook his head. "They'd have started crowing right after the first hit. These aren't some morons who trained themselves in a garage or a cave. The tactics, the efficiency, it's professional. Military. This isn't one or two loose cannon lunatics, it's a well-oiled group making a statement." He stepped forward, bony finger extended at Carpinello's face. "And that statement has something very specifically to do with

Carpinello." Then to Payne's. "With Payne. With a policy, a piece of legislation."

Thomas shook his head. "They were on zero committees together--"

"And they represent nowhere close in proximity," Jill jumped in. "Carpinello from the Maine Second, Payne the Ohio Eleventh. Their home districts almost a thousand miles apart."

"I need their complete schedules from the last five years. Every meeting, every rally, every convention these two attended together. Everything they voted the same on, *everything* since Payne was sworn in."

Thomas was already banging away on that iPad, then bringing his phone to his ear with his other hand as he made his way for the door. "I'll try their offices right now."

"Make it the last seven years."

"Copy that," Thomas said as he stepped out, the door swinging shut behind him.

Jill set down her binder, a little surprised he hadn't perused one yet. "We put all this together for you, like you asked. Do you want to rev--?"

"Did they campaign together?" Sour continued to wonder aloud, as if he couldn't even hear her. "Did Carpinello endorse Payne, or vice versa? We link these victims," he turned to Jill, boring his eyes into hers, "we can figure out who's going to be next."

She got the hint, nodding and heading for the door to follow Thomas out. "I'll see if Thomas needs any help."

But when her hand reached the knob, she couldn't help but stop. Jill knew she wouldn't be where she was today, wouldn't be alive today, if she hadn't long ago learned to defend herself. "I want you to know, I know no more than you."

"Hmm?" Sour turned back from the collage.

"About the Congressman. About why he brought you in. I recommended against it, as a matter of fact."

"That makes two of us."

"I just wanted you to know, since you don't know me at all, that I don't bullshit. He's told me exactly what he's told you."

Sour just stared back at her without a word, a habit of his it would take Jill a while to get used to.

"Okay, well," she dribbled out, "we'll get back to you when we have something."

"I know you got through Stanford." His voice stopped her when she had only opened the door a half dozen inches. "I know ROTsie was the only way you could afford to go to a school like that. I know after graduation you ended up at Ranger School. My fellow Ranger." She turned back in time to see his impressed eyebrows do a little hop. "First female lieutenant to take live fire. First female lieutenant to record enemy kills. Applied to the Bureau, but had to settle for Allied Armament security contractors, settle for busting heads on the mean streets of Detroit, until they went under. You got some sand in you, don't you, Ms. Creete? You're just a regular Annie Oakley."

But Jill didn't stand tall or swell with pride. Her record could be interpreted a few different ways, and it made her nervous whenever someone reviewed it behind her back.

Jill had been pounding on the door for five minutes when she decided to try the knob, finding that indeed, it was open. Everything in the main room was as they had left it – billiards felt still stacked with binders, walls still decorated with headshots – but his bedroom was empty, no suitcase or sign he had moved in visible on the mussed bed or in the closet.

Returning to the main house, she found Blunt and his son watching football in the TV room. Though Randy had body duty, he was on the opposite couch, also making wisecracks about the losing team.

"Did you know Manco's gone?"

Seeing his superior approach, Randy jumped up and moved behind the couch into position, while Blunt gave a quick look over a shoulder with a grin. "He asked me if he could take the plane."

"What? To go where?"

"I don't know. He just said he needed it and would be back in the morning."

"Jesus Christ," Jill spit out in a whisper as she turned away.

"Jilly," the Congressman sat forward, tapping the open couch cushion with his palm. She succumbed to the hint and came around to join him. "I know the next few weeks are gonna be tough on you. They're tough on all of us-- we can't leave our house, for Chrissakes."

"But we agreed this is what it would take-- *he* is what it's going to take to end this thing. Now I know we only hired a quarter of an FBI agent, but when that quarter comes out-- that's the quarter's gonna find these assholes. That's the quarter that's gonna--"

Blunt mimed a clenched fist going straight up some orifice, and his son giggled. "Nice, Dad!"

"So let's give him some breathing room," Blunt slapped his open hand down on Jill's thigh, but she knew to ignore it as she always did. "And if we're lucky, maybe that quarter'll turn into a half."

Jill stood, that hand falling away. "Sir," she pledged obedience – for now – and walked out.

Most Americans had never heard of Parker Poughkeepsie, but he had made himself into one of the most powerful law enforcement agents in the country. His innovative High Value Targets team, an FBI all-star squad structured like a military platoon, had become the main PR salvo in reclaiming the Bureau's honor after its string of major league fuck ups. The Director who had gotten the FBI back on track over the last twelve months was considered an interim choice, and Poughkeepsie was the safest bet to take over Hoover's old post sooner rather than later. He also, at age 49, already had three beautiful children in Ivy League schools, and a fourth who was top of her class at Sidwell Friends. And this was without even broaching how much of a rising star he was in his local ward of the LDS church.

Family dinners had always been a top priority for Poughkeepsie, but he also knew that no FBI agent with future political ambitions could be seen leaving the Hoover Building at 5 PM with the nation under high alert. He had seen the potential pitfalls of this up close a year ago, when the Director had been Snapchatted at a 'skins game a mere thirteen days after the Supreme Court bombing.

So while the Congressional Killers were still at large, Betty and Jacob Poughkeepsie would eat family dinner without him, and the man of the house would leave the office after his 9 PM delivery from some carcinogenic DC eatery.

It was a brown bag from Ben's Chili Bowl in his hands when he heard Sour's voice for the first time since January. "Dinner at 10?" that voice said, and Poughkeepsie dropped the bag right onto his driveway, the contents inside splattering out of their containers.

"Jimminy Christmas, Clay!" he exclaimed when he saw his former top agent standing in the middle of his Chevy Chase lawn.

Sour chuckled; he always loved the words that would flow out of Parker's Mormon mouth in place of cusses. "I'd say all evidence points to High Value being put on a big case, Park."

"Everyone's on it. Counterterrorism, ViCAP, Criminal. J. Edgar's whole family's on it."

"Then you can help me."

Poughkeepsie had to look up from the pavement where he was collecting his brown bag, cupping the bottom of it in a palm to keep more from tumbling out. "What? Clay? What are you doing? We had our deal. You can't come back--"

"Unless I'm working for Blunt."

That name sent a shiver down Poughkeepsie's spine, his entire future flashing before his eyes: *his kids' various graduations, the Directorship, a future political race--*

"I, I don't trust that man, Clay," he stammered. "You've gotta understand, everything's different now. The amount of oversight now--"

"You mean you're different now. You have much more to lose."

"Yes. That too."

"Park. This is the only way I get out from under this guy. *We* get out from under this guy. Do what he wants, make him happy. And then go back to the agreement we had."

Poughkeepsie nodded. Sour wasn't sure he had ever seen him speechless, but he was more scared of Homer Blunt than Sour was.

"The next time you have an active crime scene," Sour broke through his trance, "I get notified within three hours." Sour beeped open his rented sedan, but before he sat, added one thing: "Oh, and return my calls. I love you, but it's sure a pain in the ass to have to fly cross country to see you."

He slammed his door, and Poughkeepsie spiked his dinner back into the asphalt.

A SNIPER TO TRACK A SNIPER

"**M**mm," Helen Brandtley lied through a mouthful of lamb chop and quinoa. "Good tonight."

"Yes," her husband Rick sneered back as he tore a roll in two between his fingers. "Prison food never tasted so good."

As her husband gnashed into the bread, Helen looked away, trying for a moment to pretend as if he wasn't even there, as if no one was there with her, as if she was eating in blissful solitude. But it was impossible to look in any direction without seeing at least one of the four hulking private security guards in the corners, all in jackets a size or two too big so you couldn't see what they were hiding underneath.

"Rick, please. You know I don't like this anymore than you do."

Rick was feeling pugnacious. It should have been great news when they received word Helen would be free to return to Washington in a week, and yet his wife had shown no enthusiasm during the videoconference with Capitol Police. Upon the connection going dead on her MacBook screen, she didn't start talking about what flight they should book, moving back into their A Street penthouse or what pet causes she couldn't wait to get back into – no mention of getting military spending back up, or her personhood push which had had its momentum undercut by this forced, unplanned holiday. She just mumbled something about it being safer to stay right where they were. And it wasn't that Rick disagreed with that; yes, it was probably safer holed up here in North Carolina, but since when did Helen Brandtley just do what was safest?

After 27 years of courting and marriage, Rick knew his spouse well enough to know when she was lying, when she was withholding something. God bless her, Helen wasn't practiced at it, and wasn't very good at it, so she avoided it like a plague – something her constituents had appreciated and adored about her through three campaigns. And that once in a blue moon she did attempt to lie, even a small, harmless little lie, she quite simply sucked at it. There was another reason Helen didn't want to leave the newly-installed safety of this house, but whatever it was, she wasn't sharing it with Rick. He didn't have anything of his own to lie about back, so his only recourse was to do what he did best in return: be a dick about it. "But I'm not the one who chose to run for national office, am I? Oh, wait, that's right, as a matter of fact, I told you *not* to."

Helen threw her fork down across her half-empty plate with a jarring jangle. "Oh, give me a fucking break." Rick could swear he noticed the guards flinch a little, either at the violence of the fork toss, or when they heard the blue language spit off the tongue of one of the few elected officials you could actually call *respected.* "Your quote unquote foundation wouldn't even exist if I wasn't in Congress," Helen ranted. "The kids wouldn't be in Ivy League schools--"

"Helen! Are you fucking kidding me right now?"

"No, I am not fucking kidding you. It's all true and you know it."

"Oh, you wanna talk about what's *true*, is that what you want to talk about?" Rick stood, throwing his napkin down on top of his own plate. He wasn't quite that angry, no, but he needed to amp up the dramatics if he was going to achieve his ultimate goal. "I was happier *without* the foundation, without the constant fundraisers, without my picture in the *News & Observer* every other week. I was happier just owning the dealership in anonymity." He let that settle for a moment, knowing she wouldn't dare to argue with his feelings. He raised an open palm for the coup de grâce: "I-- I can't. No. I just can't. I'm gonna go watch the Wahoos."

He spun on a heel and charged for the door. Sweet Jesus, he did it. This is all he wanted, to watch his UVA Cavaliers pay a visit to the Seminoles – or watch a quarter or two at least, while they were still within three touchdowns. Unfortunately, only one of the rooms they were now allowed access to housed a television, only one of the rooms with the ballistic glass installed: the upstairs bonus room with its windows facing the expansive backyard and the golf course beyond it, rather than the street in front. And Rick knew that making Helen feel guilty about this whole situation was the only way he was going to wrest control of the bonus room plasma before she put on another episode of that insufferable *Pro Bono* on Netflix.

Rick headed for that bonus room, one of the guards stepping into line behind him. Congresswoman Helen Brandtley (R-NC) fell back against her chair, surrendering the fight.

As he unlocked the door and stepped in, Brenden silently hoped the objective of the operation had already been achieved, that the guys had finally caught views of Helen Brandtley in one of her home's many windows and done what they came to do. For just a moment, Brenden allowed himself a daydream of the boys telling him it was done, of the three of them clearing out their small office and eating their Bad Daddy's burgers on the road.

But there they still were as he walked in, torsos draped around their .50s, eyes glued into their targeting scopes. He wasn't sure Chase and Tatsumi had even heard him until he let the door whisper shut, and Tats answered, "Still nothing, Bowz."

"Ditto here," Chaser agreed.

"Well, then it's mess time," Brenden replied as he brought the large paper bag and cardboard drink tray to the folding table. Tatsumi was the first one to leap up as Brenden removed their orders from the bag and organized them before the seats to which each man had instinctively returned for all of the dozen or so meals they had already spent here. Brenden was the only one who hadn't been to sniper school, so he was burger bitch by default, and secretly, he relished that role, relieved that if everything went as planned, he would avoid having to personally pull the trigger for once.

"Wait, wait, wait--" Chase, still behind his own rifle, exclaimed from the window. "Movement."

Tatsumi leaped back down behind his own rifle.

"South window three," Chase directed his eyes.

"Got it. That's the TV room."

In one of those windows they had been watching for days, one with the blinds always drawn – all the windows had always had the blinds drawn, since the moment they had set up shop here – a long snout had just pushed its way out from behind the slats. It snorted on the glass, leaving a damp impression. Then more of the face behind that nozzle appeared: a long face; sharp, trimmed ears; then the whole athletic body of a Doberman, painted green and black by their night-vision scopes.

Chaser licked his lips, then let them settle into a smile. It wasn't their intended target, but it would kick off just the kind of chaos that could open up some opportunities for them. He moved his finger behind the guard, onto the trigger. "Drill me a big one, Tatsie," he grinned.

"There we go, boys," Rick slapped his hands together a single time as he leaned forward onto the edge of the couch. "Smack the shit out of 'em. Get that ball back." The Cavaliers were keeping it close with halftime approaching, and the Brandtleys' seven-channel surround system made Rick feel like he was on the Doak Campbell turf for every hit and every tackle.

It was so loud, in fact, he would miss the most ominous sound of the evening.

As halftime approached and the sideline reporter ran beside the 'noles coach to grill him on why his top-ranked team in the nation could only distance themselves by a field goal from an unranked squad, Rick rose and picked up the remote, draining the volume. He didn't need to hear that two minutes of coachspeak rhetoric; he would go apologize to Helen instead. She had surely already given up on Netflix by now and would accept Rick's apology, then release him to return to the bonus for the second half while she fell asleep under a blanket of policy homework.

But with the TV almost muted, Rick finally heard the whimpering as he shuffled for the door.

"Thorn?" Rick called out for his precious Doberman he had named after a dog in his favorite '80s horror movie. The whimper, that unmistakable whine of a canine begging or in pain, rose in volume as the animal realized his master had heard him. Rick rushed behind one couch, then the other – finding the bloody heap under the window. "No, no, no, Thorny, no," he pleaded as he dropped to his knees. When he put his hands beneath her, they soaked with something liquid, drawing his eyes right to the puddle of red underneath her limp abdomen. *"No--"*

"Sir!" The guard who had accompanied him to the bonus room now had a hand on Rick's shoulder, but Rick didn't even feel it. "I'm going to have to ask you to step away from the window--"

"It's gonna be okay, girl, you're okay, we're gonna get you help..." Rick sobbed. This dog had welcomed Rick Jr. to the house the day he was born, she had woken the kids on every Christmas morning and barreled into every Christmas card shot, she had laid across their youngest daughter's bed for a week of depression after that last Brandtley child had left for college...

"Sir, step away from the window right now!"

But it was too late. The guard heard the tinkle of glass, the xylophone of the shades ruffling-- and then a grunt from Richard Brandtley. His body tensed for just a second, before he collapsed on top of the dog. More blood was mixing with the dog's now, blood of a lighter shade--

"FUCK!" the guard screamed out. He had never seen a person die before. He had seen animals die on the farm growing up. And everyone had always assumed he had seen people die during his two tours in Iraq. But Rick Brandtley was the first. He went down to his knees, pawing at Brandtley's neck to confirm it, as he shouted into a wrist, "Man down, man down, upstairs bonus room, I'm gonna need medical--"

The piercing scream cut him off. Helen Brandtley was at the door, staring down at the bloody coagulation of her husband and dog.

"No, ma'am, you can't be in here, I need you to go right now to--"

But Helen was on her knees, digging them right into the soppiest, reddest bit of carpet, as she tried to shake life back into her life partner of 27 years. "No, no, not Rick, he didn't have anything to do with this--"

The guard grabbed her shoulders – "Ma'am, listen to me, I need you away from the window *right now!*" – but her adrenaline was fueling her with unusual strength, enabling her to fight him off.

"*Not Rick, you mother fuckers!*"

The guard heard three more of those pumps, heard the blinds quake three more times, a couple of slats even splintering apart, their shards tumbling to the carpet. But Helen hadn't screamed or fallen, and the guard had felt no tags on his own body. Those three shots had missed. They were lucky, but their luck wouldn't last long. "CONGRESSWOMAN! GET DOW--"

There were only three more shots. The first entered his skull through his right eye. The second perforated the guard's chest right at the heart, and as his blood spread across his white shirt, it was tinged with black from the Skoal tin he always kept in his left breast pocket.

The third bullet passed through the temples of Congresswoman Helen Brandtley, killing her instantly.

"She's the first Republican victim," Thomas whined through the tiny speaker of Sour's phone as they pulled off the tarmac of the General Aviation Terminal at RDU. "Re-upped last year for the third time in the North Carolina thirteenth. Now you had said the killers might be military-- all three victims, including Brandtley, voted to allow transgenders in the armed forces. That's the only time she's broken from the party over the last three years--"

"I thought I told you to look at everyone's last seven."

"I, I was, looking at Payne and Carpinello's, but there hasn't been time since I heard--"

Sour killed the connection with his thumb. A vote on transgender rights might link the three victims, sure – and there were no doubt some people vehemently against it – but it didn't feel right, didn't feel like the kind of issue that would inspire three meticulous military-style assassinations.

Getting to North Carolina wasn't the way Sour had intended to spend his evening. He had just last night found a local distraction that could keep him from the bottle, found it in the center of town, in the Copper Queen Hotel. Twenty-three miles south of Tombstone and eleven north of Mexico, the Main Street of Old Bisbee winding through the mountains was a clash of old west time capsule and gentrified artists' colony, with tourist saloons mixed in among galleries, tasting rooms and head shops. The Copper Queen had been the epicenter of the era of bustling mines and bitter labor wars, and legend had it, was still inhabited by the spirits of many of the workers and strike breakers the Phelps-Dodge company had built the place to house. Once on sale for as little as a dollar, it had luckily been snapped up by artisans who made it a priority to keep its unique charm intact. Sour sat in the hotel saloon, a little relieved to find it so vacant (tourist season had ended about a month earlier with the annual running of Old Bisbee's one thousand steps), breathing in its British pub aroma and nibbling on the bowl of chips the noseringed bartender had brought him. He didn't need to waste money to confirm that no one in this town would compare to the radiant Resplarda.

His eyes were drawn to the door by robust voices, and there he noticed three older gentlemen in suits greeting a fourth who gripped a huge stogie between stubby digits. Sour knew card players when he saw them, and asked if they would be open to a stranger joining. "Depends how much cash that stranger's got," one of them winked.

Sour was well on his way to cleaning all of them out when he felt his phone vibrate from his pocket, three or four buzzes in the cadence of a call. The current hand continued, and was still playing out when the phone buzzed again, this time with just the singular, quick double-buzz of a text message. As the man on Sour's left shuffled and dealt, he pulled it out and checked it under the table, reading that the missed call was from **Poughkeepsie**, as was the subsequent text that followed:

Consider this your 3 hour notice

Sour re-pocketed the Motorola and let the next hand play out, only the polite thing to do, then cashed out, collecting the numbers of the other players for the next time he felt like a game (with a brief wonder if they were giving him legitimate information after the spanking he had given them).

As he walked out to Beast, he was also ringing through to Jill's cell. She would have the plane ready to depart within two hours. But Sour could never sleep on planes, and was instead subjected to sitting back and watching Jill snooze from just before takeoff through to the Captain's twenty-minute warning to descent. It was the first chance he had had since taking on this job to properly examine her, and to admire her, he admitted to himself. She was an attractive woman, who took some care to keep a hint of sex appeal mixed in with her athleticism, the subtlest hint of make up on her eyes, her shirt buttoned just above the front clasp of her brassiere. What he had seen in her rejected application to the Bureau had concerned him, and he had made sure she knew he had seen it without also admitting that as a general rule he liked to make his own assessments of people, often ignoring their histories or résumés. In his experience, people worked harder, stayed more on their toes, if they thought they had to repair their name.

After a final hour flying into the sunrise, they descended into Raleigh-Durham in daylight. A rented black Escalade waited for them on the tarmac, and Jill drove while Sour answered Thomas's four voice mails, each left after three more months of Helen Brandtley's voting history had been analyzed.

It was about a fifteen mile drive out to the suburb of Cary, and the GPS on Jill's phone said they still had 0.3 to go when they came to a grinding halt at a logjam of news trucks and emergency vehicles choking out the wooded street leading back to the Brandtley address. Jill ripped the phone out of the cup holder and was flipping through her contacts, wracking her brain for the name of someone who could clear a path for them, when Sour threw open his door, got out of the car and walked into the mass of insanity. "Shit, wait, Sour!" she cried after him, but he was already disappearing. She had only seconds to act or she would lose him-- and her *one fucking job* was to stay with him.

She screeched the Escalade half up onto someone's front lawn, slammed the red triangle of the hazard button, and leaped out, sprinting after him. She didn't see him again for a few blocks, so she just followed the loosening of the bottleneck, until she was running up to what had to be the Brandtley house: its driveway clogged with law enforcement and government issued vehicles; the droves of media crowded right up to the rope line delineating the property into which they couldn't legally cross; and at the front door – Sour, talking to a suited young man on the front steps.

"--don't care who the fuck you think you are," he was ranting in Sour's face as Jill stepped up behind him, "this is a closed scene."

Jill touched Sour's arm. It didn't look like he was getting in, but if by some miracle he did, she wanted to make sure he knew she was there to ride his coattails inside. "Sour. C'mon, let's--"

"This one's with me," a voice boomed from just inside the house, before the one and only Parker Poughkeepsie poked out his head. His name might not have been a household one, at least not quite yet, but Jill had been studying the careers of the Bureau's most luminous figures for years now. Some people might get starstruck around NFL footballers or movie multi-hyphenates, but someone like Parker Poughkeepsie was all Jill needed for a thrill, even if his hair was thinner and his waistline wider than in any of his Wikipedia photographs. She knew Poughkeepsie was the founder of High Value Targets, the team of which Sour had been an original member, and knew that he was being positioned to perhaps become the next Director of the whole kit and caboodle. As Jill would have expected, the young agent manning the door swiveled to his right without a word, a matador move clearing the path for Sour-- and Jill, who made sure to stick just close enough to his heels that no one could mistake her partnership to him.

With Poughkeepsie as their chaperone, Jill wasn't surprised by the double-takes of young agents and evidence technicians when their small entourage passed. But what she realized as she overheard two of them whisper just behind her was that it wasn't the current FBI agent they were so impressed with – it was the *former* one, the man she had brought here:

"Holy shit. Sour Manco."

"Who the hell is Sour Manco?"

"He was in Poughkeepsie's Academy class. Manco was the first agent he asked to join High Value. But he eventually had to shit can his ass for working freelance gigs on the side."

"Freelance? What kind of freelance?"

"The kind guys like us can't afford. Let's just say if Teddy Kennedy had Sour Manco on the payroll, you never would've heard of Chappaquiddick."

The snap of a flashbulb pinched Jill's attention forward, to where Sour and Poughkeepsie were disappearing into the room at the end of the upstairs hallway. She stepped through the threshold, fighting down an immediate urge to wince at what she saw. It had been three years since she had seen a dead body, since the Aleppo firefight that cost her a career. But now here were three, three human bodies plus one dog carcass too, laid out under a window as if they were some sort of sacrifice to the sun beating in through the panes of glass just above them.

Jill did have to hand it to Sour – coroners were still snapping photos and taking swabs, agents were just dusting for prints; they had arrived as the investigation and forensics were just getting underway. None of which stopped Sour from kneeling next to the bodies, and – without gloves on – moving each one just enough to examine the entry wounds himself. "Hey-- Sir!" the nearest examiner erupted. "WHAT THE HELL! You can't touch them. Who the fu--"

"Jesse, it's okay," Poughkeepsie soothed him. "Mr. Manco is consulting High Value on this."

"That's great, but that doesn't mean he can--"

But Sour was already done with the bodies. He was standing, staring at the broken blinds now raised, so that four clean holes were visible in the thick glass. Sour touched one of the holes, a few inches removed from the other three. "This is ballistic?"

Poughkeepsie nodded. "Their freelance PSD replaced all the panes in the back of the house last week, and was only allowing them in those rooms."

"Let me guess," Sour continued. "Shooters missed four times."

The entire room froze. One gloved agent turned from the far wall opposite their window, itself dotted with four craters in its yellow paint. He didn't answer Sour, just opened a palm, revealing the four smashed bullets he had tweezed out of the wall.

"Clay," Poughkeepsie shook his head with a smile, "you mind telling us how the heck you knew--"

"They didn't miss. These holes," he swiveled back around, raising his finger back to the window blemishes, "they made on purpose. Then they fire right through them again – for their kill shots." He turned his finger back to the bodies. "One hole for the dog, then I'm betting Mr. Brandtley walks right into the same firing line. Then, three holes for the Congresswoman and her body man."

Sour turned back to the window, stepping right up to the glass and looking down at the ground below. "Sour?" Jill took a step forward, trying to break through his trance and hear what he was thinking next.

But without replying, he turned for the door and charged out.

Jill followed. "Manco?" Poughkeepsie called out from just behind her heels as Sour disappeared down the stairs.

They reached the ground floor, where one of the agents who had been so impressed with Sour motioned them to the open French doors leading to the back yard. They stepped out in time to see Sour charging through the trees lining the back of the property. "What's he doing?" Jill called over a shoulder as she picked it up into a jog.

"I take it he hasn't told you what he did with the Rangers?" Poughkeepsie asked, and Jill's blank look was answer enough. "Takes a sniper to track a sniper," he shrugged as they stepped under the shadows of the trees, finding Sour at the ornate back fence of the property, looking out onto the lush greens of the Lochmere golf club. He was at the lone gate, its sealed padlock hanging into the palm of his hand.

"Can we get this open?"

Poughkeepsie pulled out his phone and brought it to his ear, but he already was taking too long for Sour, who grabbed the spokes of the fence, pulling himself up and over it. After a soft landing on the course side, he started marching onto a perfect putting green.

"Shit," Jill cursed before mounting the fence herself.

"You're telling me," Poughkeepsie mumbled, as the call he started before Sour's escape finally went through. "Yeah, it's me. We need the back gate onto the golf course opened *right flipping now.*" As he waited, he watched Sour and Jill go; he knew there was no way he was getting over that fence.

Sour had stepped over two holes and pissed off no less than eight golfers when Jill caught up to him at a full stop. As she caught her breath, she watched him scanning the tree line, his eyes whipping back in the direction from which they had come. Then he spun one-eighty, staring at the small high-rise office buildings on the opposite horizon. Jill had heard her own sniper buddies wax poetic about all the high-level geometry and arithmetic that went into their shots, the inclusion of factors like wind and, for shots far enough away like these appeared to be, even the Earth's rotation, and now was witnessing a shooter reverse engineer all those mental gymnastics.

Sour moved again, huffing it for the office park. Jill hadn't started following when Poughkeepsie ran up, a sweating, wheezing mess. "How far you think we're gonna have to go?" she asked him.

He looked up from his knees to answer. "Sniper kill record's over a mile and a half."

"Fuck." She started jogging in pursuit again, Poughkeepsie not far behind. Sour was up ahead, again disappearing into trees, an outcropping that from Jill's vantage sat right at the base of an office building. She charged after him, reaching another fence; Sour was already on the other side, in the parking lot of the business park, crossing to that nearest building, which couldn't have been more than five or eight stories tall. She started to climb, ignoring Poughkeepsie's G-rated exclamation behind her.

Sour stopped at the front entrance of the building, looking up at the floors towering above them. Then, back to the golf course; Jill pictured his imagination taking him all the way back to the Brandtley bonus room, back to those four holes in the ballistic glass, trying to gauge the exact angle from which the shots must have originated.

Sour turned and entered the building. Jill stayed on him, into the lobby, onto an elevator. There were seven floors in total, but Sour somehow knew to depress the **6** button. As the doors slid closed, she could just see Poughkeepsie running in the front entrance, trying to catch them in time.

She followed Sour off the elevator car and onto one of those blank office hallways devoid of color or character, the most simple, boring nameplates on each door, the most exciting thing to ever occur in this corridor a hunt for a restroom with the hope you didn't need a key from one of the businesses to get inside. Sour moved down the line of doors, not reading the names, but trying to calculate the direction to the Brandtley house despite being in a windowless tunnel.

He stopped at the second- or third-to-last door, pounding on the wood as if he had no doubt this was the right place. Before Jill could even reach his side, he had raised a boot and blasted it open in one kick. Jill yanked her Glock from her waist, keeping it pointed floorward, her finger kept cautiously along its barrel, and paused for just a hair-second to read **AIRWAVES CELLULAR TOWERS OF AMERICA, INC.** on the nameplate before stepping in behind Sour.

"Holy shit," Jill whispered as her eyes found Sour kneeling next to a desk. It had been turned on its side, a blanket laid across it with a sniper rifle displayed like a showroom piece. Just beyond this makeshift shooter's nest was a tall file cabinet, also knocked over, also with blanket and rifle atop it. Sour had his eye in the targeting scope of the nearer rifle, looking through it across the width of the room and out the floor-to-ceiling windows. They didn't look like they were meant to be opened, but the pane of glass directly across from the rifles had been removed and set upright against the nearest wall.

"Why so far back from the windows?" she wondered.

"They didn't want to take any chances someone from the parking lot might look up right as the sun was shining up their barrels." Sour forced his aging bones back up from the rifle. "Aimed right into the Brandtley TV room. Go on," he nodded to Jill, "see for yourself."

"Okay," she replied, but then hesitated. She believed Sour, and found the thought of seeing that house through the scope somehow too morbid, too macabre a mere half-hour after standing over the corpses. "You were this good a shot?" she nodded at the long guns.

"I wasn't chosen for my shooting skills. I was chosen for my stalking. For knowing where my prey was going to be and when. For how well I could pick the perfect overwatch looking down on the exact patch of road our quarry was about to walk down."

Jill took a knee, but Poughkeepsie entered before she lowered her eye to the spyglass. "So those make three for three," he said after letting out a long whistle from the door.

"What?" asked Sour.

"Carpinello, Payne, Brandtley," Poughkeepsie counted out on his fingers. "Murder weapons left at all three scenes. Including the mags still half full, and plenty of extra ammo. Hundred bucks says we're gonna find the serials still legible on those guns. But zilch for prints."

"Serial numbers?" Jill asked, rising back to her feet. "So you can tell who they're registered to?"

"They want you to find their guns," Sour stepped away from them, going over all of it in his brain.

Poughkeepsie knew to let Sour do his thing, and shook his head in response to Jill's query. "Every weapon was bought over the internet or at a gun show."

"And the sellers didn't run backgrounds," Sour chimed in, as if he already knew all this.

"So you mean, you *don't* know who owned these guns?" Jill asked.

"But you do know who *sold* the guns." Sour looked up at Poughkeepsie. "What shows they sold them at."

"We do. But they're all dead ends, Clay." He pulled out his cell again as he turned back for the hallway. "I gotta call this in."

In the silence that followed, a realization suddenly smacked Jill right in the head. She moved back for the guns, her brain quickly putting her new theory through its paces. "They're civilians." She looked up at Sour, stepping closer to him, stuttering with excitement. This felt like a lightbulb, a breakthrough to her. "These are M107s. They used these instead of M82s or some other military issue. In the Payne killings, they used Bushmaster AR-15s instead of, of M4s or SCARs. It's all civilian grade hardware, readily available on the open market. These guys, they're fucking--"

"SEALs," Sour cut her off.

"What?"

"Two rifles. No spotter scopes. Only snipers who don't use spotters are SEALs."

Sour walked around her and exited. Jill froze for a moment.

Hearing the bing of the elevator opening again, she ran out after him. "But then why use these shitty--" But the doors were already sliding shut again, both Sour and Poughkeepsie inside. "Fucking assholes!" Jill spit.

FROM HIS COLD, DEAD HANDS

"Let's say you're right, they are SEALs," Jill attempted to continue the conversation twenty-four hours later. They were now back in one of her team's Escalades, driving from the Bisbee Douglas tarmac to the Blunt compound.

Sour hadn't stayed in the Cary business park for more than ten minutes after making his declaration about the Killers, seeing no reason to stick around when the evidence techs descended on that sixth floor room and tore it apart. He walked back through the golf course without a word or even a grunt, all the way to their parked rental, where he finally spoke, telling Jill to get them a hotel. To her, it felt premature to leave the scene, but he assured her with a wry grin that, *"If they find anything we need to see, Park* [Jill assumed he meant Poughkeepsie] *will let us know."* The next morning when she went down for the free breakfast of egg patties and travel size Yoplaits, Sour stood from one of the tables gripping a coffee and a *USA Today*. "We can go home now," he grumbled as he shuffled past her and out the door before she could even fill a paper plate of food.

Sour avoided her questions throughout their journey home, even pretending to sleep through their flight back from North Carolina. But now, in her car, he was a captive audience, and she was going to take full advantage while she had it. "All three of the victims voted for HR-2230 last year," she brainstormed. "That bill closed twenty-five military bases across the country. Maybe these guys were affected by one of those closings, their lives were ruined. All three victims also supported the transgender soldiers bill--"

"No."

"No? What no?"

"The answer isn't in what they did or didn't vote for. It's in their MO."

Jill let that sit for a moment, thinking it through. "The guns. They're leaving the guns behind for a very specific reason."

"I would think so."

"They're trying to send some sort of message."

If Sour knew what that message was, he wasn't going to have the chance to explain it to Jill right at this moment. He suddenly sat up straighter in his seat than she had ever seen him sit, staring out the windshield at the main gates of the Blunt property just a quarter-mile away now. "The hell's this?" he grumbled as they pulled up behind a line of cars snaking around both sides of the Vista park that served as the centerpiece of the Warren neighborhood. The line continued up the hill to the security booth at Blunt's front gates, where a legion of young, tuxedoed valets rushed to help people out of their cars, collecting keys before driving the vehicles away to be parked elsewhere.

"This is called stubbornness," Jill explained as she cranked the wheel left to bypass the queue, lowering her window to hold her staff ID out and win them passage around the valet line and onto the main driveway of the estate.

Jill had first recommended to the Congressman that he cancel this fundraiser almost two months ago, right after the Carpinello murder, and he had just scoffed in her face; he had again outright refused to call it off, this time without even a hint of humor or smile, after the Stephen Payne killing; and he had never even deigned to reply to her email about abandoning it sent thirty-six hours ago as she flew to the bloody Brandtley home in North Carolina. Blunt argued that the greater Bisbee community had come to regard his 'Blunt Barbecues' as a highlight of their hard, hot years, and cancelling one would be simply devastating for the morale of the entire district. More importantly, he didn't want to risk what it would do to his job approval ratings – or what message it would send to the local donors he used these events to butter up and make feel important. So, yes, a man who recently had three colleagues assassinated in their homes, a man whom Sour believed had reason to think he could be next – yes, that man had decided to go ahead and open his house up to hundreds of strangers, to caterers and kids, to blue bloods and bonnet hats, to juggling and target shooting.

As Jill pulled them up next to the front door of the mansion, Sour huffed out, marching through the house, past the hors d'oeuvre servers and the projection screen looping a Blunt commercial, and out to the veritable carnival filling the backyard. Jill spotted Randy and tossed him her keys, then spent the next ten minutes doing the same thing she had done throughout their Carolina excursion: tried to keep up. Sour was past the bandstand, batting aside the helium balloons of the clown, when she caught him. "Worst call this country ever made," she mumbled into the back of his ear, "two year terms for Congress. So they're always campaigning. Always looking for the next baby or ass they can kiss."

Sour ground to an abrupt halt, Jill almost tumbling right into him. Something up ahead had made him stop dead in his tracks.

"Bryce Lafayette?"

"Of course he's here," Jill answered before she even had to see the man. "Congressman Blunt has an A+ from the NRA." She stepped around from behind Sour's considerable shoulders to see Blunt chumming it up with the president of the National Rifle Association, a man as loud as the weapons for which he stood. Their wives, Peggy Ann Blunt and Paula Lafayette, stood dutifully at their sides, sharing their own conversation about their kids and dogs and charitable works. "Blunt and Lafayette have been besties for years, since they were practically kids. Blunt actually beat Lafayette at the NRA steel target national championships when they were teenagers."

"You don't say," Sour growled without taking his eyes off them.

"Blunt even had a nickname: 'The Southpaw Shooter.' Years later, on Lafayette's very first day as Exec VP of the NRA, he took time out of his first press conference to endorse a little-known Arizona state delegate named Homer James Blunt for Congress."

Sour stood and stared. Jill anticipated the line of thought that she assumed was bouncing around his brain, and tried to head his next questions off at the pass: "We can look at the three victims' relationships to the gun lobby. And there's also the NLRC, the National Right to Life Council-- Lafayette's on their advisory board. I do know Helen Brandtley was sponsoring a personhood-- Sour?!"

Sour wasn't listening to her, he was charging forward, right for Blunt, hot breath somehow pumping from his nose even though it was a sweltering desert day. Blunt clocked him when he was about ten yards away, face lighting up in his most expansive politician's smile. "Mr. Manco! I should introduce you to--"

Sour balled the fabric around Blunt's neckline into a fist, yanking the Congressman right into his face. Jill saw the other members of Blunt's detail taking note and converging, and put her hand on Sour's left arm from behind to try to pacify the situation before any of them got close enough to turn this truly ugly. "Hey-hey-hey, c'mon now, deep breaths…" she tried to purr as calmly as possible.

"What the hell do you think you're doing here?" Sour spit into Blunt's face.

"You said I couldn't leave," Blunt reminded him with a smile. "You never said anything about having guests come to me."

Sour caught himself, looking up over Blunt's shoulder to see Randy exiting from the house and eeling his way closer. Then he looked down at Jill's hand on his biceps. He tossed Blunt away for his NRA pal to catch. Blunt was able to laugh it off, turn this potential embarrassment into an indelible campaign moment. "Let's get one thing straight, Sour. These terrorists may kill Homer Blunt. But they will never stop me!" Lafayette patted his friend's shoulder in support of this defiant statement, while everyone within earshot nodded or even added applause.

Sour just headed back for the house, and after reading in her boss's eye contact the silent order to follow him, Jill continued to stay right on his heels.

There was never any doubt that Brenden would be the one to pose as the *Daily Star* photographer. He had attended intel training while Chaser and Tats were at sniper school; he had the smallest build, the least conspicuous stature; but most importantly, he was the photography enthusiast in the triad, the one who already owned some equipment and had used it enough to look legit with it in his hands.

All three of them had their hobbies, their passions, their amateur vocations. Okay, maybe Tatsumi's couldn't be called a passion; more of a sickness. He was that pyro who had never grown up, the kid in chemistry class who mixes all the volatile compounds the teach tells you (to your glee) will cause an explosion; add to that a career as a district champion swimmer, and Tats was easily the fastest planter of limpet mines in their underwater demolition training at BUD/S. Tats just loved blowing shit up, which in Uncle Sam's hands had been crafted into more than just a hobby, but a combat specialty.

Chaser was the computer expert, the gamer, the hacker, the one who grew up blasting out his eardrums with death metal as he dominated all the weaker-willed schmucks who dared cross his path in a multi-player game. If you saw his Junior year yearbook photo, you'd think he was a recurring guest star on *The Big Bang Theory.* But that summer he hit a growth spurt, and when he returned a 6'2" senior, he strutted right across the sacred school seal, an infraction that traditionally got nerds hazed by the football lettermen. (They still tried, and Chaser unfortunately had to end the seasons of the star nose guard and free safety, and with them, the school's dream of a state title.) Chaser always used to joke that he was supposed to be assigned to US Cyber Command, but that a rival gamer he had embarrassed at *Mobile Strike* had hacked into the Navy and switched out his deployment orders after Basic. *"That's why I ended up with you a-holes,"* he would often say. *"Somewhere, someone's laughing his ass off at me."*

Either way, sending the *Daily Star* photog who was assigned to the 'Blunt Barbecue' an email that looked like it was from his editor instructing him not to attend was easy-peasy for Chaser, as was hacking the credential template from the paper's servers and manufacturing a new ID with Brenden's picture on it. All three security guards who had reviewed the badge outside the Blunt compound had bought it, and the valet even believed Brenden when he said press had been given permission to self-park on the property.

Brenden had been at the fundraiser for over an hour by the time Sour and Jill arrived. He knew what he was supposed to take pictures of, but also allowed himself this moment to just *enjoy* the party, to savor being behind a camera again, to relish being out in the open again, something none of them had wanted to risk since they began their first op, on the Carpinello home in Maine. More than anything – the bigger reason than his love of photography for volunteering for this recce – Brenden just loved seeing all the children Blunt had invited, the glee in their eyes as they dug into hotdogs with abandon, their patient joy as flags and fireworks were painted onto their cheeks, their laughter as the clown made a zoo's worth of balloon animals. He hadn't been around kids, hadn't seen kids, since his wife had taken Ty and moved out, and it was a hole in his heart that needed filling.

Brenden had just taken a photo of the last outside security camera when his attention was drawn to one strange man. He must have been one of the body men, one of only five or six men here in full suits – although this guy wore his without a tie. Most concerning, he was staring right at Brenden. Like a deep-into-his-soul, no shame about it stare. It was the oldest of the guards, the one with the craggy face and the salt and pepper hair; Brenden couldn't help but notice him when he had just made a commotion over by Blunt. Somehow, the way he looked at Brenden now, drilling into him with those sad tired eyes, it felt like he was seeing right *into* him, reading his darkest secrets like a book.

Brenden spun ninety, raising his lens to capture yet another jubilant juvenile, a vain attempt to keep his cover.

Then lowering it, he snuck a side-glance back to that guard-- *who was still staring at him.*

Everything in Brenden started screaming, imploring him to get out of there. He turned all the way around and, very subtly and calmly and normally, started walking back for the house.

But he couldn't help throwing one more look over his left shoulder-- *and now that fucking guard was walking too,* following Brenden, not just keeping his distance, but picking up speed, getting closer, fore-checking any obstacles out of the way.

Brenden faced forward as he continued to walk, testing the camera strap around his neck to confirm it was secure.

He took off into a full sprint, blasting a server girl's plate of tiny little quiches aside as he neared the back French doors.

"STOP HIM!" Sour yelled from behind Brenden, ramping up into a full run himself.

Jill was seven or eight paces behind the action, as it always felt like she was, but started running herself when Sour did. "SOUR! WAIT!" She didn't know who Sour was chasing, who he wanted stopped, but she knew her job: when Sour ran, she ran.

Brenden was in the house now. He thought about pulling out the Glock he had in the back of his pants, hidden under his shirt. He wouldn't fire it, wouldn't harm an innocent, but maybe the very sight of it would discourage anyone from trying anything stupid.

But seeing guards on his left and right, he knew pulling his piece might only lead someone inexperienced in combat, in adrenaline, to start firing, to maybe hit him, or worse, someone else.

Someone like the hefty server now approaching with a silver tray, rearing it back like he intended to be the hero today and knock Brenden out with it. Brenden screeched to a stop, dodging the server's swing, then pile driving the front of his skull right into the bridge of Hefty's pudgy, flat nose. Brenden heard a crack as he leaped over the server's plummeting body, not waiting to see the blood pour out of his nostrils, instead charging up the stairs, taking two at a time up to the second level.

Brenden could hear Sour several stairs behind him, heard his breath pumping hard – he could tell he wasn't in the mission shape Brenden was in, knew he wouldn't be able to keep up.

At the top, Brenden got his bearings without slowing, moving for the double doors of the Master, cracking them asunder in one kick, then darting for the attached bathroom in back. He took a three-step run up onto the lip of the Jacuzzi, shielding his face and aiming his shoulder right for the center of the window above the large tub. His momentum shattered him right through the glass, and he landed on the clay tiles of the main entrance alcove's roof. He rolled off, prepared to drop the last story onto the brick driveway, but there was an SUV there, parked just under the sloped roof. The top of the car dented inward as he tomahawked into it; he rolled off, landing on the driveway in a three-point stance.

"Shit!" he heard Sour's voice above him, and as he stood, looked up to that weathered face looking out from the shards of the window. Brenden smiled and Sour scowled, as if that grin pierced right into his heart. Sour turned and disappeared inside, surely on his way down the stairs to keep up the pursuit.

Knowing he had only a few second's lead, Brenden moved behind the giant succulents where he had hid his bike, kicking up gravel as he started it up and got its wheels spinning. He launched off the planter bed and onto the driveway among the darting valets, flying down the drive, underhanding a guard out of his path with his helmet before dropping it over his head.

The wake of exhaust and gravel dust was just settling as Sour careened out of the house. He looked down to the main gate, watching the bike disappear around the guard shack, then down one side of the rectangle of Vista greenery. Sour cursed under his breath--

Then jumped backward as Jill's Escalade reversed at a full 30 miles an hour right into the spot in which he had been standing. Gravel crunched under the car's tires as she slid to a stop. "Get in!" she barked at Sour as she threw open his door. He climbed aboard just before she lurched them down the driveway.

"That way, that way!" Sour pointed to the right and she whipped them up the west side of the Vista, the same way Brenden had just disappeared. She tore them onto Bisbee Road, approaching the roundabout that would send them up to Old Bisbee, back in the direction of the airport in Douglas, or down to the twin Naco towns saddling the border.

"There!" she pointed ahead with her right finger, the car feeling like it would bounce off the other direction without both of her hands firm on the wheel.

She was right: Brenden's helmeted head spun around as he heard the Escalade behind him, as he realized he had been too conservative in his speed. He uprighted his bike as he flew under the Erie Road overpass, heading up into the Mules. Jill pushed the Escalade to its limits as they chugged behind him, wall of rock on their right, gaping maw of the Lavender pit on their left. His seatbelt still not on, Sour braced his right hand against the ceiling and his left on the dash as Jill drag raced them faster and faster.

"Shoot him!" she yelled at Sour as she rushed at Brenden's back tire, hoping to run him right off the road.

Brenden leaned into the bike, picking up just the one or two mph more he needed to keep an inch ahead of them. Knowing he now had no choice, Brenden yanked his pistol out of the back of his pants. *Security is fair game*, he reminded himself. *They know what they're getting into when they take this job. They're well paid, their families well supported if they're KIA-- and they should have been more fucking principled about who they went to work for!* He knew they weren't his words, they were Chaser's rationalizations in his mind, but they were all the excuse he needed right now to aim the gun behind him with one hand and pull the trigger blind-- once-twice-thrice. His hits answered any question about whether the Escalade was reinforced, ringing out not with the crackling of glass or puncturing of rubber, but the welts and whumps of impacts with armored chassis or ballistic glass. He breathed a sigh of relief even as the rest of his body was pumping with stress and adrenaline. *Good. I can't kill them. Or even hurt them. Just slow them down.*

"Fucking shoot him!" Jill screamed again as sparks sprayed up from the tire well just under her. But Sour didn't move, just kept those hands in their brace positions, just kept staring straight ahead. For a second maybe he remembered that his holster was on, for a moment he felt it bouncing up against his ribs again, but by the very next second he had remembered it had been empty since he left Bryan. "Sour--"

"I'm not armed!"

"*What?*" But Jill didn't wait for his answer, just reached down to her waist, extracting her own Glock, then slamming it into his chest. "Now you are!"

Sour didn't allow himself a moment's hesitation. Sour understood that if he sat in that car thinking about that gun in his hand and his pledge and all the reasons he had made that pledge, their chance at catching a Congressional Killer would slip through their fingers. He slammed down on the automatic window button, those few seconds it took to descend almost being enough to suck his resolve right out of him. But when it was down, he was able to marshal the strength to rise up on his feet, leaning his torso out the window, left hand slapping down on top of the roof for balance, right extending with Jill's weapon held aloft.

But Sour didn't pull that trigger. He knew if he had, this would all be over. One shot was all he needed, all he ever needed. One shot, and that motorcycle would be tumbling ass over tea kettle, its rider a splattered mess to be scraped off the shoulder.

"Shoot, Sour!"

But Sour didn't pull the trigger.

And now he was out of time. Brenden had prepped for this surveillance & reconnaissance for three weeks, he already knew what he was supposed to do if chased off the property. And there it was up ahead, his escape hatch, that break between mountains. He curtailed his speed just a hair as he approached it, bouncing his right boot on the pavement as he leaned hard to starboard and turned into the narrow Copper King Canyon.

"Hold on." Jill winced as she slammed her own brakes, twisting the wheel as she did to spin them out across the 80, coming up facing the dry estuary of the canyon. Sour held onto the roof as they bounced into the red dirt, Jill not letting up on the gas, putting the truck into a violent caterpillar dance in their desperate attempt to keep up with the bike. For almost a mile at least, it felt like the chase would take them into the deepest recesses of hell and still never end.

And then Brenden could finally make out the felled telegraph pole up ahead, another remnant from the ravine's mining past, propped between mountains on both sides like a thick, round rodent bridge. *There just might, might, be enough space underneath*, Brenden told himself. He knew it didn't matter, it was the only hope he had, and he leaned hard to the left, lower than he had ever leaned on this bike, head hovering just inches above the Mars dirt as he aimed wheels first for the tiny crevasse under the pole.

Jill saw the bike slide under the pole and slammed her own brakes--

As red dirt kicked up into his face, Sour saw the disaster approaching and dropped back into the cabin of the SUV--

 They smashed into the felled pole at full speed, the hood of the car folding up, their momentum carrying them sideways to also smack their passenger side doors against the bending, but not breaking log.

Inside the Escalade, the force of impact threw Jill forward, right into her steering wheel as it exploded out the other direction, the white fabric of her airbag enveloping her face, knocking her consciousness into black.

Brenden's bike was gone by the time Sour got out of the car, but its engine's roar still echoed off the canyon walls. He looked around at the red Mule rock surrounding their wreckage on both sides, and for a moment allowed himself to once again wish, as he often did, that he lived in a different time, a time when his quarry would be on foot or on horseback, a time when he could have utilized the tracking skills passed down through generations of his tribe, to his father's father, then to his

father, and to Sour himself, a time when he could have just followed the
hoof prints, or blood spotting, or hound the smells on the wind, across
rivers and streams, and mountains and mesas, to catch this guy, or better
yet, find the base of operations for his entire team of murdering bandits.

"What. The. Fuck."

But as Sour heard Jill emerge from the carnage behind him, he was
reminded that he no longer lived in such a time. He had never lived in
such a time. That bike was long gone by now, leaving no trail behind it,
probably even abandoned for some other vehicle already, and soon for
one that spirited their foe away to the heavens, never to be seen again.

"What the fuck was that, Sour?" Jill was now right next to him,
towering over him as he crouched down to examine those bike tracks
galloping off into the distance. "Hey, I'm talking to you. Where's your
fucking Sig Sauer you're so famous for?"

Sour rose up to his full height, but avoided her eyes as he walked
back to the car to get his phone and tell someone they needed to be
picked up.

"*Hey!* Asshole. What if he tried to make a move on the
Congressman? Huh? What if he tried to kill him right then and there in
the middle of the barbecue? You think about that?"

Sour reached in between the side of his seat and the center console to
retrieve the device where it had fallen from out of his pocket. As he
checked its display, he gave her an answer. "He wasn't there to kill him.
Just case the place. To plan." He looked up at Jill, returning the laser
focus of her brown eyes. "Now we know for sure. Blunt's next." He spun
on his back heel, starting the long trek back for the highway. "No signal
out here. Better start walking."

Jill threw up her arms, then slammed them down on her hips. And
then she followed.

Jill was eventually able to get a text via one bar of service out to Randy's
phone, and he had been waiting in another Escalade at the mouth of the

canyon for thirty minutes when Jill and Sour emerged. By the time they pulled in through the main gates of the estate, the sun was waning in the west and most of the guests had cleared out, including, Sour noticed as he returned to the backyard for the PSD team briefing, NRA President Bryce Lafayette.

But there was Blunt in the middle of it all, still consoling his wife and daughters. As Jill began the briefing of her team, Sour didn't hear a word she said, drowned out by the fuming of his own brain. He barged right through the circle of guards and marched over to the Congressman. "You apologizing to them?"

"What?" Blunt replied in confusion. "Manco, what are you--"

"To your family. For knowingly putting them in danger today."

"Excuse me-- I thought *you* were the one being paid to make sure my family was safe--"

"You knew you were the Killers' next target, and you still had this fucking barbecue today."

Blunt's youngest daughter, the one in her awkward years, gasped through her braces. "Daddy? Daddy, what is he talking about?"

The Congressman put a hand on her temple to calm her. "I'll expect an apology, Manco! That, that bastard comes onto my property, invades my home, and you accuse me of--"

"I've had about enough of your performances, Congressman. You can cut the shit with me."

Now it was Peggy Ann Blunt's turn to gasp and grimace. "Homer, who is this man--?"

"Don't worry, ma'am," Sour sneered at her. "You can rest easy at night knowing your husband is everlastingly faithful to you. He may say he's having an affair, but he's just lying about it."

"What?! Homer, do you know what he's talking about?"

"I really don't, Sour."

"Sour." Jill had now broken away from her briefing, crossing the circle to try to goad Sour out of this confrontation.

"Barbara Carpinello was a lesbian," Sour went on unabated. "She was killed with her wife of twenty-four years, and their adopted daughter. You never had an affair with her. That was complete and utter bullshit, so I'd stop asking why you were really hiring me for this." Sour crossed his arms. "Now I don't need to ask. You hired me because you knew sooner or later, you'd be next."

"Sour." Jill now put a hand on Sour's left arm again, but this time, he yanked it free.

"You listen to me, Manco. I swear to holy heaven I have no idea who these maniacs are or what they want--"

"You forget my third ground rule, Congressman? You tell me why. You've been breaking it since day one, and you're still breaking it, right to my face."

"*Sour!*" Jill finally just yelled. "We might have a photo of the guy."

His attack dog focus broken, Sour turned to Jill, to see her holding a large, professional still camera, her hand wrapped around its extended telephoto lens like it was the barrel of a bat. Jill reached back to usher forward a young woman who looked like she couldn't be older than her early 20s, and Sour scanned the badge around her neck, catching the words *Bisbee Observer.* Though he could've kept on Blunt for days, the tracker in him was pulled away at the whiff of a potential scent. "Okay, let's get every camera that was used here today." He raised his voice to Randy and the other guards gathered behind Jill. "No photographer leaves here until we've seen every shot they've taken!"

Alas, they were not destined to taste the delicious irony of catching a man who posed as a newspaper photographer with another newspaper photographer's camera. In four hours, Jill had scrolled through everything on the *Observer* photo drive, as well as the one used by the local guy whom Blunt's staff always hired for events like this one. Sour meanwhile went through all the security camera footage, as well as the raw rushes from the local stations that had sent over news videographers.

"Everyone, *everyone* got him from behind," Jill bellyached as she shut the laptop she had set up on the pool house billiards table. "He knew exactly where the cameras would be, and how to make sure no one ever caught his face."

"This wasn't his first Blunt Barbecue," Sour surmised from the computer he had been moonlighting on. "These guys have been planning each of these killings for months. And Blunt knows why."

Jill didn't want to wade into that argument, throwing back her head with a sigh. "I just work here."

Sour was about to turn back to his borrowed laptop, when crazed jabbering drew his eyes to the main pool house door. Randy was opening it, but holding someone behind him with his other hand. "Hold on, hold on, I'm telling them, hold on. Hey," he turned back into Sour and Jill. "Either of you speak Spanish?"

Before Sour could explain that he did, the jabbering started up again, and he leaned forward on his arms just enough to see a Hispanic middle-aged and mustached gentlemen in the tuxedoed uniform of a valet frothing hysterically behind Randy.

"His phone." Now able to hear the man's words, Sour shot to his feet. "He wants us to check the camera on his phone."

Jill was up too, and beat him to the door. Sour didn't mind, as he knew anyone would be faster than he would at navigating a foreign device. In fact, Jill had thumbed through to the right video on the decrepit flip phone by the time Sour reached her shoulder.

It was shot from outside, in front of the house, in the heat of the afternoon – screams indicating it was also the heat of Sour's chase of the Congressional Killer through the house. Smashing glass suddenly covered the shrieks, and the camera whipped up to the clay roof of the main entrance alcove as shards rained down onto it. Then a body smacked down onto the tiles. It rolled off, onto the roof of a parked security Escalade. The camera followed him as he leapt off the SUV and onto the ground—

"There!" Jill slammed her thumb to pause the image. "Got you, mother fucker."

Indeed, in four hours of hunting and pecking through images both moving and still, it was the first frame they'd found that caught Brenden full on, face forward. But it was also an image taken with the weakest camera they had reviewed all day, his face nothing more than a garbled, melted, pasty mess.

Sour rubbed his chin. "I could ask Poughkeepsie to get that cleaned up. But we'd never see it again."

"No." Jill was already heading for the door, pushing past Randy and the hero valet. "I got a guy."

THE 55TH COMBAT CAMERA

As each of the one hundred twenty photos bloomed to life in his darkroom's chemical bath, Brenden hung them from wooden clothespins on his drying line. He leaned in to stare into the images painted red by the room's work light. The ones of the estate's security measures – its cameras, its windows and doors recently reinforced to gird for attack – he then pulled down and set aside; those, the boys would study ad nauseam over the coming days.

There was another interesting one: one of the locals in a golf shirt chatting it up with Blunt. Brenden hadn't noiced until now the Budweiser, the golden SEAL trident pin, on the local's lapel. He was a SEAL, or had been one at one point in his life. Brenden touched his heart, as if he could feel the tattooed eagle – flintlock, anchor, and three-pronged spear gripped in its talons – through the fabric of his tee.

When all the other photos had been collected, he realized only the children remained on the photo line, the children getting their faces painted or running with balloons. As he stared at each still, his mind transposed *Christina* into each and every shot. Christina was getting her face painted; Christina had a fistful of balloon string wrapped around her fingers to keep a bundle from sailing off into the heavens; Christina had cotton candy on her nose. But when Brenden's gaze moved to a shot of a teenage boy hanging from one of those pins, his mind was suddenly wrenched back to the memory not of Christina--

"You fucking killed my mom."

--but of the Payne boy, Daniel Payne, levelling his smoking shotgun down at Brenden as he lay prone across kitchen tile.

Brenden had been the highest ranked of the three members of his renegade little band, the Lead Petty Officer of their platoon before the head shed put them on what turned out to be permenant shore duty. It had been Brenden that had convinced Chaser and Tats they had to embark on this quest against four useless, lying, windbag politicians, it had been Brenden that had gotten them lathered up and bloodthirsty for revenge, Brenden who had mapped out how they would scout each hit, when they would do them, in what order.

But in the Payne kitchen, just in the way the boy pierced Brenden with those eyes, Daniel Payne had sucked from him any and all inspiration to complete this vengeance.

And now, looking at all these children, Brenden realized the inspiration hadn't returned since that night, since that kitchen. His own boy, his Tyler, was out there somewhere. Sarah Beth didn't know what he and his Teammates were up to, but she knew Brenden well enough to know he was in a dark, dark place. After he punched that hole in their bedroom wall right next to her head, he wasn't surprised she stormed out of the house, dragging Ty by the wrist, and had refused to reply to any of his calls or texts asking where they were ever since. He knew treating him like this, keeping his son from him like this, must be illegal, but he also knew going to a lawyer right now, going to *anyone* outside of the circle right now, would be really fucking stupid.

Besides, he had figured out where she was. An old friend, uninformed of the Baumans' separation, had written Brenden an email that had exposed her: *"Got the invite, Bowz. See you Sunday."* Brenden now knew where they were, or at least what they would be doing this coming weekend. Getting there, getting down on his knees before Sarah Beth and begging for her forgiveness, explaining to Ty he was sorry but now he was back in his life and was never going away again; shouldn't *that* be his mission now?

He had talked the others into this mission. He had led them right to the verge of completing it. And now he could barely even remember why. He remembered the thrill, the rush, the high he got when on an op, when shooting and killing people. Could it just be that they missed *that*? Could it be they had just invented an elaborate excuse to get back into action after it became clear the Navy might never take them off stand-down?

Maybe he could talk Chaser and Tats into ending it now. But how would he even begin?

"Can't believe there's still someone who wastes his time with this shit," he heard Chaser chuckle behind him. How had he not even heard Chase come in? Was he that lost in his own thoughts, that lost in these perfect, beautiful, cherubic faces? At least Chaser knew to make sure the mudroom light was extinguished before breaking the seal of the garage door. He had learned that one the hard way, ruining some of the shots Brenden had taken after posing as a gas company employee and convincing Barbara Carpinello he needed to update her meter.

Brenden loved the meticulousness of the darkroom arts, the care that had to be paid until the images finally rewarded you by fading into existence. He had stuck with real, tangible rolls of film even when technology had passed them by, and even though he hadn't even been introduced to them by choice – his mom had bought him his first camera from the Salvation Army nearest their house without even realizing how outdated it was. She probably thought Brenden would tinker with it for a week before tossing it in his closet; she didn't realize film would become one of his obsessions, one of his passions.

As Chase stepped up next to him, Brenden let out a whisper. "They saw me."

"Huh?"

"They saw my face." Maybe this was the way: play up that everything was unraveling, that it was all falling apart, that they were on the verge of getting caught. Maybe that was the way he could talk them out of what they were doing.

But he had forgotten that Chase had seen his closed eyes in Payne's kitchen, and probably even noticed his finger off his trigger in surrender. "You know," Chase spit back at him, "I've about had it with you forgetting why we're fighting this war."

Brenden turned to stare back into Chase's demonically crimson pupils. He could smell his hot Wild Turkey breath; they had each eased whatever reservations they had with what they were doing in their own ways: Chase with cyclical benders, Tats with unending swims (he was probably on one as they spoke), Brenden with good ol' fashioned stress and depression, like his mama had taught him.

"You think I'm so blind I haven't noticed what you've been like lately?" Chase continued his rant. "It's too late, Bowser. The die has been fucking cast. Eleven times over. Don't forget why we're doing this. Don't forget--"

But Chase didn't get out that last word before Brenden's hand was around his throat, his thumb in his Adam's apple. He slammed Chase's skull back against the stone wall of the garage.

Brenden didn't need to hear the last word of his sentence. He knew the word, the *name*, Chase was going to utter next. "Don't you ever say that ever again. You understand me? I will *never* forget her. *Ever.*" He bounced Chase's cranium another time to emphasize the seriousness of this. "We clear?"

Chase didn't answer, but his eyes did. They weren't just full of tears, they were full of fear. Brenden had established control again.

He released Chase, to collapse onto his hands and knees in a coughing fit. Brenden calmly picked up his tongs and dipped the next photo paper in chemical. No, he wouldn't talk the others out of one more attack. And when the anger was pumping in his veins again, the elation of hate of violence, Brenden had realized Chase was right. The die *had* been cast, irrevocably cast.

As they mounted the stairs up to the second floor of the Motel 6 repurposed as affordable apartments, Sour sniffed at the atmosphere. "How do you know this guy?"

"Rangers," Jill answered, reaching the top of the stairs and knocking on the nearest door. "What?" she barked back at his stare. "They didn't have pothead Rangers in the '80s?"

"The '90s. The *late* '90s."

Before she could retort, the door ripped open in a puff of smoke. A tall, rail-thin, ghost-white apparition emerged through the mist as if he had just been introduced onto a Vegas stage. With his hair unwashed into stringy dreads and giant night-vision goggles strapped across his eyes, he struck Sour as some sort of space alien that had chosen Jamaica as his first stop on Earth. "Jilly Creete? Hol-ee shee-it!" He lifted the goggles to his scalp to reveal his bloodened eyes, then grabbed Jill's right shoulder, pulling her into a hug. "Talk about someone I didn't expect to show up on my doorstep!"

"Doesn't smell like you're still with your girlfriend, Java."

"Ah man, she kicked my ass to the curb two years ago."

Sour cleared his throat, less because of any clock they were on, but more the searing angle of the midday sun beating down on their unshaded perch before Java's door.

"Java, Sour. Sour, Java."

"Sour! Cool name, bro." He reached a hand from out of the mist, but Sour didn't take it.

"You said if I was ever in a bind, Jav…" Jill explained.

Java stepped aside with a grand sweep of his arm, welcoming them into his very humble abode. "Shit yes, of course. Tell Java everything."

Within minutes, they were seated before his work desk, his numerous computer monitors glowing off their cheeks as he hunted for USB access on the bottom of the valet's obsolete flip phone. Sour blinked to keep his eyes from watering and swallowed to try to fight down the coughing fit he was sure the smoky ambience would eventually inspire. When thumbnails of the media content of the phone finally populated one of his screens, Jill leaned forward, fingering the frozen square of video from Brenden's escape. "That one. We need the clearest shot you can get us of the guy in this video."

The video expanded to fill the full monitor and Java let it play out in slo-mo, the glass raining down onto the roof given an almost snow-like sparkle, the screams of the party-goers warped like they were screening a horror film underwater.

And then, Brenden's feet appeared at the top of the screen, descending into frame at a snail's pace – his knees, his thighs… "Stay on target," Java droned nasally, "stay on target!" Jill recognized the quote from the attack on the Death Star, the original Death Star, not the second or third rip-off versions. Java let it roll through Brenden's landing onto the SUV, then the driveway. He slammed a key, suspending Brenden's image only an imperceptible frame or two off from where Jill had frozen it on the phone itself the night before. "Domino mother fuckers!" he quoted another film, this time *Boyz N the Hood*, though Sour would miss this and every other cinematic reference Java would make that night. Sour noticed his keyboard looked like any other computer's, except many of the keys had colored squares glued on top of them to indicate their functions specific to video editing. Java hit one key, then double-tapped another, rewinding and advancing the frames back and forth until he was sure he had the best one, the one on which he wanted to work his surgery. Playing those colored keys like a master pianist, he zoomed way in on Brenden's face, then slammed one more key, sitting back as the gunman's blurred face filled with new pixels that would soon bring more clarity to his features. "You just give Uncle Sam's little bitch here a couple minutes to work her magic," he added, giving one of the humming drives under the desk a little love pat.

"Uncle Sam?" Sour confirmed.

"Bet yo ass, Homes. John Q. Taxpayer bought me all this shit. Why you think I signed up for the 55th Combat Camera? Most Rangers get an M4, I got an Avid."

The truth was, PFC Javier Micelli wasn't authorized to have this editing system in his home residence, but his Lieutenant had come to trust Java's instincts as both a filmmaker and editor so much, he didn't bat an eye when the boy said he needed to take a system home to stay 'in shape.' It was the mission of the 55th Signal Company (as they were officially known) to utilize the very latest in cameras, sound equipment, editing software, the whole nine, to provide state of the art, on-the-battlefield documentation wherever the Army went. It was on such a mission that Java had met Jill, and recorded her side of the events that led to her discharge. Java had thought her fate a grave injustice; he tried to have his film entered into the official record of the incident, but it quickly became clear how important it was to certain higher ups that the narrative of a female CO botching a hostile engagement not be challenged. Ravaged with guilt, it was then that Java had promised Jill he would lend her a hand whenever she might need it in the future.

"Say hello to your little friend," he laughed, giving the *Scarface* line the appropriate splashes of both Cuban and Pacino accents. Brenden stared back at them, his close-cropped brown hair, piercing blue eyes, his lightly-pocked cheeks from a rough adolescence, now all clearer and easier to discern than at any point of their chase.

Sour stood, tapping on Brenden's 1080p face with his finger. "Can you print this?"

"How soon you think the plane can get up here to Phoenix?" Sour had asked as they returned to their car in Java's parking lot. It was only after Jill had made the call and confirmed it could be on the Sky Harbor tarmac in under an hour that he warned, "I don't know who's expecting you at home, but you might want to let them know we're gonna be a couple days."

Jill was growing tired of Sour's need-to-know approach, which he of course continued when they boarded the Cessna, heading straight up to the cockpit himself to ask the pilots to get them to one of the airports in the greater DC area as quickly as possible. And he did it again upon their sunrise arrival, ignoring Jill's questions about where they were going until she was behind the wheel of their rental and Sour instructed her to head for the J. Edgar Hoover Building.

Jill guessed they were there to see Poughkeepsie, but it was the principle of the way she was being treated that rankled her the most, and with only a couple hours of sleep during the night flight under her belt, her impatience started to crack through her usually steely façade as they made their way across a floor of agent cubicles, nearly all empty for the weekend. "Hey," she barked from a couple paces behind him. "You mind telling me our objective here, before we just waltz into Poughkeepsie's office? Huh? Sour! I'm talking to you."

He entered Parker's office before he had to answer, and Jill stepped in right behind him. Like most of the floor, it lay vacant at just before 0800 local, and realizing Sour wasn't planning to answer any time soon, Jill stepped to the window to stare out upon its spectacular views of the National Mall. "This isn't something we could have done over FaceTime?"

"Yeah, Sour," she heard Parker Poughkeepsie groan from his door, "You know how many people I have to lie to, to escape to Washington on the Sabbath?" Jill moved out from behind Parker's desk as he brought a steaming mug of coffee around the other side and took his seat. "Couldn't we have done this over FaceTime?"

"What the hell's FaceTime?" Sour answered.

Jill snorted. "Don't you have a teenage daughter?"

Poughkeepsie stared daggers into her, for what reason Jill didn't know, then loudly emphasized, "*Never mind*."

"One of them was at Blunt's home yesterday," Sour moved on.

"Okay. What? Who? One of who?"

"The Congressional Killers."

"What?" Poughkeepsie rolled his chair forward, raising an open palm and planting his elbow into the desk. "Hold up. At Blunt's house--"

"He was holding a fundraiser."

"Yesterday? That lunatic held a fundraiser at his house *yesterday?*"

"Friday," Jill corrected.

"He's still a lunatic."

Sour held up a manila envelope that until this moment Jill had been too tired to even realize he was carrying. "We got photos of the guy."

"Wait," Jill panicked. "Sour-- we weren't supposed to share those--"

"You haven't known this man for very long, Ms. Creete," Poughkeepsie said. "He's not here to share them. He's here for his favorite pastime: gloating right in my face."

"Actually, I'm here to give you everything we've got," Sour smiled. Poughkeepsie reached thumb and forefinger for the envelope, but just as he laid flesh on it, Sour ripped it back. "*In exchange*-- for the list of gun shows and internet sites all the murder weapons have been purchased at."

Jill opened her mouth to continue her protest, then caught herself, trying to think through Sour's plan here.

"I told you we already wrung out those rags." Poughkeepsie crossed his arms over his chest. "But sure. Fine."

"And one other thing." Sour held the envelope aloft again. "I want confirmation we're right, that this is actually one of them."

"Okay. And just how the heck do you propose to get that?"

The FBI had given Emily Payne the choice of where to live. Or at least, they had let her believe she was getting to choose. As luck would have it, her first choice was her northeast Ohio second cousins, who lived off a road in such rural Amish Country, it had never even been Google Earthed. The house afforded with its wide-open view out onto miles of rolling hills and a road traversed mainly by horse-drawn buggies the secureness necessary to protect her. The Congressional Killers had taken out Barbara Carpinello's daughter, they had murdered Emily's brother Daniel, they had even shot down the Brandtley *dog*, so the Bureau had to assume the Killers wouldn't rest until they had finished the Payne hit with little nine-year-old Emily. And besides, she was the only one who had seen the three Congressional Killers face-to-face.

Sour was impressed with the strength she exuded when her lawyer showed her into her Uncle Art's dining room. (Art was really a *cousin* of her mother's, but Emily and Daniel had always called him Uncle because of his advanced age.) Sour and Jill waited across the polished wood table previously used only for birthdays, Thanksgivings and Christmases. "Now, Emily, if you don't feel up to this..." her lawyer prefaced before he pulled out her chair for her.

"No, I want to do this. I want to help." Sour was glad she had rebuffed him; he knew this jackass wasn't *her* lawyer, just a stiff suit whose law firm of Aldermen & Rich Guys (as Sour had always referred to high-profile DC firm Alterman & Richbourg) had selected to be present because he was the only lawyer who had ever had any interaction with the family. Sour knew he had only represented Payne in campaign finance disputes and a sexual harassment charge; he had never even met Emily before today.

As Emily took her seat, Jill opened the manila envelope and pulled out the 8x10 glossy blow up of Brenden that Java had printed for them. She wasn't sure why Sour had handed it to her when they walked in, until she noticed him looking behind her to the small video camera stationed in the corner behind them, one of Poughkeepsie's requirements for arranging this meeting. Sour rose up and lifted his chair under him to move it to the right just an inch or two – an inch or two right into the camera's line of sight, blocking it from their lone photo of the Killer. Jill could've sworn she heard some sort of angry impact, some Disney version of a blue streak being sworn, from back in the kitchen where Poughkeepsie had set up his monitor, but she stifled any grin from popping out. Poughkeepsie had joined them in Blunt's plane on its flight to Holmes County Airport not because he wanted to, but because with such short notice they weren't going to get permission to land more than one plane there in the next twenty-four hours; Holmes County had only one runway, after all. But Sour wasn't going to let his old colleague see even a corner of their photo until they had gotten their complete half of the bargain, the confirmation they needed out of Emily.

"Emily?" Jill prodded after Emily had stared at that photo of Brenden for a minute or two, at least. "Do you recognize this man? Was he one of the men that came into your home, Emily?"

Another minute passed. Jill thought perhaps it was because the girl just wanted to make doubly and trebly sure this was the guy before fingering him. *Smart girl,* she murmured in her mind; even at her young age, she was aware what her IDing this guy would do to his life (assuming they could find him) and wasn't letting any hunger for vengeance push her to hastiness or carelessness.

"No," the girl finally answered, pushing the photo back to Sour and Jill's side of the table. "I've never seen him before."

Sour stared back at Emily. Jill's reaction was bigger, words stuttering out of her mouth. The way he had acted in the house when they had noticed him, his elaborate escape, *I mean, the guy pulled a fucking nine on us and opened fucking fire--* he had to be one of them. "But-- Emily, are you sure…?"

The A&R lawyer was already standing. "You heard her," he barked as he pulled Emily's chair back. "I'm sorry she can't help you."

Jill was confused, but knew there was nothing they could do. She wasn't about to interrogate a girl who had watched her family's slaughter less than a month earlier. She stood too. "We very much appreciate your time, Emily. If you think of anything else that might help us--"

"I can protect this man, Emily." Everyone froze and looked down at the table, where Sour was the only one who hadn't yet risen.

"Sour--" Jill said, putting her hand on the back of his chair.

"That's what you're worried about, isn't it?" Sour looked up from the photo, bringing his eyes right into Emily's. "What's going to happen to this man?"

No one missed the in-take of hard, fast air sucked into the deepest recesses of Emily's gut; much more than a gasp, it was a full-body shock. She lowered back down into her chair, without moving her stunned, tearing eyes off Sour's.

"I have a daughter too, Emily. I know how confusing grownups can be sometimes."

Jill noticed this tone she had never heard before in Sour's voice; this was the tone he used with his daughter; this was his nurturing, fathering voice.

Emily brought her hand to her cheeks, realizing there were flowing tears there that needed to be wiped away. She tried to hide her churning emotions with a joke, a smile. "Sometimes?"

"I just want to talk to this man, Emily. Ask him why he's doing these things. Hurting all these people. Like your family. He *did* hurt your family, Emily. Didn't he?"

Emily rocked her fists down into the surface of the table, the tears now just sobbing out. "No! He's the good one!"

Sour put a forefinger on the photo, and pushed it towards her again. "So he *is* one of them, Emily?"

Emily for the first time looked to her lawyer for a bail out. "I, I didn't say that, I'm so tired, I'm confused, forget what I--"

"If I don't get to him first, Emily, these men all around you, these men with guns, they're going to *kill* this man."

The lawyer's nostrils flared and he grabbed Emily by the arm. "Listen, pal, I don't appreciate the way you're treating this poor girl! C'mon, Emily, you're done here--"

Emily slammed down her open palms as she stood, making an even louder impact than her fists had moments before. "You can't let anyone hurt him! He's the one who saved me!"

For another moment, no one moved, just letting the revelation settle. *The guy was in Emily's house for ten minutes and whatever he did, he gives her a fucking ten minute case of Stockholm Syndrome,* Jill thought. She was impressed with Sour's performance, drawing this out of the girl's deepest emotional wells so quickly.

But when he reached forward and patted Emily's hands with his own, she realized that maybe it wasn't performance at all.

"I won't, Emily," Sour whispered. "I promise."

Sour and Jill met Poughkeepsie in the kitchen, where in spite of Sour's cockblocking his camera, he kept his part of their bargain, handing over his own manila envelope. "Gun shows and vendor names for every murder weapon," he explained as Sour accepted it between two fingers. The FBI agent then opened his own palm, like a kid waiting for a hand out at See's.

Sour laid the black cylinder of a zip drive in Poughkeepsie's hand. "What the heck is this?" the g-man demanded.

"Every photo and video taken at the fundraiser," Sour answered with a grin.

"Hey. You gave your word--"

"And I kept it. He's in there. I promise."

"This is gonna take us hours."

"You better get started then." Sour moved past Poughkeepsie, headed for the front door, and Jill was practiced enough by now to stay in step with him as he walked out.

"I better find him in here!" Poughkeepsie's voice thundered off the linoleum behind them. "I don't find him and I will arrest you for obstruction! You hear me, Manco? Hey, wait--" he realized as Sour was pulling open the front door. "Where do you think you're going? Aren't you my ride?"

Sour shrugged. "We're headed back to Arizona, actually."

Sour stepped out first, so Poughkeepsie aimed his attack at Jill. "You tell your cute little assistant here where your nickname came from, Clay? Huh, Miss? He tell you it's because all he cares about is sour mash?"

Jill closed the front door, shielding the surrounding properties from his rant, then rushed to catch up to Sour at their sedan. "I hope you know what you're doing. When he does find that photo, he'll plaster it all over the networks."

"It's Sunday, right?" Sour asked as he sat down in the car, ripping open Poughkeepsie's gift.

"Yeah?"

"Then we've got no more than four or five hours to find the gun shows these sellers are at this weekend."

CROSSROADS OF THE WEST

It was just after Noon in Ohio when Sour and Jill started perusing the list of gun vendors the Congressional Killers had used, and not even ten minutes later that they realized all the guns had been purchased within the state of Nevada at gun shows managed by Crossroads of the West, a small family-owned company that organized multiple shows each weekend across California, Utah, Nevada and Arizona. That made it after 11 AM Pacific time when the Blunt Cessna took off from Holmes County, and already nearly 4 PM when it touched down in Reno. Sour and Jill had confirmed in the air that one of the sellers the Killers had frequented would indeed have a table at the Crossroads of the West show that weekend in the Reno Convention Center, but that gave them barely two hours to find his table before the show closed and they were forced to wait another week for him to pop up – assuming he would even choose to sell at another show the very next week. (He didn't have a storefront, or he would have been required to run background checks of the Killers and every other person who bought from him; just operating small tables at shows, he was able to legally present himself as a gun collector just looking to make trades with other enthusiasts, and thus exempt from any background check rigmarole.)

Strolling between the tables on the Convention Center floor brought Jill back to childhood weekends with her father. The elder Creete had a walk-in closet off his den, and its walls displayed an impressive collection ranging from a vintage Nazi Luger to the latest model Israeli Uzi. Jill remembered sneaking in there before he had deemed her ready, looking up at all the guns with wonder, even daring to reach out and touch one or two. Two years later, when she turned 13, she had to act surprised and honored to be let in, when in actuality she had already

memorized every piece over several covert visits. She credited that
collection as a first inspiration for her future career.

But it had been years since Jill had attended a show with her father.
On this visit, she noticed things she hadn't in the '90s: an undercurrent of
violence; rage in every passing conversation; distrust of anyone who
wouldn't spend their weekend at a fine gathering such as this one.
Among the expected stars & bars and Don't Tread on Mes for sale were
also tucked swastika banners or images of President Salas with 'Wet
Back in Chief' splashed in red across his chest; every conversation she
overheard was about how secret forces were rumored to have been
planning a mass revolt in retaliation of the President rigging the election,
or how the militia that had recently met its bloody demise in Michigan's
Huron National Forest had been a false flag operation; and for every two
or three tables of pistols and assault rifles, there were also sales stations
devoted to Prepper literature, to handbooks and video tutorials outlining
the steps every American should be taking to prepare for the inevitable
socio-economic collapse that would soon befall the country.

"Can I buy you one of these?" Sour's voice broke her reverie, and
she followed his point to a shotgun painted hot pink.

"You better buy a Kevlar ass-pad then, Sour, 'cause I can tell you
what I'm gonna be aiming at first." Sour grinned at her – perhaps a first
– before moving on, continuing to scan the laminated display cards
identifying each vendor. Jill stayed a step or two behind him as she
talked. "You know why Americans don't go to church anymore? This is
our religion now. This is so much more real than religion ever was. This
is the only thing no one's been able to take away from us. Our jobs have
been taken, our opportunities have been taken, all by the intellectuals
running our inner cities – those same elites who want to take all this
away next. This right here, events like this every Sunday across the
country, these are our last stand, our OK Corral, our last bastion of
identity – and the people here won't let anyone take this away, unless it's
over their dead bodies."

But Sour was in his own meditation by now. He was no longer
walking through the Reno Convention Center, but was now back at the

Post Oak Mall in College Station, approaching that escalator again, the one Eddie had descended. That was his name, Abby's boyfriend. Abby and Eddie, everyone had gotten a kick out of that, or so Sour had been told, like they were a fucking '50s rom-com sitcom.

He had only seen Eddie once, in the morgue after that security guard had taken off his jaw. But now, he was seeing Eddies everywhere. Eddie had bought his gun at a show just like this one. There weren't just camo caps and cowboy hats here, good ol' boys, hunters and military enthusiasts, there was a new, younger generation of pimpled, Homecoming-dance rejects with purpled hair or sloppy tat sleeves. They now seemed to outnumber the sportsmen, the soldiers, even the conspiracy theorizing rednecks. Short and skinny Eddies, tall and fat Eddies. So many fucking Eddies, looking for the gun or eight they would use to show their classmates how fucking legendary they were. There's a fucking Eddie posing with an AR-15 for his buddy to take his iPhone photo like he's holding a ten-pound trout. There's three fucking Eddies showing off their 3-D printer, bragging to a potential customer that a young woman recently snuck a plastic, 3-D printed pistol into the Supreme Court and nearly assassinated the Chief Justice.

"Sour." Now it was Jill's turn to get Sour's attention. She had broken away from him, three or four tables up. She nodded down to the card on the table's right corner: **SAVAGE FIREARMS, Carson City, NV.**

The friendly, mustached man who looked to be in his 30s was closing a deal on a Beretta as Sour stepped up next to Jill. Sour knew it would be best to ease into things, and picked up the nearest gun, not even mindful of make or model, squinting to look down its sightline. Jill backed away, pretending to peruse the table across from it; they had agreed in advance to not make Savage nervous by ganging up on him, that Sour would take the lead, and though Jill's instincts were now questioning this course of action after noticing the older man's space out, she decided to let him ride it out… at least for now.

"Good news is," the man that Sour assumed to be Jason Savage smiled as he walked over, "that one's only had one previous owner." He leaned across the fold-out banquet table with a whispering grin. "If I could afford to be choosy, though, I wouldn't touch Hi-Point with a ten-foot pole." He chuckled, giving Sour some space, turning back to the two young blonde girls in matching pigtails, engrossed in some cartoon on an iPad. "Darcy and Carrie Ann, homework time."

"You got any Sigs?" Sour asked as he set down the Hi-Point.

Savage turned back with a smile. "You know what to ask for. The Beemer of handguns." He took a step to his right, then returned with a P320, much stubbier than the P220 Sour had left back home in Bryan.

When Sour took it from Savage, an old, comfortable chill ran through his body. *There's that weight. The weight of the damage to human life it's designed to inflict.* Sour knew without even asking that this was a 9MM weapon, not the .45 caliber he preferred. He could just *feel* that sort of detail when he lifted a gun.

"You also can never go wrong with the Glock," Savage continued, always selling, bringing a Glock over. "It's not the Beemer, but it's the Toyota. Never break down on you."

Sour didn't take it, but kept the P320 laid across his two hands. "And I can just walk out with this right now?"

"You look like a guy who's licensed to conceal carry?"

"You're very perceptive."

"You buy that gun, it's in your pocket a minute from now.

"See, this is just a hobby of mine," Savage smiled, and Sour could have sworn he even winked. "Something I like to do for friends, fellow collectors. So I don't have to bother anyone with things like backgrounds or waiting periods."

"That what you told this guy?" By now, Sour had put down the Sig and pulled out the manila envelope, the same one he had carted from Arizona to Ohio and back to Nevada. He opened it, laying the Brenden blow-up on the table.

Savage's entire demeanor changed, like the smile had been wiped off his face with sandpaper. "I've never seen him before in my life."

"You haven't even looked at it."

"I've already been through this with--"

"Look," Sour smiled, setting his hands down between two guns and leaning across the table. "I just want to handle this as quickly and as painlessly as possible. Unfortunately, you stepped in some pretty serious shit here. I want to help you scrape it off, so you don't track it all over the rest of your life." Sour let his eyes dance over Savage's left shoulder, to his daughters. The gun seller caught this and tensed every muscle in his frame. "The gentleman in this photo has used some weapons purchased from you in eleven murders, including three members of the United States Congress."

"And I. Don't. Remember. Him."

"How can you say that if you're not even looking?"

"I was looking for that badge you're not showing me. This conversation's over." Savage turned to admonish his daughters for not obeying him, for not getting into their homework, no matter how few minutes their Pixar movie might have left in its running time.

Sour licked his top teeth under his pursed lips. Cutting his losses, he turned and walked away, out of the convention center. Watching him disappear into the bright, descending sun out of the cargo doors that had been opened so sellers could start hauling out their wares, Jill considered taking a run at Savage herself, but decided to catch back up with the man she had been told to stick to like glue.

"Sour-- wait. You're just gonna walk away?"

"No, that's not all I'm gonna do."

"Okay, then what else? We only have--"

"We're gonna wait."

Brenden stayed near the back during the Baptism; the last thing he wanted to do was upset Sarah Beth or make the ceremony about him. As he watched his son's head go under, his eyes moved to his wife's, slowly dripping pearls down onto her cheeks. Brenden caught a gasp in his throat; he realized he hadn't seen her happy in so long. And he was happy too, that she had finally gone through with it. She had wanted to

get both Ty and Christina baptized since they were born, but Brenden
had been the holdout, always skeptical of organized religion. This bone
had become even more contentious after Christina was gone, and Sarah
Beth was filled with terror that their daughter wouldn't be getting into
Heaven because they had never done it. Brenden tried to convince her
there was no way a sweet little angel of perfection like Christina, who
never hurt anyone or anything in her life, wouldn't get into Heaven, but
Sarah Beth's ability to listen to reason had by that time been demolished
beyond repair.

But watching Ty's baptism on this Sunday, Brenden found he wasn't
filled with any sort of bitterness that Sarah Beth had now gone through
with it without his permission. Brenden knew it made her happy. And he
was also comforted that, if their final op resulted in failure or tragedy,
the church might provide a place of solace for his wife, of structure for
his son.

Brenden exited the church early so he could get back in his Explorer
and wait for the guests to spew from the church, then follow the
procession to the after-party. He was soon parking down the street from
a familiar house, the two-story English Tudor that Sarah Beth had grown
up in, still owned by his parents-in-law. Brenden knew how aggravating
SB found her parents after even just a long weekend with them – that's
why she had moved down to San Diego with a couple girlfriends right
after high school. That's where Brenden had met her, in a bar in Old
Town, where he was celebrating his completion of BUD/S. He doubted
Sarah Beth could stand staying with her parents, but wasn't surprised she
had returned the kids to the Riverside area so she would at least have
help nearby when she needed it. And the large, two-story house they had
bought for peanuts in the '70s – back when young couples like Brenden
and Sarah Beth could afford houses that size in Southern California –
was perfect for this sort of celebratory gathering.

Brenden came in with caution, making sure to keep his distance not
only from Sarah Beth, but her mother or father, and even Myra, the
Guatemalan housekeeper they had employed for over two decades now.
He wanted to approach Sarah Beth at just the right time and place, so she

had a moment to catch her breath and process that he was there, and wouldn't explode on him. He desperately wanted to avoid any embarrassment for her in front of all her friends and members of her parents' church.

It wasn't until after 4 or 5 that he saw his opening, Sarah Beth carrying Ty over to the buffet table to fill a plate of food they would share. Brenden didn't know why his son needed to be carried; he had noticed the boy being clingy all afternoon; that didn't used to be like him. But when Ty saw Brenden, he screamed, "Daddy!" and leapt from his mother's arms, running to embrace his father. Brenden fought back tears, knowing he would need his composure to convince Sarah Beth to let him stay.

"Bren. I didn't know you were…" she trailed off.

"I know. But I couldn't miss… I want you to know, I'm so happy you did this."

"I'm glad. You should probably go now."

Brenden could feel the rest of the party hushing up on all sides of them. "Please. I-- I need you guys right now."

"Brenden. Just go." It was strange to hear Sarah Beth use his first name, even though they had been married over a decade. She had met him out amongst his platoonmates, and had adopted their name for him, Bowser.

"You heard her, Brenden." That was her father Joe approaching, placing the hand not holding a plate of food on the small of his daughter's back for support. "You guys will have more opportunities to talk. But today isn't--"

"*Please.*" Brenden wasn't giving into the crying, he wouldn't let it crack his voice or affect his breathing, but he could feel the tears pouring down his face. "I'm lost without you guys. You have no idea-- Please, SB, whatever you do, you can't take the rest of my family away from me."

"I'm sorry, Brenden." There it was again. Sarah Beth was holding her ground, even though her own cheeks were by now also drenched.

Brenden nodded, setting down Ty. His son screamed, but his grandfather put down his plate to pull him back from his dad. Brenden turned and walked out, and returned to his Explorer.

And returned to the mission. Now it was all he had left.

The Crossroads of the West show had been closed for over an hour, the Convention Center parking lot emptied of all the sedans, trucks and SUVs of its customers, populated only with the vans and trailers which sellers refilled with the wares they had failed to sell. Jason Savage's small table was one of the fastest to empty, and he had almost returned everything from his rolling cart to his trailer when both his twin daughters sprinted up to him with real terror in their eyes.

"Daddy, Daddy!" one cried.

"What's wrong, girls?"

"You're gonna lose your job?" the other chimed in.

"What?" Jason chuckled. "Of course not. Where'd you hear that?" But when Jason turned back to his open trailer, it all made sense. Just inside stood that man who had harassed him an hour or two before, that man who had tried to show him a photo of one of the alleged Congressional Killers. "Hey, what the hell you think you're doing?" Jason exclaimed. "That's trespass--"

"You move a lot of product, don't you, Jason?" Sour whistled as he admired the boxes and boxes of artillery, ammo and accessories locked up behind grates and padlocks covering every inch of the walk-in trailer. "That is your name, right? Jason Savage?" Sour smiled as he stepped down out of the trailer. "I want to make sure I get it right when I tell the ATF how many guns you're actually moving without a Federal Firearms License."

Jason stepped right up into Sour's smug face. "I don't know who the hell you think you are, but you stay away from my daughters, you understand me?"

The click of a camera whipped Jason's eyes over to Sour's right hand, aiming his phone into the back of the trailer. Sour brought the device down between both hands and started thumbing something into its keypad. "You think you could hold your horses for a second while I text this photo to my ATF buddy? I'm not used to these things, I gotta concentrate."

"Is that some sort of threat? You realize how many friends I'm surrounded by right now, mother fucker?"

The girls gasped in unison. But Sour didn't look up, just kept typing. So Jason reached forward to take the phone out of his hand--

Sour grabbed that hand before he could get it anywhere near the phone. He ripped it behind Jason's back, so hard and fast he thought he felt his arm popping right out of the socket. Sour slammed him down on top of his clean-up cart, knocking a couple items to the ground with a violent rattle.

"No! Don't hurt our Daddy!" the girls wailed.

"Go around to the front of the car, girls. Daddy's got this under control. Just give us a minute to talk business."

But the girls didn't move. "You heard your daddy, girls," Sour added. "Run along." He gave Jason's arm an extra thrust of force, enough to make the seller yelp out in agony. "Or he'll always remember it was your fault I broke his arm."

The girls darted away, whirling dervishes of tears, probably to try to find someone to help, Sour realized. But it didn't matter. It would be too late. He would only be here a minute or two more. He reached around over the top of Jason's head, poking fingers in each of his nostrils, yanking his whole skull back like a hog. He leaned forward into his ear, whispering, "I don't give a shit what you did or didn't tell the FBI. I can do things to you they can't. And for the record" – he yanked back even harder, making Jason squeal like the sow he was emulating – "*that* was a threat."

"Okay, okay! He bought two ARs and three pistols off me! All cash!"

Sour released Jason, kicking the cart out from under him as he did, so that he fell onto his hands and knees on the asphalt, concrete gravel embedding into the soft skin of his palms. "Tell me everything you know about him."

"I don't know anything! He was just a nice, friendly guy. Look, I've only met him twice, at two shows. Vegas and--"

"Barstow. He's so friendly, and you never asked his name?"

Jason sighed, reaching for a satchel on the lower rack of the cart. He used the top rack to pull himself to his feet, then opened up the laptop from the satchel on top of the detritus still littering it. After calling up a spreadsheet on his screen, he dug for a pen and pad of paper, and scribbled something down for Sour. "I don't know his name. But he wanted to be on my mailing list, so he knew whenever I was going to be at a show."

Jill checked her watch for the eighth time, then opened her door, just as Sour was also opening his to get back in the vehicle. "Long piss," she commented.

Sour held out a small piece of notepad paper between two fingers. Jill took it and read the scribble on one side:

Chris512@yahoo.com

SOME TEN MINUTE MEETING

The BLAM was followed by a ping, like the final cymbal crash of a drum routine. The pistol's echo off the Mules had woken Sour, and as he lay there staring at the poolhouse ceiling, each shot was followed by the satisfying tinkle of connection with a steel target, a ting almost matching the sounds of those old cans young Blancocito would blast off fence posts and boulders with his six-shooter.

"You think you're some kinda gunfighter, don't you? Through and through."

It was more than a tinkle, actually. Sour smiled as he felt each satisfying, full-bodied thump of a .45.

He emerged from the pool house, scanning the horizon until his eyes found Blunt, taking left handed pistol shots at a round target from a hundred yards out, each shot rattling a quake through the round piece of metal. Jill was at his side, hands on hips, as was Thomas, in full business suit with ubiquitous iPad under an arm. Noticing him at his door, Jill waved Sour over. He grumbled, but slipped his feet into a pair of furry slippers embossed with gold **B**s.

"You mind explaining what I saw on *Morning Joe* this morning, Sour?" Blunt said between shots, not even lowering his gun or breaking his gaze from his distant target. BLAM-ping.

Sour didn't know what the hell he was talking about, but Jill's bulging eyes behind Blunt's back clued him in: their security still of Brenden. Poughkeepsie had found it. It had made it to the networks. "You weren't supposed to assist the Feds, Sour. You were supposed to beat them."

Sour didn't answer, his gaze locked on Blunt's bouncing pistol as he continued to fire. It was a beautiful piece, and Sour felt his right palm moisten with the desire to feel its weight in his grip.

"Congressman," Jill interjected, not wanting to see these two in a cockfight, not when (at least) one of them was armed. "We *had* to give them the photo. We had to give them something to get the gun show li--"

BLAM-ping. "Right. The gun show list that led you to an email address with no name registered to it." BLAM-ping. "An email address that's never been accessed from two IP addresses in the same state."

Now it was Sour's turn to glare at Jill; she had already briefed Blunt on the email's dead ends, and given him way more information than Sour would have preferred at this juncture.

BLAM-ping. Blunt's pistol popped open, coughing out its last shell casing. He lowered it to waist, squinting to count his hits in the distance, still not acknowledging any of his employees with his eyes. "How much time does this give us?"

"As we speak," Sour replied, "literally thousands of tips are flooding in to the FBI tip line. Take them twenty-four hours minimum just to sift through those and come up with the couple names that have real potential."

Blunt sighed as he turned to the folding chair next to him, dropping the weapon inside its case. "You want a name?" He held out a hand to Thomas, who cued something up on his iPad screen before handing it over. Blunt confirmed what he wanted on the monitor, then passed it along to Sour. "Here's a name."

The top of the screen was decorated with the official banner of Blunt's Congressional office. Below it, a header reading, **Daily Diary of Congressman Blunt for March 1st, 20--**

"What am I looking for here?" Sour looked up to Thomas.

"The third meeting of the day," Blunt explained. "11:20."

Sour moved his eyes back down to the screen, finding next to 11:20: **Mtg. in 507 Cannon w/ SEAL Team 3 members, NAB Coronado, CA: Lead Petty Ofcr (E6) B. Bauman, E5 C. Hodell, E5 J. Tatsumi. Set by Office of H. Brandtley. Also Joining: B. Carpinello, S. Payne.**

"Brenden Bauman," Blunt pre-empted Sour's next question.

"What?"

"The one at the barbecue, with a camera. If I'm remembering them correctly, that was Brenden Bauman. He was originally from North Carolina, and had some family connection to Helen, that's why he set the meeting through her, rather than one of his California representatives. She asked me to join. This was--"

"March last year-- that's twenty months ago."

Blunt nodded. "Explains why, on Friday, he seemed so-- *familiar,* but I wasn't able to place him exactly. So when our security shot was plastered all over every news and talk show this morning, I called Thomas and asked if he thought he'd ever seen him before."

"I remember them. And I think you're right, Sir, this one was Bauman, he was the highest ranked of the three."

Blunt grinned. "The minds of the young, Sour, I tell you."

"You met with them about what?"

Blunt shrugged. "Scroll down that page, you'll see how many meetings like this we take each day. That one probably lasted no more than ten, fifteen minutes tops. From what I do remember, his SEAL team had just gotten back from the Middle East. Bauman had won a Purple Heart, and was the local rep for a group lobbying for the VA to speed up their claim times for PTSD therapy."

"And were you able to help them, Sir?" Jill joined in. "Did they ever follow up?"

Blunt looked to Thomas, who piped up on command. "I will confirm this, but we probably did what we do with all VA-related matters, referred them to Rebecca Whitford--"

"She's the Chief of Staff for the VA," Blunt explained. "She used to work for the President, very reliable young gal. I can't speak for the others, but I never saw those three SEALs again. Until last Friday."

Blunt returned to his gun case, finding a new, full magazine to load into the butt of his pistol. Sour looked away, chuckling from deep in his gut. "Excuse me, Sour." Blunt looked up, right hand tightening around his gun's handle with aggravation. "There something funny here?"

"So you expect me to believe that these men are going to all this trouble, *killing Congressmen,* because of what happened in some ten minute meeting almost two years ago?"

Blunt took two hard steps to cross right into Sour's face. Well aware of the gun still in his hand, Jill was right behind him, with a word of caution. "Congressman…"

"I've about had it up to here with your fucking attitude, Sour." Spittle flew from Blunt's tongue to Sour's nose, but he didn't flinch. "I'm not paying you to analyze why they're doing this. You know what I'm paying you to do. So go do it."

Blunt whipped to his target and ripped off his entire clip without a breath, floating the steel piece parallel with the red dirt like it had been caught in a flash hurricane. When his pistol again exhaled with emptiness, Sour had already disappeared back into the pool house.

Few Americans were aware that, located just a mile and a half down the Silver Strand isthmus from the landmark they might most associate with San Diego – the historic Hotel del Coronado – lay the main gate to one of their country's most important military facilities, Naval Amphibious Base Coronado. Over five thousand armed forces personnel were stationed there, including SEAL Teams One, Three and Five, and it's even where the introductory Basic Underwater Demolition/SEAL course (BUD/S for short) required of every new SEAL was held. The home address Brenden Bauman had left with the Congressional office of Helen Brandtley twenty months earlier was located not within the boundaries of the base, but in a nearby gated community, avenue upon avenue of identical three bed, two-and-one-half bath stucco homes run by Lincoln Military Housing, independent owner and operator of several such colonies near bases. Sour was relieved when Thomas relayed this information to Jill during their flight from Bisbee, as getting access onto an active military base would have been considerably more difficult than tracking down Albert Dunne, manager of the Lincoln complex – and a civilian – and dropping the names of a Congressman and the FBI to intimidate him into seeing them immediately upon their arrival.

"I don't think I've seen any of them in-- shoot, it's probably been a few weeks," Dunne explained as he read the list of names from the Congressional meeting twenty months past on Jill's iPad. "Not Bowser, or Chase or Tatsumi. Those are their names, Chase Hodell, James Tatsumi."

"Maybe they're on a deployment?" Jill dug.

"No, they haven't--" Dunne tried to drape his words with some false ignorance, but he clearly knew more than he was letting on. "They haven't been deployed in a couple years."

"Since this meeting?" Sour said, leaning over to tap down hard on the iPad.

"Since before it."

Sour and Jill traded their standard worried looks – these SEALs had had more than enough time to perfectly plan and rehearse and execute the three attacks.

Dunne tried to calm his nerves by busying himself, turning to his desktop computer, calling up a spreadsheet. "No, that's what I thought, they're not on another deployment. They're supposed to just let us know when they're going to be gone, and they haven't done that. I don't know where they've been."

"Is it possible they're just keeping to themselves, not leaving their homes?" Jill asked.

"That's not how things work around a Lincoln community, Ms. Creete. You see everyone at the gym, or at the pool with their kids. We even have movie and game nights. No, these guys-- if they were here, I definitely would've seen them a couple, few times a week."

"Do you know anything about their last deployment?" Sour pried.

"I'm not authorized for that. We just ask to be notified so we can help keep an eye on things. You know, neighborhood watch, maintaining the units. Especially important for the ones who don't leave families behind to do it for them." He paused, looking away with a side thought. "Come to think of it, I haven't seen Sarah Beth or Ty – Bowser's wife and son – in a few weeks either."

"What about Hodell or Tatsumi?" Jill jumped on this. "They have families we could speak with?"

Before the manager answered, his eyes clouded over for just a moment, just long enough for Sour to realize he was wrestling with a difficult answer. "No, Chaser is divorced actually. And Tats-- um, his wife, she passed away three or four years ago."

"Oh no," Jill empathized.

"Yeah, she was so sweet. It was very sad."

Sour knew they weren't hearing the whole story, and he respected this man for protecting the privacy of his tenants. He also knew it was futile, and he would get the whole story before they left this facility.

"We're going to need to see inside the Bauman residence," Sour grunted out as he stood.

"What? I'm, I'm sorry, I didn't get-- Are you with some form of law enforcement or--"

Jill looked up at Sour too, again in the dark about how he was going to get what he wanted.

"I'll cut to the chase, Mr. Dunne," Sour continued. "We know you're well aware that these three men you have living on your property are the Congressional Killers."

Dunne pushed back from his desk with a deep gasp. "Excuse me?"

"You've known the whole time that Brenden Bauman, Chase Hodell and James Tatsumi killed Congresswoman Barbara Carpinello. They killed Stephen Payne, and they killed--"

Dunne grabbed his landline. "I think you better leave--"

Sour slammed his fingers down in the phone's cradle, keeping it disconnected. "We walk out of here without seeing Bauman's place, and we'll have to go to the media. We'll have to tell them you're being investigated as an accomplice for letting these guys use your facility as their tactical base of operations. Do you like your job, Mr. Dunne?"

"No. I mean-- *yes*, I like my job. But I had no idea they were planning this. If it's even them. It couldn't be. These are just the nicest guys. Family men. You're lying to me."

Sour shrugged. "Well, then, your job should be safe. You know the news media, they would never run a lie."

Seven minutes later, Dunne was flipping through his large ring of keys as he led them across the cobblestone driveway and down one of the several cul-de-sacs. "Five minutes, that's all I'm giving you. Then I'm calling the real cops."

Reaching a door, he thumbed a code into the keypad next to the doorbell. The light above the buttons flashed green, but he tried the knob to no effect. "Deadbolt," he murmured, finding the right key on his ring and shoving into the lock above the doorknob. But the second Sour heard the click of it unlocking, he stepped forward, putting a hand on Dunne's chest and pushing him two steps backward. "I beg your pardon--"

Sour was pulling something out of the small leather pouch on the back of his belt, unfolding it in his large hands, unsheathing the blade of a butterfly knife. Holding it with his right hand, he put his left on the knob, pushed it down, and opened the door just a crack. He stuck his blade through the small opening of the door, raising and lowering it until it collided with *something*-- a razor-thin wire tied to the inside of the door.

"Sour?" Jill pressed for info. "What are you--?"

Sour reached in to grab the wire with his left hand, then sawed at it with his blade in his right – one stroke, two – until the wire snapped off the door. He held it taut, rising back up to his full height, folding up the knife on his leg, returning it to the holster above his right glute with one hand.

With a huff, Dunne pushed past him, throwing open Brenden's front door. "I'm sorry, but this has gone on quite long enou-- *Oh my fucking God.*"

Jill stepped in behind him, following his gaze to the open kitchen across from the front foyer. "Fancies himself quite the chef," Sour mused behind her.

Dominating the center of the kitchen were several industrial-sized bags of ammonium nitrate. Above them, a wire held a grenade suspended in mid-air-- a wire that Jill followed right back to Sour's hand. It was the wire he had cut off the door.

"Mr. Dunne, if you had opened that door--"

"I would have levelled the whole complex." As Dunne started to sweat and panic, Sour walked to the kitchen, carefully coiling up the wire in his palm so the grenade was kept elevated at all times. "This, this isn't right. I've got to call someone, I-- I shouldn't have let you in here. I've got to call MPs, base security, the cops, call someone--" He stumbled out, a delirious, raving mess.

By now, Sour could grab the grenade in mid-air, bringing it safely over to the counter. "How much time you think we've got?" Jill asked with a nod back to the front door through which Dunne had just stumbled out.

"No more than five," Sour replied, moving down the one hallway to the double doors at the end, which Jill figured must be the master bedroom.

Jill took the other door, finding a den. She went right to the photo of a Navy man in dress whites, confirming it was indeed Brenden, the same Brenden she had seen at Blunt's and chased into Copper King Canyon. Next to it was a framed photo of a SEAL Team in some armpit locale, posing in their battledress in front of a Blackhawk. And then a candid of Brenden flexing his bare pecs to show off a new tattoo: the trademark SEAL insignia, an eagle gripping a trident, anchor and colonial pistol in its talons.

"It's him," she called out to Sour. "From the party. Blunt was right. We got the right guy." She went to his desk, opening each drawer, finding nothing more than office supplies, files of utility and rent bills. "What am I looking for?" she called again, but Sour still didn't answer.

She was out of that room in under two minutes, wanting to make sure she gave herself time to review the entire home before their set deadline was up. "Sour?" she called out, even stepping back to those double doors, but not spotting him in the master either.

"Up here," his voice called down from the stairs on the other side of the kitchen. Jill crossed to them and was halfway up when Sour appeared with his arms crossed at the top step. "You should see this." Jill reached the apex – there were doors on either side of the short hall, with a bathroom at the end. Sour turned into the door on the right, pushing it open with one arm to allow her entry past him.

The room was all pink, decorated with boy band posters, awards and trophies, a couple soccer team photos. The bed still had a small family of stuffed animals arranged around the pillows. "What, you never seen a little girl's room before, Sour? I thought you had a daughter."

"I do. I just don't remember Dunne mentioning that Bauman has one."

WHAT TO KILL
AND WHAT TO EAT

Thirty months before Clayton Manco and Jill Creete entered her bedroom, Christina Bauman was a third grader at Ridgewood Elementary School, located less than a mile northwest from her family's home on the Strand. On the morning of May 12th, Brenden Bauman walked Christina and Tyler to school just as he always did when he was on shore leave, all three of them in shorts and flip flops, their uniform most days of the year.

With just a month remaining in her third grade year, Christina asked Brenden if she would be allowed to walk herself to school as a fourth grader. Brenden said he and her mother would talk about it, but she had to promise to always make the walk with at least one other friend. He suggested the daughter of James Tatsumi, a fellow member of his SEAL unit; Brenden and Sarah Beth had coincidentally also just put in a request for Christina to be placed in the fourth grade class taught by Tats's wife.

Ty was more concerned with whether the Padres might finally win the NL West; Brenden warned his son to be cautious against getting his hopes up when it came to the Pads.

At 8:39 AM, Christina's class was in the middle of a math lesson when Evan Watson entered their classroom carrying a Bushmaster .223-caliber assault rifle and a 10MM Glock 20SF pistol. He opened fire first with the assault rifle, killing nine of the eighteen students and injuring several others before they could hide. He dropped the empty gun and pulled out the Glock, which he carried to the fourth grade classroom across the hall. After killing only three more students here, he was tackled by the teacher of this class, Mrs. Tatsumi, but was able to shoot her in the skull before she disarmed him of any weapons. The wound killed her instantly, but Mrs. Tatsumi's distraction allowed the rest of her students to escape before Watson could get any more shots off.

Watson pursued the fourth graders into the hallway, where he took heavy fire from the SDPD SWAT team which had just entered the school, and retreated back into Mrs. Tatsumi's classroom. Watson later testified that it was at that moment he decided to take his own life using his Glock, but by stunning him with a flashbang grenade, SWAT was able to storm the classroom and disarm him before he completed his suicide attempt.

Watson was pronounced guilty of thirteen counts of first-degree murder and nineteen counts of attempted first-degree murder. On the day Clayton Manco and Jill Creete entered the bedroom of Christina Bauman, Evan Watson was serving seven consecutive life sentences at Napa State Hospital five hundred miles north of them.

Christina Bauman would never walk herself to school. Thirty months before Clayton Manco and Jill Creete entered her bedroom, she had been one of the twelve Ridgewood Elementary third and fourth graders killed by Evan Watson.

"The shooting occurred on May 12th," Sour was explaining, but the Congressman was already at his office wet bar, pouring himself a full, neat tumbler of Johnny Walker Black. It was 9:49 AM. "May 12th, 5/12."

"'Chris512@yahoo,'" Jill connected the dots. "Chris for Christina."

Blunt didn't respond, or even turn back to them.

"The three SEALs you met with in Helen Brandtley's office had all lost children at Ridgewood ten months earlier," Sour continued. "And Tatsumi lost his wife too. Now you didn't really forget that when you recognized Bauman at the barbecue. Did you, Congressman?"

Blunt tipped back his drink, left hand on his waist.

"You didn't forget that they scheduled that meeting to plead with you to propose new gun control laws. Including more mental health monitoring. No sales to anyone on the terror watch or no-fly lists. And background checks on all sales at gun shows or over the internet. Like the show where Evan Watson bought his Bushmaster and Glock from Jason Savage."

Blunt moved around behind his desk, facing them to pull out his chair and take a seat.

Sour stormed up to the desk, spitting across it, towering over the politician. "Answer me, goddammit."

Blunt looked up into Sour's eyes. "I did sponsor that bill, Sour. I was the only Republican to sponsor it. But Evan Watson didn't have anything in his background. He had never been flagged for mental health issues. He would have walked out of that show with those guns anyway. That bill wouldn't have changed a damn thing in this country--"

"We'll never know, will we? Because it ended up three votes short. If you had gotten your buddy Lafayette to stick to his support for it... He had promised to be the first NRA President to support background che--"

"That was in the heat of a Supreme Court confirmation battle. He was pulling out all stops to get a Justice he liked on the Court. He needed a joint resolution with the one he had supported in the Senate. It was just politics. Are you getting this, Sour? That ten minute meeting with those SEALs, I had long forgotten about that, we all had. It was Bryce asking me to support the bill, that's why I--"

"But as soon as the bill passed the Senate, the day it got to the House, Lafayette burned it in effigy. You all did. Carpinello didn't vote for it. Payne didn't vote for it. Brandtley didn't vote for it. And you didn't vote for it—"

"It wasn't the same bill. It had been porked up and watered down—"

"You voted against a bill you yourself had sponsored. You four promised Brenden Bauman, James Tatsumi and Chase Hodell you would change this country in honor of their children. Then as soon as they turned around and walked out, you shot them in their backs."

Suddenly, Blunt was on his feet, spiking his glass into the hardwood. "Oh, now you're going to tell me how I should be voting on bills? You, the scumbag who never saw a law he couldn't break? How do you think I should have voted on Lilly Ledbetter? Huh? How 'bout the Iran deal? Please. Tell me."

The shrapnel from Blunt's glass missile was still settling, the liquor dripping from three different edges of his desk. Sour didn't answer. Blunt was just getting revved.

"You know what it takes to be a Republican today in America and vote as I did on these issues? It takes sacrifice. It takes picking my battles. It takes voting against a gun control act that wouldn't have made a damn bit of difference anyway. Because let me assure you, that bill passes, and it doesn't matter how many years I've known Bryce Lafayette, he takes his NRA money and his four million Twitter followers and his mailing list across the street, and gives them to some Tea Party whack job to primary me. And the next thing you know, we've got ourselves another elected official who thinks every bill brought before Congress is a UN conspiracy to create a world government. So, no, I don't always vote the way you, or Brenden Bauman, or Rachel-fucking-Maddow thinks I should. But unlike the three of you, I'm a political animal, and I know what I have to kill and what I have to eat in order to survive. And that, in the long run, is what's best for the great people of Arizona's Second Congressional District."

Sour just stared back, neither man blinking, for what felt to Jill like several whole minutes. Finally, with a tap on the desk with his fingertips, Sour turned and headed for the door.

"And just where do you think you're going, Sour?"

You broke my rules," he answered without looking back. "We're done."

Blunt was laughing. "Is that right? You are just way too easy to control. I put one ex-con on Fox News and you're right back in your truck on your way west. I buy the College Station Waterford and order them to evict your daughter, and you're right back in your truck on your way west."

Sour had stopped with his fingers on the door's handle. Blunt sauntered over to the oil painting of his copper miner daddy, an energized grin on his face and pep in his step. "See, I don't think you understand the stakes here. You don't know what I promised this man as he lay dying." He put his fingers around one side of the frame, pulling it back off the wall, revealing a heavy armored door, a keypad above the knob. "I promised him I would never be a slave like he had been. A slave to Phelps-Dodge, a slave to his union. I promised him I'd be a self-made man and I'd never work for anyone in my life. I promised him I'd someday buy this house. I promised him I'd spend my life running *everything*, Sour. I promised him I'd be President someday." He typed in a code, and after a beep and a click, pulled the door open to reveal a small, hidden room on the other side. From his vantage point, Sour could make out a large safe, a rack of rifles sitting upright in gorgeous oak; it was a custom panic room.

"So here's what's not going to happen," Blunt's voice echoed from within. "Those three whack jobs who blame me for their children's deaths at the hands of some teenage psycho? They're never going to make it to prison." Another keypad beeped away as he entered another code. "They'll never explain on *60 Minutes* that the reason they went on this killing spree is because they came to me, they told me about their children, they gave me the answers of how to cure all the world's woes, and I did nothing about it." There was a release of air, and Blunt pulled open a waist-high drawer. He searched for something with his eyes and finding it, picked it up in his right. "That, my dear Sour, is something that's just not going to happen. You're not going to let it happen. Because if it does, I'm shutting down my new care facility in Texas as fast as the law will allow and promptly throwing everyone who lives there out on the street where they probably belonged in the first place."

Blunt stepped back out of the safe room, crossing to Sour. "You're going to kill Brenden Bauman, Sour. And Chase Hodell. And James Tatsumi. You're going to kill all three of them." He held out whatever he had retrieved from that armored drawer for Sour to take. "And you're going to use my gun to do it."

Sour looked down. In Blunt's palm sat the gorgeous, pristine Sig Sauer P220 he had used for target practice, its long chrome barrel so spit-shined he could almost see his reflection in it. Sour did want to pick it up, he did want to feel that weight in his hands again, yearned to feel its recoil tingle up his arm.

But instead, he looked up in Blunt's eyes, said flatly, "Go fuck yourself," and walked out of his house.

Sour had gotten his ruck sack re-packed, and thrown it in the bed of the Beast by the time Jill found him in the driveway. "Hey, you're not leaving."

Sour didn't feel he needed to answer. Just getting in the cabin of the truck and roaring her to life should be response enough. Jill stormed to his window, which remained halfway down as he had left it three weeks ago to keep her ventilated. "That's it? You just quit? Look, I know you consider me about as smart and as useful as tits on a boar, but together, we've made such strides on this. We're right on the verge. We can figure this out, I know we can."

Sour released the parking brake, then arm wrestled the gear stick into first. Jill knew she had only seconds to talk him out of this, and walked along the vehicle as he chugged down the long driveway. "I would love to know what happened to you. I don't know if you became this brooding dickhead the day you signed up for the FBI, or the day you got suspended, for whatever the fuck that was for—or whatever it was that happened that made you choose to never go back, and just waste away on your shithole of a farm—" By now, Sour had reached the bottom of the concrete ramp, waiting for the gate to swing open, giving Jill time for one last salvo: "But here's a word of advice: if every once in a while, you acted like a human being and *let other people in*, you'd probably find it easier to figure out situations like this." The gate was now open wide, but Sour didn't look over at her or respond to her diatribe.

But he didn't drive off either. This startled Jill, sure she would never get through to him.

Then she realized it wasn't her that had stopped him. He was digging into his pants pocket, burrowing for his buzzing phone. After reading its glowing face, he brought it to his ear. "Manco."

For several seconds, he just listened. Then he lowered it, but still didn't drive off or betray even a whiff of emotion. He just stared blankly out the dusty, bug-splattered windshield he had insisted to Blunt's house staff he didn't want cleaned.

"Sour, you okay?" Jill inquired. Not getting even a flinch of acknowledgement, she stepped closer, surprised to find herself for the first time worrying about him. "Sour, who was that? What did they tell you?"

"My daughter. She's been having terrible seizures for the last several hours. They found a blood clot in her brain. She's going into surgery."

They both digested this, Beast's idling rumble filling the space between words until Sour spoke again. "I've gotta get home."

"Wait!" Jill slammed her hands down on the sill of his open window before he could move his foot from brake to gas. He looked over at her. Didn't she realize he would drive off with her hanging from his door if he had to?

But the point she was about to make was indeed a good one. "You'll never get there in time."

RANGERS, LEAD THE WAY

Jill and Sour didn't share a word the entire flight from Bisbee to Easterwood, giving her time to call into Blunt and tell him she was borrowing the Cessna to follow up on a promising Bauman sighting. No, Jill assured the Congressman, she hadn't spoken to Manco and didn't know where he had gone after fleeing the estate.

Jill also texted Lynchie from the air; she would be in his neck of the woods for the next couple of days. How about a beer or some barbecue?

Jack Lynch had been one of the Rangers under her command in Syria. Theirs had been a confused relationship; he loved to flirt with her when they were off-duty or cock his right eyebrow with condescension whenever he was saying, "Yes, Ma'am," or sometimes even, "Yes, Sir." It was the type of casual insubordination that should have driven her berserk; it would have with most men, but Lynchie wasn't most men. He was a damn good Ranger, and he was sexy as hell.

Knowing that he had joined the Brazos County Sheriffs after leaving the Army, Jill first thought about reaching out to Lynchie when she and Randy came to Texas to initially recruit Sour, but there just hadn't been time for any horseplay outside of the mission at hand. She knew this time she might be staying a couple of days, until either Abby Manco woke up or Sour calmed down. So as soon as her iPhone connected to the Cessna's Wi-Fi, she texted Brazos County's newest deputy.

Upon landing, Jill drove Sour to College Station Hospital and walked inside with him, but let him pull ahead with Abby's recovery room in sight. Jill didn't go further than the door, leaning just against the frame so she could see Sour sit down next to his inert daughter, cords and IVs snaking in and out of her comatose body. She could just see him raise Abby's left hand to his mouth and kiss it, when in her pocket her phone shook with the double-pulse of a text, hopefully that sought-after response from Lynchie.

Sure, she had some skepticism of his invitation to just meet at his house, then "figger it out from there." She assuaged herself that that was always easiest, and cheapest, even while deep down being well aware of his true intentions.

Jill didn't mind those true intentions. She hadn't misbehaved once when she was a Ranger, and look what that pristine record had ultimately gotten her. They were consenting adults, and she wanted exactly what Lynchie wanted.

She stayed dressed in her uniform of a blouse and blazer, dressing it up just a little with more make-up and some pumps. Lynchie answered the door in t-shirt and cowboy boots, but that was just fine with her. "You really just want a beer, Lieutenant?" he smiled from the kitchen as he held up a bottle of Patron.

Shot one, they caught up on life. Shot two, reminisced about their time in the Suck. Shot three, Lynchie got into how cute he always thought she was, his right eyebrow cocking up that same way it did whenever he Yes Sirred her. Shot four was poured but never brought to their lips before they started necking like tipsy horndog teenagers.

She opened her shirt for him and he put his strong, rough hands on her, across her stomach, onto her back, up onto her shoulders. He pulled her in and kissed her chest, breath picking up with pure, drunk lust. Lynchie pulled his tee off over the back of his skull with one hand and Jill ached as she ran her fingers along his tight chest. Before she could debate how far this should go, he had a hand down the front of her pants, coaxing her own moisture around the rest of her opening. He took the back of her hair with his other hand, pulling her ear into his mouth. "You gonna let me do what I always wanted to do to you?"

"What was that?"

"What every man wants to do to a woman that tries to order him around. You gonna let me?"

She was almost finishing on his fingers, barely able to pant out, "Oh yes," before he had turned her over and yanked down the back of her slacks and panties. He slapped her ass hard with an open hand and Jill moaned with pleasure. He reached between her legs for some juice, then rubbed it all over himself, using it to ease himself into her from behind. But not the behind she had expected or desired. "No, stop—" she grunted out on his third thrust, but his fingers were in her teeth before she could say more.

"You don't get to order me around anymore, Lieutenant." he replied, then kept thrusting six, seven more times. Eight.

Jill grit her teeth. She couldn't get one image out of her head: Sour kicking down the door, charging in and pulling Lynchie off and out of her, throwing him to the ground, then stomping his head in.

But Sour never came, and Lynchie finished inside her, collapsing his full weight onto her back with ecstatic release.

After a breath or two, he rolled off and she sat back on the couch next to him, dissatisfied and more than a little disgusted, mostly with herself. He grabbed a Marlboro from the pack on the table, and as he sat back to light it, all she could do was stare at his pathetic member dribbling onto his thigh as it shriveled back to its resting shape. "You're a fucking asshole," she whispered, but for some reason didn't move, didn't sit up or pull her own clothes back on.

"No, but I just fucked yours," Lynchie giggled.

Jill nearly vomited. What had she been thinking? Hadn't she remembered Lynchie hadn't even come to her defense when she was court martialed? No, he hadn't testified against her, but those Rangers who said nothing almost did as much damage with their silence. Why did she let him off the hook for that, why text him, why come here when she knew he had contributed to her discharge? Was she that desperate, that pitiable?

She knew the answer. She didn't deserve better.

Lynchie leaned forward to down his fourth shot. "You never even told me what brought you to Texas, Jilly." Jill didn't know why she didn't stand up and walk out, why she carried on with him as he turned their post-coital into a full-blown conversation: he had heard she went to work for a contractor, but what was she up to now? And what was she doing in College Station of all places?

Jill gave way too much in return (whether because she was overtired or had this need to make Lynchie respect her, she couldn't be sure): She was now head of security for a Congressman, and was here to support a colleague named Clayton Manco whose daughter had just gone into emergency surgery.

"Holy shit, Jilly, Sour Manco?" Lynchie interrupted. "I thought he had retired after what happened to his family."

Jill looked up from his dick to his smug fucking dickhead face. "What happened to his family?"

Jill heard the clunk of a vending machine releasing its wares before she even rounded the corner into the hospital cafeteria. She stood at the door and watched Sour, the only soul in the whole cafeteria, take a seat four tables away, unwrapping his breakfast burrito with fingers almost too fatigued to function. His back to her, he didn't see her approach, didn't realize she was there, until she put a hand on his shoulder and told him, "I know what happened." He looked back at her with confusion, and she came around to sit right next to him. "Another Ranger from my battalion, he's now a Brazos County deputy. He knew why you moved back from Washington. He told me what happened to make Abby like this."

Sour had by now taken a bite of his burrito, and though the machine that had spit it out had promised to do so piping hot, the center was cold and wet. He stood and took it to the microwave, and Jill swiveled in her seat to call after him. "I hope you know—you're a good father, Sour."

"And how the hell would you possibly know that?" he asked without turning back.

Jill didn't counter until the microwave had beeped the end of its cycle, and Sour had returned to the table for bite number two. "I always wanted to be a Ranger. Just like my dad. I didn't do ROTCie to get through Stanford, I got through Stanford because how could I turn down an opportunity like that? I used ROTCie as my excuse to go into the Army, when no one thought that's what a Stanford girl should do. It was a commitment, an obligation. I would go into the Army and I'd be the first woman to make it through Ranger school, the Ranger school my father said a woman could never complete, the Ranger school my own older brother failed at. Becoming a Ranger was the proudest day of my life. 'Rangers, lead the way,'" she repeated the final stanza of their creed. "I'd still be over there if I could, still over in Syria. But one day we're sweeping a street in Aleppo when our point man steps on an IED and goes up in pieces. AKs erupt from windows all around us."

"I know what happened."

"No, you don't," she pointed in his face, like he was every man who had ever doubted her. "I got us out of there with only the one casualty. But our point man, turns out he was a colonel's son. That colonel gets four men in my unit to testify that I was reckless sending us down that street without an EOD sweep first. A couple guys came to my defense, but most just stayed on the sidelines. Yeah, I know this must sound like all the grapes in the fucking sour patch, but that's why I'm no longer a Ranger."

Jill took a deep breath, swallowing some hard memories. "I thought that was the end of my life. But my dad, he wouldn't let that be the end. He called everyone he knew, everyone he ever met, until he convinced an old buddy at Allied Armament to hire me. Then that company goes under for all the dirty shit they did, and I look even worse. My dad made all those calls again, he even wrote letters to every politician in our whole state. *He's* the one who got the Congressman to take a look at me. He's how I know a good father when I see one."

His burrito finished, Sour folded up the discarded yellow wrapper it had come in, deposited the origami on his plate, then wiped his fingers and mouth with a napkin. "Does a good father move to a different state just because things don't work out in his marriage?" he replied rhetorically to her compliments. "I thought just because I knew where they were, they were safe. But that's not enough anymore. You can't just know where your kids are, you have to *be there*."

Jill stood. She knew her mission here was a hopeless one. "You're not coming back to Arizona are you?"

Sour just shook his head. Jill placed her hand back on his shoulder, for a second again picturing him saving her from Lynchie. Then she turned and left him there.

Poughkeepsie just happened to call at the perfect time. Sour would have ignored his call if it had rung through while he was in with Abby, but he had stepped out for a consultation with Dr. Schwartz, the surgeon who had operated on her. With the sun coming up, Schwartz had returned to the hospital after a night's sleep, making this Sour's first chance to meet him. He promised that Abby was in no pain, and that they were going to keep her sedated for a few more days, giving her a chance to heal before she started moving her head around too much. "It might be a week or more, Mr. Manco. My suggestion is you go do something that completely takes your mind off Abby, and off worry mode."

"You don't have children, do you, Doctor?"

As Schwartz went on his rounds, Sour ducked into the head to piss before returning to Abigail's side. He was just washing his hands when the phone buzzed in his pocket.

"Clay, I just woke up," Poughkeepsie's voice crackled through the line. "I just got your text. These three names—"

"They're who you think they are. You can shut down the tip line, Park. I'm folding. Table's all yours."

Sour for a few moments received only silence in response, and wondered if Poughkeepsie had already hung up to sic his High Value pit-bulls on these leads. "Clay," Poughkeepsie finally chuckled. "You know I always think about the role you played in getting me to where I am today. I want you to know I haven't forgotten it."

"And who do you have doing the Judiciary Committee's dirty laundry and keeping you on their Christmas card lists these days?"

"Playing it straight, above board, it's worked for me since you left."

"I understand," Sour shook his head, knowing full well when he was being condescended to.

"No no no, I'm saying this is a luxury *you* gave me, Clay. Without you, without the work you did on my team – and off it – I'd still be just another junior field agent. There would be no High Value Targets team without your contribution."

"You know us Mexicans. Willing to do all the dirty jobs you're not."

"Clay-- This isn't why I called-- Look, it's gonna take us today and tomorrow to get the warrants, then go tear their homes apart, only to realize they haven't been home in weeks. Then the interviews start. The credit card checks, the hours of Waldo-hunting through security footage. This is gonna take us time, Clay. You know that. You could be using that time."

Sour didn't answer. His brain wanted to say he didn't want to use that time, that all his time would be spent at Abby's side now. But when he saw Dr. Schwartz crossing from one room to another down the opposite end of the hallway, his heart reminded him of the doctor's orders. *My suggestion is you go do something that completely takes your mind off Abby.*

Parker's last words solved the debate between brain and heart. "You understand what they're doing better than anyone, Clay."

PEOPLE ARE ABOUT TO DIE

Thomas was waiting beside Randy's Escalade when Homer Blunt emerged from Temple Kol Hamidbar. "It's Manco, Sir," Thomas nearly shouted as the Congressman crossed Canyon Drive. "He said he's been trying you all morning."

Blunt glared at Thomas, reminding his assistant with his eyes that he needed him to activate the speaker phone and hover the device near his face so he wouldn't have to operate it himself. "I take the rules of Shabbos very seriously, Sour."

"You're close with Governor Clark," Sour's voice answered through the phone speaker.

"Of California? What does that have to do with anyth--?"

"Are you close with him or not?"

Blunt didn't like where this was going – these days, he heard California and he of course thought immediately of the three Congressional Killers – but he was also sure he had to appease Sour if he wanted to get him working again. "I made some appearances in his state when he was running, tried to explain to his constituents the mess Antonio Salas was making in Washington and what a mistake it would be to re-elect the Lieutenant Governor he had left in charge. Clark gives me more credit than I probably deserve for his win. He suggested my name to Brad Benedict when he turned down his VP slot himself."

"You're gonna call Clark when we hang up. You're gonna tell him exactly what I tell you to tell him. Then, you're gonna do two other things for me."

"You want your check now." Blunt had counted on this demand coming, and was prepared to negotiate a compromise without completely surrendering his leverage.

"I don't want your campaign money. I want Abby's next five years at the whatever-the-hell-you're-calling-it-now covered. First thing tomorrow morning. All in one lump payment."

Blunt crossed his arms over his chest. "Okay, I do that for you—and what's my guarantee you won't be in Mexico by tomorrow evening?"

"You can afford to take that chance."

Blunt nodded. He wanted, *needed* Sour back, no matter the cost. "All right. What's your second thing?"

Guy, the lone flight attendant to crew Homer Blunt's Cessna since he purchased it seven years ago, was just leaning over to pull the air stairs closed when Sour heard Jill's voice punch up from the tarmac. "Don't you dare close that door!"

Guy stammered just long enough for Jill to shove past him and on board the plane. "Ms. Creete, I'm sorry, I was told this flight was only--"

"Oh no. That mother fucker may fire me, but he's still paying for my ride home to Arizona."

Jill threw her bag down on one seat, plopping across from Sour on the other side of the aisle. Guy had flown with Jill long enough to know he wouldn't win an argument with her, especially not when she was fired up like this. He nodded and pulled the stairs closed so they could get under way.

"That's right, you fucking asshole," Jill spit across to Sour. "Blunt just fired me. And I know it's because you told him to."

"C'mon," he tried to brush off her concerns as paranoia.

"He *told* me it was because you told him to. What, you really hate me that much, you'd get me fired from the only job I could get?"

"You've been drinking," Sour observed.

"So?" Jill stood and marched over to the liquor cabinet next to the mini-fridge. "Isn't that what unemployed people do?" She grabbed three mini-bottles in one hand, and had sucked one of them dry by the time she had returned to her seat.

Sour couldn't help but grin at her. She tossed a bottle into his lap. "Drink with me. I saw how you live. I know you can't get enough of the sauce."

Sour saw it was Patron, and his tongue tingled. But he still managed to deposit the bottle in the nearest drink holder. Jill just shook her head and drank down the one still in her hand.

"People are about to die," he finally offered her in explanation. "And I don't want you to be one of them. I noticed in Phoenix, when I said you should let whoever needs to know that you were going to be away for a few days – you never called anyone."

"Maybe I texted… people."

"I figured, where you are in your life now, you could survive with a little time off. That's why I made Blunt fire you. You'll be without a paycheck for a few weeks, just until Parker calls you."

Jill's eyes shot up into Sour's.

"Him, or someone he tells to call you. Not this week, maybe not next, but when he has a slow moment. To set you up with an interview."

They were now in the air, the ascension of the engines settling as they found their cruising altitude.

And suddenly, Jill was on top of him, straddling him, pulling his mouth into hers, thrusting her pelvis down onto his crotch.

"What are you doing?" Spittle flew off Sour's words as he pushed her lips away.

"Isn't this what you want?" she answered, continuing the grind. "Isn't this why you did all that for me?"

Sour lifted her up and threw her back onto her seat, where she landed with a thud.

Jill leaned forward, picking up that third mini-bottle, the Patron. She chugged it down despite the fact (or maybe because) it reminded her of Lynchie.

"What I just did-- I'm really fucking wasted, Sour. I'm much more professional than that. I hope that's not going to make you call Poughkeepsie and tell him you changed your--"

And he was on top of her, like a rabid animal. It had only been two or three weeks since Resplanda, but for a machine like Sour, the hunger built up quickly. He gripped her jaw in his rough palm and pushed his lips into hers with the full power of his soul. He pinned her legs back with his thighs, thrusting the hardness in his slacks up and into her most sensitive areas. "Wait, wait," she panted, "not so fast, my pants—"

"Just come with me," he growled in her ear, and that's what she did, all down the inside of her pants like a high school student on her first dry hump. She wasn't sure Sour actually joined her – he didn't grunt or gyrate – but he still gave her the best orgasm, the strongest orgasm she had experienced in years. And he collapsed back against his own seat like *something* had drained from him, even if it wasn't his total essence.

Several moments of silence passed before Jill broke the awkwardness. "Now that we're not working together—when this is all over—I know you probably don't—"

"That's right. I don't," he firmly confirmed.

"Well, if you ever considered it, I'd consider it with you."

Sour looked out into the clouds. The awkwardness now thicker than even before, Jill looked out her own window.

"So, um, anyone need anything?" Guy asked as he emerged from the cockpit.

Sour stayed in the clouds. He never did get the chance to tell Jill that he might consider what she was proposing, once Abby was awake. Once this was all over.

The FBI's search of three military homes on San Diego's Silver Strand dominated the news and buried almost everything else worth reporting.

But one of the Congressional Killers did see the story of Evan Watson's transfer, just as Sour knew one of them would. He correctly guessed that at least one of them would be so riveted to the aerial news footage of their front doors, to the endless video loops of bomb-sniffing robots and kevlared High Value agents going in and out of their homes, that when the Watson story was thrown out as a pre-commercial tease, the Killer or Killers watching wouldn't be able to resist sticking through the two minutes of reverse mortgage and pharmaceutical pitches to see what the hell new news there could be on the young man who had murdered all their children and even one of their wives almost two years before, a lifetime of news cycles ago.

One could argue that it was fate that decreed Brenden would be the one who saw the Watson report first, Brenden who would call his compatriots into the room to see the full report. Since their first eye contact in Blunt's backyard, it had been as if Brenden and Sour's destinies had been intrinsically, almost cosmically, intertwined.

What a strange opportunity this presented, Brenden thought to himself as his fellow SEALs also took in this news. Just days from completing their mission, from their final op, a planned remodel of the Napa State Hospital would force the move of the killer of their children to a different facility. Brenden had already been doing some hunting, some Googling and GPSing on his phone: Watson would be outside of maximum security walls, guarded, yes, but relative to the rest of his past and future prison career *out in the open,* for probably somewhen between one hundred ten and one hundred twenty minutes. For just under two hours, they would have a better chance to exact revenge – not symbolic or message revenge like they had been chasing for weeks, but real, thick-as-blood, honest-to-goodness vengeance – upon the man who had murdered their children. The man who had shot Tatsumi's wife in the head.

The man who had murdered Christina.

"No, no, no, we can't listen to this," Chase shook his head, traipsing out of the room. "We can't allow ourselves to be distracted from our—"

"*Distracted?*" Tatsumi was incredulous. "Isn't this what we should really want?"

"And will we ever have another chance to get it?" Brenden finished his thought in a whisper.

EXPOSED LIKE THIS

The air was as crisp as you would expect for a morning in California's northern reaches, but Sour still felt his pits perspiring with anticipation. He crouched down next to Cody Bremner, the man positioned to be most likely to get the first clear shot at Bauman, Hodell or Tatsumi.

Evan Watson would be brought out on the east side of the colonially spired main building of the Napa State Hospital to a procession of police vehicles which would then proceed off the seventeen-acre campus via Palm Drive North. Sour had come prepared for party crashers, borrowing five members of Blunt's personal detail, all but two of his full-time security staff (or all but one, once you subtracted Jill from the rolls), and these men had even at his request recruited three other buddies for the day. Sour had stationed these eight men in various points around the hospital roof with .338 caliber Accuracy International rifles. None of them could properly be called snipers – none had the training or ability for that rarified title. Sour knew that even out of practice he could surely out-shoot all eight of them. But with the parking lot laid out only four stories below them, Sour didn't need world class military snipers, just capable, trustworthy men. And Cody Bremner was one of those; former Marine, former Tucson beat cop. Sour knew the scope of Bremner's long gun was most likely to be the first to catch the Congressional Killers in its sights when they came for Watson. And they *would* come for Watson.

Media and law enforcement filled the asphalt below them, as if tailgating for a concert or football game, but twenty minutes after Watson's scheduled exodus, there had still been no sign of him or the men Sour had predicted would take this opportunity to make an attempt on his life. "Stay alert," he reminded his improvised team through the mic on his wrist, then pulled out his warbling phone to check its display.

It was an unnecessary formality; he already knew it would be Blunt, checking in for the third time since Sour had arrived atop this building.

"You got any updates for me?" his voice came through with that echo of the speaker phone on his office desk.

"Still waiting. No Watson. No Bauman, Hodell or Tatsumi."

"I don't like this, Sour. Sitting here exposed like this—with only Randy. All my guys a thousand miles away with you—"

"You wanted Randy. You chose Randy."

"I wanted Jill. But you wouldn't let me have her."

"Look," Sour let some exasperation through, "you want me to finally get these guys, this way is the only way."

"From your lips to God's ears."

"This man killed their children. This might be the last time he'll be exposed like this for the rest of his natural born life. They'll be here."

Chase was behind the wheel and Tatsumi in the back. They had removed the middle row of seats so Tats could do what post-family Tats liked to do most in all the world: get his bombs ready. As Brenden climbed into shotgun, he could feel their hot glares of impatience, especially from Chaser, before he backed them out of the tandem parking spot their SUV had occupied for over a week. They didn't say anything; no one ever said anything when they were this close to Go time.

Brenden didn't like this car, didn't like that they had no familiarity with it, that they weren't using their bikes. But they had pledged early on to make every direct action unique, so that no one would be able to plan ahead for them, no one would be able to predict, even if they had figured out who they were coming for next, *how* they would be coming. Brenden didn't like the decision they had made, who to target today. Chaser was right, Watson was a distraction from their mission objectives. Going after Watson probably meant they would never get their shot at Blunt, and would muddy the entire message of their quest up to now.

But Tatsumi had a point too. This would probably be their only chance at real, solid, inarguable revenge.

They had started something more important than simple revenge, Chase countered, something bigger than them, and they had to finish it.

The tie would be left to Brenden to break. Brenden saw Chase's points, but he also knew he no longer daydreamed of sex, nor his Padres winning the World Series, nor any of the things young men were supposed to daydream about. He hadn't thought of any of those things in close to two years. He daydreamed now about strangling Evan Watson with his bare hands, about crushing his skull like Prince Oberyn's on *GOT,* about slicing his body apart with a fully-auto M4, about cutting off all his fingers and toes and his limp little dick on a butcher's block.

This op was the first time they weren't unanimous, that they had settled a decision two votes to one. That lack of unanimity filled Brenden with unease. 0.667 would be a historic batting average, but they didn't get strikes or foul tips in the game they were playing.

Brenden shut his eyes and said a silent prayer. It was a SEAL tradition before ops, but one their little band had forgone, maybe because they knew God was no longer on their side. Brenden didn't clasp his hands, but put one of them on his SEAL trident pin, hoping it could somehow send some clarity into his veins. Brenden's prayer was not for success of the misson, but that wherever he ended up, Sarah Beth and Ty would know he loved them.

"Randy!" Blunt screamed after he had punched the call with Sour dead.

"Sir!" Randy bounded into the room with his favorite toy, his Ruger .357, already pulled from his belt holster, pointed into the floor. "Everything okay in here, Sir?"

"Just making sure you're not falling asleep on me out there, Number Twelve," Blunt replied without making eyes with him, his own too buried in the patch of floor across which he paced back and forth.

"No sir," Randy smirked at the latest reference to the retired Eagles quarterback. "Red alert and ready," he assured the Congressman as he backed out of the office, holstering his five-shooter, closing the door behind him once again.

The buzz near the door was the first sign it was happening. Cody Bremner sensed it before Sour did, tensing up and announcing, "I think he's coming."

Sour saw a flash of orange jumpsuit beneath them and brought his right wrist to his lips. "This is it."

Even from forty-plus feet above Watson's head, Sour could hear the questions screamed from the press corps as they tried to encroach further and further into his path to the armored prisoner transport van which awaited him. "Mr. Watson! Mr. Watson!" "Do you know why you're being moved?" "Do you have any regrets about what you did?" But Watson didn't answer, indeed, didn't even look up as he was dragged and yanked and pulled.

"Steady," Sour implored his men. He knew the ones with a clear view of Watson must have been gripped with a swirled mix of emotions. The sadistic fucker who had gunned down nine nursery school kids for fame or sick pleasure was a sitting duck in the scopes of their rifles that from here might be able to take his head clean off. Half these guys were of the age that they probably had little third and fourth graders of their own, little cherubic smiley faces like the ones that filled the news for weeks after Watson's rampage. "When he goes down, no quick reactions. Find the shooters first. Let me assess. Wait for my order."

Sour didn't realize that Cody Bremner might have been the most conflicted of all of them. They were all former military, but the military had been his lifeblood since he was pulled out of his mama and laid down in that hospital warming tray. The son of a Navy man, Cody had grown up moving from base to base, and the news reports of a gunman murdering the children of servicemen in the school nearest their base filled Cody with daymares of how horrific it could have been if his own schools had gotten shot up when he was a young boy. Sour caught Cody adjusting his sweaty trigger grip out of the corner of his eye, and put his hand on the man's shoulder, keeping his voice low enough and far away enough from his comm to give him some personal assurance. "Hold tight."

"One shot." Cody licked his lips. "One pull of the trigger and I could make this world a much better place."

"And you would get to enjoy that world from a ten-by-ten cell. It's not worth it. They're going to do him for us."

After a beat, Cody nodded. And waited.

They all waited – until Watson was stepping up into the back of his transport van. Through his scope, Cody could see him being chained down to the bench inside, an instant before the backdoors of the vehicle were closed tight. One of the hospital guards slapped his open palm onto the right door to signal the driver they were good to go, and the white vehicle started to pull away.

"What the fuck?" Cody exclaimed.

Complaints from all the men were filling the tiny speaker in Sour's ear before he processed what had just happened. "They're not coming here," he realized as he stood up to his full height.

"No shit," a faceless voice agreed.

"They're going to Stockton. We've got to get out of here! We've got to beat them there! We gotta haul ass, now!"

Cody already had the neck yanked from the body of his gun. His personal record for taking apart a service rifle was under fifty seconds. Too bad no one was around with a stopwatch right now.

"People are about to die, people are about to die… about to die…"

The floorboards of Jill's house creaked and groaned as she paced and paced and paced, the full length, then the full width, then the length again, of the small edifice. She paused for a sigh and a look out the front windows, down onto the Old Bisbee Main Street tucked between Mules. She knew she should be saying goodbye to that little town down there, packing for a move to Quantico, but instead, couldn't take her eyes off the news coverage of Watson's transfer, or the FBI searches of the Congressional Killers' homes. She restarted her pace, trying to piece together what the hell Sour had meant, what the hell he was planning. The other members of Blunt's detail loved her; they had all promised to keep in touch and had texted over the last couple days with updates on what Manco had them doing. Their notes just made her feel more uneasy, queasy, even. Nothing about Sour's plan felt right, especially when she thought about the cryptic clues he had dropped on the Cessna. She knew he was taking everyone but Randy off the compound and with him to California and—

"Oh fuck, Sour." The realization hit her like a Mack truck. She stopped for just a moment, then rushed for her phone, her fingers shaking as she scrolled for Randy's number, pulling open her front door with her other hand as she brought it to her ear.

"Yo! It's Randy, leave a--"

Fuck! She was moving so fast, she didn't even realize she had forgotten her piece until she was seventy-plus steps on her way down to her Civic in the Courthouse parking lot. She killed the connection, and rushed back up and in for the holster. *Fuck shit fuck!* In the drunk-hungover hybrid she had arrived in yesterday morning, she hadn't left it in its usual spot, on the left barstool. In the bedroom, the bedroom, it had to be in the bedroom.

The black Escalade nearly knocked Officer Lewiston off his motorcycle as it charged by him on his left, dominating half his lane, its two driver's side tires fully over the yellow center line, spitting up dust and debris as it pulled in front of him and blasted off into the distance. The cop checked his speedometer – their procession was going almost 70, which meant that car, and the three that followed soon after it, had to be pushing 90. "Please let me run this hot dog down," he implored into the procession's reserved channel.

"That's a negative, Lewiston," the rebuke came through his helmet speakers. "Do not break formation, repeat, do *not* break."

Once they were out on Highway 12, Sour had given permission to – check that, *encouraged* – Cody to put pedal to metal, then barked at the other drivers behind them to strap on their big boy underpants and keep up. Though Watson's procession had made good time, every car in their path pulling over at the sound of their sirens, Sour and his men reached the procession and passed them before they had even merged onto I-5 south.

"GO!" Sour yelled.

"I'm going ninet--" Cody yelled back before he noticed Sour was actually speaking into his phone.

"Shouldn't it be over by now?" Blunt barked into Sour's ear.

"They weren't there. We're en route to the second facility."

Sour heard the Congressman curse again, then a crash of his speaker phone going off the desk before the line went dead. No time to call back now – they were just pulling into the lot of the Stockton hospital, and who knew how many minutes before Watson's caravan came in behind them. They parked haphazardly across five spots on the far end of the lot, far from the reporters that had already set up near the doors Watson would enter through.

Sour commanded, "Go-go-go!" as they all got out of their cars and attempted to re-build their rifles on the fly. He even noticed a couple guys looking at their phones to re-check the map of the facility on which Sour had marked all their roof positions; they had scouted this building once, three days ago, but hadn't talked it and walked it and rehearsed it ad nauseum like they had the Napa hospital. Stockton was a much newer, starker, more industrial complex, with many more buildings, and Sour hoped he had enough men if it was indeed here the Killers decided to strike. He only had enough men to cover the four buildings bordering the parking lot. It should be more than sufficient, as long as the cops running the transfer didn't find some reason to alter the plan of where they would drop Watson off.

"ETA ten," Chaser broke Brenden's trance from the driver's seat. Brenden looked back and saw Tats loading his 40MM little babies into his vest, then locking and loading his Bushmaster.

Brenden reached back into his messenger bag for a tin of black greasepaint. He lowered his sun visor and opened the mirror, its tiny lights reflecting off his lifeless eyes as he blacked out every inch of his pale skin.

"Here they come," Cody spotted, and Sour crouched down with him to watch the procession of police vehicles they had passed only miles ago making its way down the long drive to the parking lot.

"Same drill," Sour reminded into his wrist. "Wait for my mark."

As the police vehicles found parking spots, a couple hospital orderlies were clearing a path to the door, and Watson's white van spun around and backed into this open space. It stopped fifty feet short of the steps up to the hospital entrance, its backdoors pulled open, reporters filling the void between those van doors and the hospital doors opposite it with the same exact queries their colleagues had asked just ninety minutes and eighty miles earlier.

"Hey-hey-hey, what's this?" Cody exclaimed. He had moved his scope up off Watson and the reporters and back to the entrance to the parking lot, where a '90s model, dirty white Explorer was making its way down the same path Watson's caravan had traversed only moments before.

Sour put a hand on Cody's back. "Steady."

"Holy shit." Cody took a hand off his gun to wipe the sweat from his brow before it dripped down into his sightlines. "This is it."

"Steady," Sour implored again, but this time into his wrist.

The Explorer got as close as it could get, before a couple ChiPs officers intercepted it. Its hazard lights came on as it froze in a no-man's land between regular parking spots.

Cody moved his finger off his trigger guard, down onto his trigger.

All the men were doing the same from their own roof perches as the doors of the SUV all opened in unison—

And a gaggle of young people dropped out, wrestling large signs out of the car behind them. "Killers-should-die!" the first woman pumped with her fist.

"Hold your fire, hold your fire!" Sour came up to full standing again, both arms raised high above his head.

"Killers-should-die! Killers-should-die!"

Watson was in the hospital before the protestors could even get close to him, the doors sealing tight behind him.

Sour saw Cody's shoulders melt around his gun in frustration, and heard in his earpiece the sighs of defeat from all the men. "What the fuck we do now, Sir?" Cody asked.

"I've got to get back to the plane," Sour answered, then sprinted for the stairs, not waiting for Cody to rise or take apart his rifle.

"Hey, wait—" Cody pleaded, but Sour was already gone. He would have one of the Escalades off the property before any of his men even descended from a roof.

Everything was proceeding as Sour had suspected it would. And he had to be alone for what was going to happen next.

Randy had no idea who Evan Watson was. Oh sure, he knew that Sour had taken the rest of Blunt's PSD to California, to the prison transfer of that school shooter. But he wasn't sure why the Congressman would allow him to do that, wasn't sure why Watson would be important to the Congressional Killers and therefore under Sour's purview. He wasn't watching MSNBC or Fox News when the transfer went off without a hitch, he was watching his 'skins on *Monday Night Football*. (Yeah, that was the worst part of Blunt's Randall Cunningham nickname; that Cunningham had QBed one of the teams Randy had grown up loving to hate. But what the hell, Randy wasn't about to mess with his health insurance by telling a Congressman what he could call him.) Blunt had already said over the intercom that he was going to bed, so Randy was taking advantage of the ginormous plasma in the Great Room, keeping the volume low enough to avoid disturbing him.

The Redskins had just fumbled it away thirty yards from the end zone, so Randy cursed out a little "Mother fucker!" before answering Jill's call. "Jilly Vanilli, what's happening?"

"Randy! They're coming there!"

"What?"

"The fucking Congressional Killers, they're coming there right the fuck now!"

Randy sat forward, muting the game. "What the hell are you--?"

"You've just got to trust me, Randy! They're fucking coming to the house!"

Randy pocketed his phone without saying goodbye, without even extinguishing the line, shoving his holster onto his belt, yanking out his Ruger, thumbing the hammer back and ready. *Everything's going to be fine, deep breaths, one step at a time.* He tried to tamp down his most frantic thoughts, and turn them instead to procedure. He would cross to the front door first to make sure it was locked, then proceed to the master keypad to light up the alarm, then the security room for a check of the monitors, followed by a sweep of everything with his own two eyes. 'skins were down two touches anyway. Maybe him not watching was just the change in luck they needed. Randy could see the front deadbolt was locked, but put fingers on it just to make sure.

That's when the front door exploded inward, one hundred seventy-seven pounds of flying, pure solid oak tackling him back into the wall.

YOU WEREN'T SUPPOSED TO BE HERE

"Three minutes."

Randy wouldn't know it, but that was Chase's voice he heard as he lay under the fallen front door. He kept his eyes locked shut and counted footfalls: six feet padding in, three invaders total – who else could it be but the Congressional Killers?

He waited and listened while they surveyed the Great Room, then split up, one rushing up the staircase just above Randy's head, the others around opposite corners, deeper into the caverns of the house.

Randy extricated himself as quietly as he could from under the splintered pieces of oak, gripping the left side of his ribs as he stood. He was sure the impact of the door had broken two or three of them, but was too grateful it had also cloaked him during the entrance of the marauders to complain. He looked down at his hands, now pasty white from the dust and plaster spit up by the explosion. His right hadn't lost its grip on his Ruger, just tightened if anything. He raised it, swiveling its orifice in every direction as he moved for the hole where the door used to stand, also darting his eyes to the floor to make sure he wasn't about to step on any debris that might crack or crunch under his weight. No, he wasn't stupid enough to pursue three gunmen into the house in a vain attempt to save Blunt. Randy was one man, against three guys he understood to be SEALs. Getting the eff out of Dodge, and as fast as he fucking could, that was the smart play, so he could return with reinforcements. It would be sad if the Killers got to Blunt, Randy might even shed a tear, but let's be real, Blunt was a paycheck, not worth the sacrifice of one's own life.

He was just stepping through the threshold to safety when he heard Tatsumi's voice behind him. "You breathe loud."

Randy whipped around, eyes rising to Tatsumi standing just behind the banister on the second floor above him. The SEAL's face was the last thing Randy would see before meeting five quick rounds from Tats's Bushmaster with his chest.

"Shots fired, shots fired!" Tatsumi heard Chase yelp over his headset.

"We're good," Tats replied, already moving down the upstairs hallway. "One guard down. Great Room clear." He hadn't gone downstairs to check Randy's vitals; there wasn't time if they were going to clear this entire estate in their allotted three minutes. But he had eyeballed an entry wound on Randy's throat as he was going down. There was no way anyone would survive that.

Tats shoved his AR barrel into a room on his right, then another on his left. There were just offices up here, one which looked like a mini-campaign HQ stuffed with worn signs from years past, another which had been converted into a gym. He opened every closet, looked under and behind every potential human-sized hiding spot, but turned up nothing. "Upstairs clear," he spit into his mic with disgust, returning to the stairs.

"I'm not finding anyone either," Chase replied through his headset. "Bowz?"

"Nothing."

"Shit, he's not here." Tatsumi was by now stepping off the bottom step, back on the ground floor. "Fifty seconds," he noted with a glance to his watch.

"Try the kitchen again, Tats," Chase recommended, "in case I didn't get every cabinet or drawer. This asshole hasn't left the property in six weeks, he's in here somewhere." Tatsumi was way ahead of him, already turning into the kitchen as Chase said the words.

Tatsumi wouldn't see who was already standing on the other side of the kitchen island before a single fissure of red popped open in the center of his forehead – and everything went black. He plummeted backwards, and Jill heard his skull connect with the tiles on the other side of the cooktop. She came around the box of cupboards and appliances, the tinny, frantic barks of the dead man's fellow invaders getting louder as she got closer to his headset.

Jill used her right fingers to confirm an unmoving carotid, then rose back up to aim her Glock down the mouth of the nearest hallway. She began side-stepping her way into the northern wing of the house. There were two more Congressional Killers to go, and she had fourteen rounds left.

Brenden was in what he thought had to be Blunt's office. There was the humongous desk, the wet bar, the white board covered with little magnetic nameplates representing the votes of each of his fellow members of Congress. But more than anything, it was the giant oil painting of some sort of miner. Brenden knew from Blunt's self-absorbed attempt at small talk in the first seven minutes of their meeting in the Capitol that this must be his father. Blunt couldn't help himself, crowing about how far he had come, the ignoble origins he had had to overcome to get where he was today. *Try having your fucking child shot dead in her fucking classroom,* Brenden had seethed in his mind as Blunt prattled on.

Brenden fixated on this painting now, wondering why it had to be so large, why that was really the size the Congressman had commissioned. Sure, maybe it was just what Blunt's ego required, not something lifesize, but larger-than-life. Or was there perhaps a more practical reason?

Brenden rotated his rifle onto his back, then pulled the survival knife off his belt. He shoved its tip right between the elder Blunt's eyes, and knew upon contact what he would find on the other side. He chuckled as he zippered the blade down, slicing this miner open from third eye to twin balls. Brenden shoved the knife back in his belt, and for just a moment stared at that slit he had opened. *I should fuck that slit,* he thought—

Brenden caught himself, reminded of the young man he used to be, that angry, pimpled, pugnacious little dick that had signed up for SEAL training. That Brenden, he just might have pulled out his cock and shoved it in that slot and left something special behind for Blunt because why the fuck not. Sarah Beth had changed him, Christina and Ty had evolved him beyond *that* Brenden. But what had happened to his daughter, to his family, erased all that evolution. Evan Watson had transformed him back into the animal he used to be, the rabid creature Uncle Sam had tamed, and though he was still good at hiding it, he did find himself morphing back into a depraved monster on each and every one of their Congressional Kills.

Brenden stuck his fingers through the slit, well aware before he tore the two sides of it wide what he was going to find. When he had made that initial puncture into the painting, his knife tip should have embedded into the wall behind it. But instead, it stopped, sending a vibration up his forearm like it had connected with steel or metal.

Jill's single gunshot rang out from down the hall, from in the kitchen. Brenden crouched behind Blunt's desk, rifle out, as defensive a position as this room would allow him. *That was a nine*, he thought. *Could've been one of ours; could've been a Glock.*

Brenden was about to inquire into his teammates's safety when his eyes were caught again by that gaping hole he had left in the middle of the ornate frame around Blunt's daddy. Through the open wings of parchment, a single metal door had been revealed.

Jill was barely halfway down the hall when the .223-caliber hailstorm started. She crouched and turned back for the kitchen, her peripheral vision just catching a fleeting silhouette through the smoke and flying shrapnel of one of the Killers traipsing for her with Bushmaster at full rat-a-tat.

She sprinted back behind the island, slipping onto the bloody floor next to Tatsumi's corpse. The wood of the cabinets all above her head splintered and burst, the one with the glass display doors raining down onto her back. The porcelain from the Blunt family china displayed within also cascaded off her spine.

And then just as it began, it ceased. After the shrapnel had settled, Jill heard the unmistakable thok of a hollowed out magazine dropping to the floor. Before the next one could go in, she raised her Glock just above the top of the isle and unloaded four rounds blindly in the direction from which the fire had originated. She pulled her gun back down, not wanting to waste too many shells. She cursed under her breath, hearing no grunts of pain, no connection with flesh or bone, just wood and adobe.

"You know why we're here!" Chase's voice screamed from down the hall, between the sounds of fresh ammo being shoved into his gun. "We just want Blunt! Stand up with your arms raised and we'll let you walk out of here!"

Jill wasn't stupid enough to reply with anything but silence. She kept herself down with Tatsumi, waiting for the inevitable response: more gunfire, tearing this once-gorgeous room even further to shreds.

And that's when she noticed the grenade launcher lying prone next to the corpse. She searched the Rhodesian rig of pouches the Killer wore around the abdominals area of his body armor, finding his stash of 40MM grenades. This one must have been their breacher, she thought, their mortarman; he looked like he had come prepared to bring down a bridge or level a skyscraper. As she waited for the second barrage to end, Jill slid a shell out of Tats' gear and slammed it into the side of the weapon.

When the barrage ceased, she rose up to her full height, firing Tatsumi's H&K in one fluid motion. She saw the shell hit the far wall of the hall, then ate tile – she didn't know enough about explosives to guess how much of a punch that projectile she had just hurled would pack, or to even be sure she would survive the subsequent explosion. She just knew it was her only hope of survival.

"Oh fuck m--" she heard Chase mutter, before he was cut off by the loudest sound she had ever heard, that sound itself almost instantly replaced by a droning buzz that covered all other noise.

Ninety seconds later, in fact, all she could still hear was that unending Emergency Broadcast Network whine. She knew she was at a disadvantage with one sense dulled, but also knew she couldn't sit there like a duck any longer. She rose with Glock levelled, approaching the pile of building materials that now blocked the mouth of the hall, the dusk sun just peeking its last light through a new gap in the ceiling. She climbed over and traipsed through the rubble, until she came upon Chase, still finding breaths despite the wood shard impaling him between the ribs, despite the bubbly blood pouring out of his mouth with each belabored gasp.

"Put them on." Jill tossed a pair of flex cuffs onto Chase's chest, not letting herself get disconcerted by the underwater timbre of her own voice.

His hands moved in response, even though neither his eyes nor his head could, finding the cuffs, picking them up between his fingers.

"I said, put them on." Jill accentuated her point with another jut of her Glock.

But Chase didn't put them on. He just held them for a few seconds--

"No, don't!"

--before his right hand whipped down to his waist, to the Glock holstered there--

Jill stamped him right between the eyes with her sixth shot of the day.

She turned, leading with her gun again as she continued her interrupted dance deeper into the mansion. Two down, one to go.

After all the shots, at least two clips being emptied, then a grenade burst that rocked even this far end of the house, not to mention the random shots of a Glock here or there, Brenden knew some shit had gone down. The radio had been silent for over three minutes now; best case scenario, that meant the guys had the drop on someone. Maybe they had just gone silent until they slew their prey. Hell, maybe the explosion was just Tats ripping a rat hole short cut between rooms just to show off.

But, worst case, they had been forced into eternal silence.

Either way, their initial three minutes had been up two minutes ago. They had agreed upon a protocol before the Carpinello hit: no more than three minutes at any location, and at the end of the three minutes, there would be no hot extracts; everyone who could get out *would* get out, even if it meant leaving a man behind. They all knew this was suicide shit they were attempting, that they were bound to lose one of their number sooner or later, and the most important thing was not any "No man left behind" bullshit, but that someone survived to complete the mission, to deliver their full message to the world. If they only got one or even three of these assholes, would anyone even understand? But get all four, *these* four, the four who had welched on the gun bill – that was the only way they would be heard loud and clear.

Brenden wrestled with the protocol now. He couldn't call for the guys on the comm without giving away his own existence and maybe even theirs. That left him two options: go back down the hallway from whence all the violence had been heard, or go out those two glass doors opposite the desk he was still hiding behind. He wanted to go down that hallway, he wanted to get them out of the shit, but he also knew they wouldn't want him to. He wasn't a corpsman, a Navy medic, none of them were. And hospitals were no longer an option. Even if he saved one or both of them, if they'd sustained any injuries whatsoever, he would probably have to leave them behind anyway. Brenden wished getting that metal door behind the painting open was one of the options, but he would need Tats to do that, and he had a bad feeling about Tats; Tatsumi had gone silent even before Chase had. Brenden realized it would be a bitter irony if he, the one with the biggest doubts, was the lone survivor, if he was the only one left to take out Blunt. But he silently promised the guys he would do just that, that he would stow all his personal baggage and finish it, even with his last dying breath.

Brenden rose, and with his rifle aimed at the mouth of the hallway, sashayed for the glass backdoors. Keeping the gun raised with his right hand, he reached his left over for the handle without looking at it, pushing it down, then pulling the door towards him.

"Stop right there."

Brenden turned from the hallway to the glass doors, looking out with confusion into the darkening red expanse—until the motion sensor lights snapped to life, illuminating Jill and her raised Glock moving closer to the house.

Jill breathed a sigh of relief that Brenden had done as she had guessed, as she had hoped: he had assumed she would be coming from the hall. He had left his rear flank open. "I know what you carry," she continued. "Bushmaster and Glock, both on the floor, now."

Brenden reached over to pull his Bushmaster's strap off his right shoulder, then lowered the long gun to the floor. He opened the holster snap on his waist, pulling out his pistol and laying that next to the rifle. "Might as well surrender that knife, too." As he complied, Jill was stepping in through the threshold into the house. "Now, hands on your head. Back up, one step at a time, nice and slow." Brenden did as she asked, giving her space to step deeper into the room. She didn't bother to close the door to the outside behind her, not wanting to distract herself even in the slightest. "Good boy. Now on your knees."

Brenden dropped to his right knee, then his left, not even cognizant that he was now almost directly in front of the tattered remains of the oil painting he had defaced. "You going to kill me?" he asked. "You can go ahead and kill me. I'll be with my daughter again."

Jill smirked, pulling her phone out of her back pocket. "I'll be quite content knowing you'll never take a comfortable shower again."

But before she brought it to her ear, Brenden could hear the hard click of a lock being opened behind him, then a breath of air whispering through the hairs on the back of his neck as a door was thrown open. The padding of older, less athletic feet—

"Congressman, what are you--?"

--and then the hard metal of a gun barrel being pushed into his brain stem. "Put the phone down, Jilly." Brenden knew that voice. It even made him smile.

"Sir, you really shouldn't be—"

"I said put it down!" Blunt yelped from behind Brenden's shoulder, betraying his tensed nerves.

The girl's right, Brenden thought. *Moron shouldn't be doing this…*

"This is my home, and I will be the one to end this!" Brenden felt Blunt's hot breath on the skin just behind his right ear. "You hear that, Bauman? This time, you're not leaving my house alive."

Blunt was a corpulent, bloated piece of government pig shit. Brenden was a SEAL. Brenden was faster first thing in the morning with a ten pound hangover than Blunt had ever been in his life, than he ever would be again. Brenden wanted Blunt's gun and he took it. Brenden wanted Blunt in a headlock, and he put him in one, drilling his own pistol into his temple.

"No! Congressman!"

But the girl-- Brenden was worried about the girl.

"Shoot him, Jill!"

She had somehow taken out Chase and Tatsumi. Blunt was child's play for Brenden, but the girl was a variable he had to worry about.

"Jill! You've got to--"

BLAM-BLAM-BLAM.

Brenden ripped three rounds off from Blunt's gun before the girl could get a shot around her employer. Her shirt burst with red, and one of the glass doors behind her exploded as a bullet found its way through her.

"NO!" Blunt howled.

She stumbled back, her Achilles tripping over the leftover frame of the door. She landed flat on her spine on a bed of glass and cement. She tensed as if she would find the strength to get back up, then released it in surrender.

"No. No, Jill, I'm sorry…"

"On your feet," Brenden spit into the ear of the sobbing Congressman. "Let's go." He took hold of Blunt in the roughest way he could think of, a hard grip around the throat, dragging him back towards that rubbled hallway and the front of the house.

Sour wouldn't arrive for another two hours. It had taken him over an hour to get back to Napa where he had left the plane, then over an hour and forty-minutes in the air, plus another fifteen to get off the plane, get back in his Beast and drive her from Bisbee Douglas back out to Blunt's estate.

Sour found what he expected to find after that two hours: the front gate pushed aside, its motor disabled; the front door blown off its hinges; Randy's corpse discarded over a great room love seat like a slimy rain slicker tossed off when its wearer walked in the door. Poor Randy. Sour liked Randy, but Blunt had to choose one man to stay with him, and Randy was that guy, collateral damage in this terrible, terrible game.

It was in the kitchen that Sour started to find his prediction amiss. The cabinets, the center island, everything was shot to shit, with a dead SEAL's body in the middle of the floor. Sour confirmed it was the Asian one, it was James Tatsumi, then moved onto the hallway. Something even harder had hit the hallway, not to mention the second SEAL, whom Sour found impaled on some plywood.

Chase Hodell. And James Tatsumi before him. Who had fought these guys off? Sour instinctively reached into his jacket and touched his holster, before remembering there hadn't been anything in that holster in over a year now. What was he going to find in the back of the house – the third SEAL, or Blunt?

He poked his head in Blunt's bedroom, finding it empty and immaculate.

The office next to it was too. Or at least, that's what Sour thought until he felt the breeze from the far wall and turned to the back French doors, finding one left ajar, relieved of its pane of glass. Resting on the bottom sill of the door frame, two feet clad in comfortable but classy women's work shoes.

"No," Sour mumbled as he charged to the door and through the frame, ignoring the glass crunching under his knees as he knelt beside Jill, lifting her head with his left hand. "You weren't supposed to be here."

Her eyes fluttered, then blinked. "Sour," she smiled as meekly as she vocalized.

"We're getting you out of here."

Feeling his other hand go under the small of her back, realizing he was lifting her, she put a hand on his chest to try to stop him. "No. Blunt... Bauman took him."

"I don't give a shit about Blunt."

Jill's eyes started to roll back up into her skull, and Sour put her down, trying to slap some consciousness into her as tenderly as possible. "Hey. Hey. Stay with me. You gotta try to stay awake, just until—"

Jill shook her head. "I'm such a liar."

"What? You're not a liar. You're probably too honest," Sour smiled, remembering their last flight together.

"It's against the natural order of things," she said not to him, but up into the heavens, into the vastness of her life flashing before her eyes.

"What are you talking about?" Sour asked, slapping her again, worried she was delirious and losing it. "Stay with me..."

"When I got discharged... my Dad didn't really stick by me. 'This is why women shouldn't be in the military.' That's what he said to me. 'It's against the natural order of things. They're just going to get more men killed.'" She rotated her face back to his, looking up into his eyes one last time. "I cold called Allied Armament myself. *I* cold called the Congressman." She fisted that hand on Sour's chest, balling up his jacket between her fingers with the last strength she possessed. "That's how I know… you're a good…"

Her lips didn't move again. Neither did her eyes.

Clayton Manco closed those beautiful eyes with a shaking finger. A droplet of tear landed on her cheek, the first he had let fall in nearly a year.

Sour shrouded Jill with the comforter from Blunt's bed. Then Sour went out to his Beast, retrieving the rucksack he had hastily packed when he thought he was leaving this place for good.

He went back inside and emptied the office bar's decanter of tequila, pouring it down his open throat like he had found the waters of Shangri-La. That initial light-headedness of a drunk lowering itself onto his consciousness didn't fill him with warm euphoria, but transported him to a different time and place, reverting him back to the man he used to be.

That's when he saw it lying in the middle of the giant Chinese rug covering the center of the floor, just a few feet in front of the metal door to Blunt's safe room.

"You think you're some kinda gunfighter, don't you? Through and through."

Sour bent to pick up the Sig Sauer. It wasn't his old friend, but a relative of his oldest friend, a close enough simulacrum that he knew he could trust it implicitly. He didn't know how he had missed it, reflecting the room's overhead lights like a freshly polished diamond on the ring finger of a newlywed.

As he rose back up to his full height, he could feel the weapon become not only a part of his hand again, he could feel it course energy through his veins, eradicating any aches and pains and giving new strength to his every joint and cranny. He had known all along, from the moment Blunt asked to hire him – no, from the moment he saw Jill and Randy standing in his front yard – that this moment would come. He couldn't involve himself in an affair of guns without being sucked into the affair himself. Eventually, he knew he would himself be compelled to drink in the hot adrenaline rush that only the firing of a gun at another living being brought to your breast and to your temples. Sour knew the dark controlling souls that resided within these guns, knew the dark magic in which they congressed, and knew it was the guns that had twisted events in a conspiracy to drag him into the conflagration.

Could he feel in the gun's weight that it wasn't full, that it was missing some shots? Or did he just somehow know this was the gun that had killed Jill? He really couldn't feel that minute difference, could he? Is it possible this gun spoke to him? Did it *tell* him it had killed Jill? Did it apologize?

He stepped into the panic room, turning for the lone drawer Blunt had left pulled out, the foam slot that usually served as this weapon's bed left empty. Around it, more slots, for fuller magazines. Sour took two, filling the empty leather pockets hanging under his right armpit.

And then he slid the gun itself into the pocket under his left.

He returned to his rucksack, removing the small laptop his daughter had once picked out for him, setting it down on the bar to open it. He clicked the icon to life as Frazier, the FBI computer tech, had once taught him. A map of Arizona filled his screen, a single red dot proceeding west across the bottom of the state. Sour let out a tiny mental smile at the memory of Frazier. He had been High Value's resident gadget guy, might still be for all Sour knew. He would have to ask Poughkeepsie sometime if 'Queer' was still around. That's what Sour had called him, 'Queer,' after James Bond's 'Q.' He never seemed to mind, but now Sour had to wonder.

He shook off those regrets, digging back in the ruck for the white ear buds Frazier had also told him he would need, finding the correct hole on the left side of the computer's base to plug them in. He placed the tiny speakers in his ears, but at first, all he heard was the drone of tires on road, plus an occasional hard bump or two, building in intensity and frequency, like someone was knocking on something. Finally he heard a voice:

"You let me out of here, you mother fucker!"

Knowing it was working just as it was supposed to, he pulled out the buds and set them down on the bar. He crouched to open the cabinet doors underneath all the bottles, digging through glassware until he found a flask, engraved to Blunt from one of his kids. Sour didn't read the exact words, just unscrewed its top as he stood, finding another bottle of brown booze with his other hand. He had once told Blunt that mezcal was his drink, but he didn't really give a shit, he just liked getting drunk. He opened up this other bottle, this Dewar's or Johnny Walker or who the hell cares, and poured it sloppily down into the mouth of the flask, spilling over its sides, but getting enough in that it soon bubbled over. He took a pull off the top so he could close it cleanly, then used a fistful of cocktail napkins to wipe it down.

Sour tossed the full, dry flask into his rucksack, then replaced the earbuds in his hearing canals. *"—hear me, you coward?"* the voice inside them was saying. *"You let me out of here so we can settle this like men!"*

Sour eyed the route the red dot was taking, now through Tucson and continuing west toward the next city big enough to be marked on this map.

Beyond that city, beyond Yuma, lay the border with California.

Sour knew where that red dot was going, where Blunt's voice was being taken. Might as well make his way out to Beast, he thought. In this final act, his own timing had become more important than he had thought it would be.

THE DEATH OF
THE SOUTHPAW SHOOTER

As he tightened the third strand of parachute cord locking Blunt to the desk, Brenden finally spoke. It was a standard elementary school desk, a metal and plastic chair connected at about rib-height to a writing surface shaped like an upside-down L. After forcing him down into the desk, Brenden had tied the Congressman's right arm behind his back, to one of the pipes linking back rest to seat. Crouching down, he then locked each of Blunt's ankles to a leg of the desk chair. It was while tying down Blunt's left leg that he finally spoke. "This was her third grade classroom."

Blunt looked over in horror. He knew he had been in the trunk of Jill's car for hours; she had left her Civic zagged across the driveway in front of the house, key in the ignition, providing Brenden with a more convenient escape vehicle than the one the Team had left parked down beside the Vista park. Blunt had lost track of time in that trunk. He realized they were parked in a school parking lot when Brenden threw the trunk open, and knew he had been dragged into a classroom – one for very young students by the look of the decorations. But it wasn't until Brenden spoke those words that Blunt knew which classroom this was, *whose* classroom, and began to understand the morbid reason he had been brought here. Blunt looked out the wall of windows on his left at the sun starting its morning climb over the playground grass and asphalt, and started to shake with tears. He knew no janitor would be coming to unlock the doors, no early bird teachers to go over the day's lesson plans; he knew from his own kids' schedules that Christmas break had started across America, and no one would be coming to save him from this final Congressional Killer.

Brenden tapped his fingers on the flat, shiny surface of the desk. "They had to get her a special left-handed desk out of storage. Just like this one. Yep, that's right, she was left-handed, just like you, Homer." Brenden leaned over, resting his palms on top of his thighs. "You do remember telling me to call you Homer?"

"Yes, yes, of course I do, Brenden," Blunt choked out with his last fleeting gasps of hope. "We had a connection. I heard everything you said in that meeting. And I've been working on it. Politics is hard. I just need a little more time and I'll be able to—"

Without betraying even a breath of emotion, Brenden grabbed Blunt's remaining free extremity, his left hand, slamming that palm-down on the desk, wrapping several revolutions of the parachute cord around his wrist and the desk, so tight Blunt could already see his skin reddening even in this dawn light. "No, Brenden—wait, wait! Your anger is with Evan Watson. *Evan Watson* took your daughter from you. Not me—"

A desk one row up from Blunt's shook as Brenden slammed a tool box down on top of it. He flipped open its top and started digging and clanging through the tools like he had a task as mundane as tightening a door handle to complete. "Evan Watson is sick, Homer," he replied, keeping his eyes on his tools. "Mentally ill. He couldn't help what he did." He grinned when he found what he needed, the banana yellow handle of a box cutter. "You could," he finished his thought as he extended and protracted the blade a few times to confirm it wasn't rusted shut.

"What--" Blunt stuttered, "what the hell are you--?"

Brenden took one step forward, rearing back, then in one fluid motion stabbed the blade full force into Blunt's left biceps. Blunt screamed out at the impact, then shrieked as Brenden yanked it out as fast as he shoved it in, leaving a wound that geysered out blood like a champagne bottle just past the stroke of New Year's.

The SEAL leaned forward, confirming his blow had landed where he had wanted it to. "That's your brachial artery, Homer. Should give us a couple more hours together." He stood up to his full height with a wink. "Wouldn't want you to miss this." He returned to the toolbox, thumbing the blade back into the box cutter without even wiping it, tossing it back in to begin a search for something else.

"Miss?" Blunt blubbered. "Miss what?"

Brenden looked up with his most satisfied, relaxed smile of the past three years. "The death of the Southpaw Shooter."

Brenden again found what he was looking for, gripping a fist around the straight wood handle of a hammer. Blunt's chest pumped with hyperventilation as Brenden brought it back over to his desk. "The death of--What does that mean? What does that mean, Brenden?"

Brenden slammed his free hand on top of Blunt's on the desk, holding the Congressman's left forefinger extended with his own digits. Then, with four or ten quick blows – Blunt couldn't keep count through the searing pain – smashed Blunt's forefinger with the hammer. It lost shape and went flat as he pulverized the bones inside. The organs inside gushed, filling the flab of skin with internal fluids.

Brenden kept Blunt's hand locked down as he took a break from his task, like a hard-hatted foreman chatting about last night's hockey tilt with his men on the worksite. It was at this point in an interrogation that the questions would start, that's what Brenden had learned in his intel training. But this torture session wasn't an interrogation; it was to be a moral sermon.

"Did you know, at the time the Second Amendment was written, citizens with guns were required to bring them to periodic public musters? That's right, they would have them inspected, and have to prove they knew how to use them. If they couldn't, they were required to take additional training. They even, believe it or not, had to register the guns on public rolls."

Brenden's grip was already positioned to hold down the thumb next. He gave it even more whacks than the first finger, just to make sure he demolished every square centimeter of its extra width and girth.

"Gun powder had to be stored safely," he continued his history lesson after the thumping had again quieted, "and separate from your gun, even though that meant it would take longer to load in the event your home was attacked."

The middle finger was next, and by now, Blunt could only gurgle out a meek response, unsure if this was because his pain receptors were already overloaded, or the arterial blood loss was starting to set in. Brenden was able to destroy this finger with fewer blows, the entire hand now immobilized and unmoving, any initial fight in Blunt smashed out of him.

"Guns weren't allowed in any building in Boston, and the second-most common reason for arrest in frontier towns after drunk and disorderly was the carrying of concealed weapons." Brenden chuckled and shook his head. "Not many people realize that even in Tombstone, just twenty-three miles from your hometown, Congressman, site of the most famous gunfight in American history-- even in Tombstone, it was illegal to possess a deadly weapon without a permit."

Next was the ring finger. Brenden didn't even bother to remove Blunt's wedding ring, just demolished it into another deformed shape lost in the mass of numbed, purpled skin.

"In other words, ever since this country began, we've had gun control. And every step of the way since. The founding fathers you and Lafayette and your ilk worship so much – *they believed in gun control.* Even the NRA itself supported gun control measures, in the '30s, in the '60s… until they realized how much more powerful an organization, how much richer, they could become by being total absolutist obstructionists. Preying on everyone's fears. Gun control has never led to mass confiscation by the government; no one's ever even proposed that or wanted that. *We* didn't want that. Gun control has never led to the emasculation of the American man."

Brenden shook this off, realizing he was letting his passion distract him from his goal. He adjusted his hand to hold down that final finger, the pinky, then shattered it under four rapid-fire blows. He let go of the whimpering Blunt's hand, returning to his toolbox for more digging.

"You had a chance to do something historic," Brenden scolded without looking up. "Something good." He lifted the upper tray up and out of the toolbox, setting that aside. "But instead you had to make sure another gun control measure met another painful, humiliating death." Brenden held up his final tool in the light, the jagged teeth of a twelve-inch hacksaw gleaming in the morning rays.

Blunt shook his head in denial. "No, no, please Brenden, that law, it, it just wasn't right. It wouldn't have saved your daughter if it had been in place. We can do better, Bren--"

Brenden grabbed Blunt's tongue between two fingers, lightly tapping it with the teeth of his saw. "Careful. I was hoping to have a constructive conversation with you, Homer. But you're going to have to stay on topic. Not obfuscate, or turn to talking points."

Blunt nodded compliance, and Brenden turned his attention back down to the Congressman's destroyed left hand.

"You promised me, Homer. Don't you remember? As we were walking out, you put a hand on my shoulder and stopped me. And you leaned in and whispered, 'I promise, Brenden. We're going to make your Christina's sacrifice mean something. I promise.'" Brenden slapped the saw blade against Blunt's chest like he was rough-housing a beer-drinking buddy. "What, you don't remember that?" he even smiled. "You don't remember saying her name like that?"

"I, I do, Brenden, and I promise, if you could find it in your heart to forgive me…"

"You don't remember using my dead daughter's name in one of your lies?"

Blunt just stared at him, knowing when he heard those words that there would be no forgiveness, no mercy, no survival in his future.

Brenden whipped the saw blade down into the base of Blunt's forefinger, sinking its teeth into his melted flesh. And though Blunt had stopped feeling that hand when Brenden had bashed it into oblivion, he now felt it again, felt every push and pull and tear and rip as Brenden sawed into his skin and into his bone.

The sky flashed its first strobe of lightning, before splatters of a muggy Southern California rain began to land not only upon Beast's windshield, but the wooden, hand-carved sign just beyond it:

Ridgewood Elementary School. K-12.
Safety. Kindness. Responsibility.

Sour stared at those faded letters, not because he was reading it, but because it was the most convenient thing to look at from where he had parked. He wasn't thinking about the meaning of the words, or even their irony when one considered this building's recent history. Nor was he considering the dark tales that would one day be told about this particular early morning. Sour was just listening to his earbuds, to Blunt screaming and pleading and begging that Brenden stop.

The hammering had been easy to hear; Sour now had to push the buds in a little deeper, had to pump his laptop's volume, to hear the rending of flesh and bone that had replaced that pounding. He knew what he was hearing, recognizing the sound of meat being cut open and butchered from when his padre used to do it after a hunt. But this slaughter was different, performed with a dull blade, perhaps to maximize the pain. Sour's daddy would always cut around the bone, but now he heard Brenden wrestling through cartilage and marrow. Sour counted the bones, the impact of each amputed cylinder of flesh landing on cold, smooth floor. He had to keep count, because he had to know when to intervene.

Sour took another swig off Blunt's flask, like he was digging for the bottom of a lap-riding popcorn tub at a Saturday afternoon movie. He heard yet another plop, this one with the extra ding of Blunt's wedding ring. *Ring finger,* Sour thought. *My count's correct then.*

Of course his count was correct. In mere minutes, he would have to insert himself into this matinee.

The Southpaw Shooter had nothing left but a blood-soaked stump at the end of his left arm, one tiny finger sticking erect off its far left edge. Brenden held down the stump, hovering the crimson blade above that final finger, before pausing for a breath and a thought.

"A couple days after the shooting, I took Ty, my son, to school on this temporary campus they had set up out there in the parking lot. We were just sitting there in the rain, looking out at these three pathetic double-wides where he'd spend the rest of the school year. I didn't know what to say.

"So I just touched him. And said, 'You'll be safe, Son.' And he turned to me with this, this something in his eyes I had never seen before. Something you're not supposed to see yet in a child's eyes. And he said, 'How can I ever believe you when you say that? You were supposed to keep her safe. And you didn't.'"

Brenden broke. For the first time in months, maybe since Christina's funeral, he couldn't stop the tears from flowing down, even inflecting sobs into his voice as he continued. "And I just started crying. He was right. I was a SEAL, and I couldn't protect my own daughter. Not in our own country, I couldn't protect her. So I just broke down, I just *sobbed,* right in front of my son."

Brenden stopped himself, sucking in composure with a deep nasal inhale, then backhanding the moisture from his face. He brought the saw teeth back down to where that final finger met the rest of Blunt's left hand. "We will never cure the world of evil, Congressman," he said, and Blunt looked up to realize he was staring right into his eyes. "And we will never write a perfect law that will eradicate all gun violence. But our job, as parents, as men, as Americans, is to do everything we can, every little thing in our power, to make this country as safe as we possibly can. If we are presented with the opportunity to save even one life, we have to seize it. You had that opportunity, Congressman, to save many lives. And you threw it away. The next person in your position to have that opportunity must know they can't throw it away. They must know they have to do something."

Brenden sawed, and Blunt just panted out grunts of pain. The full-bellied screams, the howls, had long ago left him. He just sobbed, until he felt that final finger disconnect from his hand and drop down onto the linoleum between his feet.

"BRENDEN!"

A rumble of thunder underscored the voice booming in from the hallway door behind them. Blunt thought it only a part of an imagined fever dream, until he noticed Brenden also tensing. "S-S-Sour," The Congressman's lips somehow whispered.

Brenden returned to his toolbox, tossing in the hacksaw, before removing the Glock from the back of his belt. As he passed the Congressman's torture desk, Blunt heard the SEAL chamber a round into the pistol, just before his footsteps disappeared into the hallway.

The silhouette stood before the doors at the far end of the hall, his jacket dripping from the morning rain. There was a silent flash of more lightning – for a moment making the man look like a ghost from a choppy, sepia silent film. With the hall's overhead florescents extinguished for the holiday week, Brenden couldn't see his face, but he knew who this was, even if he didn't know his name. His voice sealed it – the same voice he had heard calling after him as he was chased from Blunt's barbecue.

"It's time to end this, Brenden," that voice projected off the lockers lining the walls. "You've punished Blunt. You've delivered your message. Let's put the gun down and call the police."

Brenden took a step forward, Glock leading the way. "You don't know anything about what I'm doing here."

"Actually, I do," Sour explained. "I know exactly the rage that burns in your soul."

"You don't know anything about me!" Brenden shook, just before the thunder corresponding to that last lightning flash rattled the building.

"A teenage gunman destroyed my own family," Sour explained, surprised that even the adrenaline of the moment could keep any crack, any weakness out of his voice, especially when it came to this topic he hadn't discussed in so many months. "I know all the emotions, the thoughts, the dreams that drove you to do what you're doing. And I was going to let you do it." Now it was Sour's turn to take a step forward. "But tonight, you went too far. One too many innocent bystanders fell tonight."

"It's called collateral damage."

"It's called murder. And you know that. That's why you spared little Emily Payne, isn't it? Stephen Payne's little girl, Emily?"

Brenden felt his palms sweating now, and adjusted his grip on his gun, left hand to the handle, right on top of it.

"You were the one with doubts, weren't you?" Sour poured it on, sensing he had exposed a weak spot, a chink in this knight's armor. He took another step, continuing to test the SEAL's resolve.

"Stay the fuck back!"

Brenden actually retreated a half-step on that declaration, a tell that Sour was getting through to him.

"There's always one, Brenden. The one telling the other guys you're taking this too far."

"Put your hands up."

"Tell me I'm wrong, Brenden."

"Your hands on your head, right fucking now!"

Sour raised his hands, but just to shoulder level, not all the way to his skull as ordered, keeping them hovering, and primed to act. He could feel his heartrate lowering, his breath slowing the way it used to do when he was lining up a target – that odd reaction he always had to situations that would make most human beings fill their pants with excrement. Even if his mind was unsure how this was going to end, his system was preparing itself for the inevitable.

"She called you the good one, Brenden."

More lightning strobed the door's windows just beyond Sour's shoulders.

"I said *on your head!*" Brenden screamed.

"I know there's still good in there."

"You wanna see how good I am, mother fucker? Huh? You want me to prove you wrong by blowing your fucking brains out?"

"Brenden, I'm warning you. If I have to fill my hand, you will die."

"You know so much about me, don't you realize who you're talking to?"

"I do. I know how good a killer you are."

"Then put your--"

"I'm just better."

"--HANDS ON YOUR HEAD, MOTHER FU--"

"YOU WILL DIE IN THE SAME SCHOOL BUILDING CHRISTINA DIED IN, BRENDEN!"

"DON'T YOU DARE SAY HER NAME TO ME! YOU DON'T GET TO SAY--"

The thunder boomed--

And Sour's right hand charged into his jacket.

Brenden squeezed off four rounds in quick, semi-automatic succession.

Blunt flinched on each echoing report. Perhaps his body didn't move in unison with every shot, his limbs far too drained of energy for that, his arteries too emptied of blood. But his soul did. He knew enough about guns to identify the five shots. He was the Southpaw Shooter, after all. And one of the two guns to discharge was his own, after all.

Four shots had come from a Glock, and just one from the Sig Sauer P220 he was sure Sour had retrieved from his home office back in Bisbee.

Four shots to one. Blunt didn't know why he sobbed; didn't know why he even cared if Sour saved him after the pain and humiliation he had endured. But he did. He had let himself become hopeful that Sour was going to save him.

And then he heard the four Glock shots to just one from his Sig. He heard the impact of a body out there on the linoleum. And he knew he was never going to be saved.

A GUNFIGHTER,
THROUGH AND THROUGH

The next lightning flash lit up the smoke wafting from Sour's barrel like a dry ice mist accentuated with laser lights. He tucked the P220 back under his armpit, then walked for that classroom from which the dead SEAL had emerged. Sour didn't pause to check himself for his own wounds, having counted out all four of Brenden's bullets landing behind him: two against brick, two puncturing the glass of the school's double-doored exit.

He stooped to confirm the hole leaking red above Brenden's right eye, and that the life had completely left those white orbs themselves. Brenden was gone. Sour was about to stand when a glint of gold gave him pause. He removed the SEAL's trident pin, that trademark insignia of an eagle clutching an anchor, tri-pronged spear and flintlock pistol, and pocketed it as he stood to continue to the classroom.

"Sour…" Blunt was already rasping before he even rounded the corner. He had recognized the click and clack of Sour's alligator skin shit-kickers as he marched down the hall and over Brenden Bauman; that's when he knew he was wrong, that Sour's one shot had beaten Brenden's four. "I told you you'd do it." Blunt forced a smile across his dry, cracking lips. "I told you you'd kill that bastard."

Sour crossed to Blunt and leaned over him-- but rather than undoing one of his parachute ties, he reached into Blunt's left pocket and retrieved Tippy, the cat pendant he had borrowed from his daughter. *"Wear this always,"* he had said to Abby six years ago. Or was it seven now? *"And Tippy will always be by your heart."* Tippy looked almost as new as on that day, no worse for the wear of the long political drama to which she had borne witness.

"I kept that." Blunt forced a proud grin across his lips. "I told you I would. Long as I have that, you'll know where I am. That's what you said. And I never stopped believing you."

Sour pocketed the pendant and turned for the door, each boot clicking and clacking twice more before Blunt could call after him again. "Sour-- wait, wait! My arm. This wound." He motioned with his head down to the inside crease of his left arm, where a snail trail of dark crimson extended out of his flesh and down onto the floor. "This is an artery. I can't remember which artery. You have to call an ambulance. I don't have much time."

But Sour hadn't turned back around, and didn't rush to help his employer.

"Sour…?"

"Last year. I didn't answer when you asked me why I wouldn't come to work for you. Why I quit the Bureau, why I wouldn't come back from Texas."

Sour looked up. If Blunt could have seen his eyes, he would have seen they were lost in these memories. "When I was recruited to DC, to the High Value Targets team, Diane didn't want to leave Texas. She had her own political career just ramping up. She couldn't leave that behind. So I said fine. We weren't that happy anymore anyways. I left Abby with her and I went to DC by myself."

Sour had Tippy back out in his hand again, and looked down into her face. "The next time I visited, I had this pendant a gadget guy at the Bureau had souped up for me. I thought as long as I could always look up on the computer where Abby was, I was being a good father.

"I knew nothing about being a good father, because I knew nothing about her. I didn't know she was struggling in math, that she had to listen to jazz when doing her homework, or that she'd recently stopped speaking with her best friend.

"And I never met her boyfriend. *Eddie.* I had no idea she even had a boyfriend. I never got my own read on the guy, or warned her to watch out for the creep. I would have just looked into his eyes and known, this kid is sick and unbalanced. He's the type that might do something demented, like go buy a gun. And I'd know what he might do with it when he does. He's so unhinged, this one, when he sees Diane at the mall, he's not going to think it's because she's Christmas shopping on December goddamn 20th, he's going to think it's because she's following him. In his sick fucking little personal paranoia, he's going to believe she's following him because she knows he's got a gun in his pants and knows what he's going to do with it. I would have known he would kill Diane with that gun, before mall security could get there and take him out.

"If I would've been there, I could've consoled Abby right away. I could've told her there was no way to know he bought the gun to use it on her, not her mother. Or if that were the case, her mother would gladly give her life a thousand more times to save hers. I wouldn't have been on the road somewhere in West Virginia or Tennessee when she went driving around at a hundred miles per hour in a blind rage, so upset and devastated and angry it was worse than driving drunk. I wouldn't have let her get in that car, the one she drove straight into a tree."

"Sour, I… I'm sorry. I never had any idea…"

"The boy only shot one person. So that didn't qualify as national news. Diane and I had never officially married, so she never took my last name. There was nothing linking me to her that would give you any idea."

Sour looked up again, clearing his throat. He turned and walked back to the wall of windows. The rain had broken, the sun starting to peek through the breaking storm clouds. "I had killed twenty-one people with guns up to that day. I sat in church and swore I would never pick up another one ever again."

"Sour…" Blunt hadn't heard his last few sentences, now going over and over a dark realization which had been settling in his mind since Sour revealed the provenance of that cat pendant. "If, if that cat's a tracking device-- Is that what you're saying, that cat's a tracking device?

Then when did you start tracking me? How long have you known he had brought me here?"

"I've been sitting out in the parking lot for the past two hours."

Blunt wheezed, suddenly unable to breathe. "You knew... you knew they'd come after me. You knew they wouldn't be at Watson's prison transfer. Didn't you? You knew they'd come after me when my security was all..." Blunt nearly dry heaved, and knew he might well have full-on vomited all down his chest if he had any strength left. "...when it was all with you."

"I had a hunch," Sour confirmed, and turned for the door for the final time.

"Wait, Sour, wait! You can't-- I'll die. I'll bleed to death in here."

"You won't be the first," Sour reminded him.

A SPECIAL ELECTION

Sour made the drive back to Bryan almost straight through, nearly thirty hours including his one stop, a detour up to the Salton Sea, to toss away Blunt's gun and flask. Though investigators would be able to trace the bullet found in Brenden Bauman's skull to a gun registered to Homer Blunt, they would never know who had fired that gun. If these items of his were ever found, Sour's fingerprints would be long washed away by the salinity of this endorheic body of water, and Sour would have scrubbed his hands multiple times over before anyone might examine them for gunshot residue.

Of course, Poughkeepsie would know who had fired that gun; he would recognize Sour's handiwork. It was Sour who had texted him to get to the school six hours after he had driven away, more than enough time for Blunt's brachial artery to bleed out, he felt sure.

And indeed, an hour later, when Sour was already well into Arizona, his old colleague's voice punched through his daydreams from a radio news report. *"In separate actions taken by the High Value Targets team, both here and in the southern Arizona home of Congressman Homer Blunt,"* he was explaining to reporters, *"the so-called 'Congressional Killers' have finally been brought to justice. Sadly, Congressman Blunt was himself a victim of the Killers."*

Sour grinned, glad that Parker was going to be able to wring a win out of his off-the-book actions once again, just like the old days.

"Agent Poughkeepsie! Agent Poughkeepsie!" the reporters battered him over the radio. *"Did the Killers leave any sort of clue, any note or manifesto, explaining the motive behind their violent rampage?"*

Sour's radio filled with dead air for a moment, before Poughkeepsie replied, *"They didn't. But looking at the four members of Congress they targeted – and we are now confident these were the only members of Congress they were targeting – we believe it was in retaliation for the failure of last year's gun control bill."*

A sense of peace descended upon Sour's breast. The SEALs had accomplished their mission. Their souls could rest peacefully. They deserved to have their budweisers, their trident pins, hammered into their caskets like every SEAL before them, but Sour knew they might not even be buried now.

Sour didn't go home when he reached Bryan. Disgusted, confused and despondent about how easily he had been drawn back into violence, into bottles and guns, he didn't end his journey back in the driveway of his ranch, but at the parking lot of his church, San Rafael.

The doors were unlocked despite the clock on his dash reading past 4 AM. Sour took one of the final pews, his eyes moving to the candle flickers reflecting off the Christ's emaciated torso. But the Christ didn't fill him with peace. He never had. He filled Sour with a deep, muscle-constricting rage. If there was a God, if there was a Jesus and a Holy Ghost, it was He who had made Sour a depraved murderer. It was He who had placed Diane right in the path of Abby's boyfriend on that day he had carried a loaded gun into the mall, He who had placed a tree right in front of Abby as she drove.

It was this God who gave Brenden the jump on Jill.

Sour stood with a primal cry, shoving the pew in front of him with all his strength. It fell forward, toppling the next one, and the one before that, until the entire row was dominoing face first to the floor.

Sour marched up to the altar, grabbing it and yanking it straight up. It was lighter than it looked, basically just a hollow wooden box, and it landed on its side with a startling crash.

Sour turned to the crucifix next, towering above his head. The condescension glowed from Jesus's face. Sour felt his hands tensing with the anticipation of more willful destruction, and grabbed around the wooden waist with both hands--

"Señor Manco!"

Hearing the voice behind him, Sour froze, but didn't lower his hands from the body on the cross.

"Is this your new way of confessing?" Father Tito asked as he moved up the center aisle behind Sour.

Sour lowered his hands, but still couldn't turn to face his priest. His shame, less in what he did here on this day than the sins he had allowed himself to commit over the past few weeks, was too great. "He's not interested in forgiving me, Padre. He won't give me any mercy."

"Of course He won't! He gives it as soon as you give it to yourself, Clayton!"

Sour turned to face Father Tito, just taking the step up to the small stage to stand next to his church's most frequent visitor. He was in a bathrobe embroidered with the logo of Jesuit Prep in Dallas, where he had been assigned before his transfer to Bryan. "And when God gives us forgiveness, or even grants us happiness once again, He does it in such small little moments. If we're not paying attention, we miss them."

Sour's gaze lowered as he thought about this. He wasn't sure he believed Tito's words, but his tone had at least calmed the burn of his rage.

He turned and stepped off the stage, bending to right the first pew. Tito joined him, and the two of them had the church put back together before the sun rose again.

Sour checked his watch when he stepped out of the church into the dawn light. Visiting hours would just be starting.

He had gotten the call on his drive back: Abby was awake again. She was okay, Dr. Schwartz pronounced, and could be transferred to a care facility. Sour knew his daughter would never be okay again, but was relieved she was at least conscious.

He drove straight to the Waterford, almost passing right by the giant new **COMFORT HILL** sign. He walked to Abby's room, seeing through the tiny window on her door that she was still asleep. He let himself in, moving to the picture frames on her window sill, where he again lifted the photo of her squeezing the dying Tippy, and deposited the cat pendant where it belonged.

"Welcome home."

Sour whipped around. Abby's eyes were open and she was staring right at him.

"Did you just say--?" he stammered back.

She didn't respond, just blinked back at him as she always did when she was calmed.

"Abbs, you just said something!"

But Sour didn't need confirmation; he knew what he had heard. With a yelp of joy, he grabbed her head and pulled it into his chest, sobbing from deep in his lowest ribs as he held her tight.

"Where are you taking her?" O'Laughlin exclaimed when he found Sour out in the parking lot, Beast's bed loaded down with various suitcases and duffels around small stacks of moving boxes.

"Not sure yet," Sour smiled as he finished belting Abby into the passenger seat. She hadn't spoken another word, and wouldn't for months. But she also didn't protest as he loaded her into the truck, and that small victory was a huge one for him.

Her words the day before had been a wakeup call, a sign that she had awoken from her surgery a new person, and ready for a new phase in life. As Sour sat in his house that night he realized he too was ready for that phase. As long as he was in that house, his body yearned to fall back into its old habits, pushing and prodding him to head out to a liquor store for sweet medication.

But more than that, it was the guns. As long as he shared a house with that safe in the garage, he knew the day would come when he would again be compelled to use the guns. The guns would never leave him alone.

Sour spent all night packing up just what he would need to start a new phase somewhere, then brought a couple unformed boxes over to Comfort Hill to help pack Abby up too. He knew caring for her wouldn't be the easiest task he had ever tackled, but it was the one God intended for him, and he wasn't going to avoid it any longer.

"But, Mr. Manco," O'Laughlin chuckled in confusion, "I figured you knew. She's all paid up. The next five years…"

"Sounds like you've got a scholarship to offer somebody who really needs it," Sour replied as he folded up Abby's wheelchair and tucked it in the bed between boxes. He closed Beast up, then came around to get behind the wheel, pausing to offer O'Laughlin one more thought: "I will come back in a few months to meet the scholarship recipient."

"Of course!" O'Laughlin tittered nervously. "We'll see you then!"

Sour got in, started Beast up, and backed her out. The radio was in the middle of a news report when it popped to life.

"--announced he will run in the special election in Arizona's second district for the seat vacated by Congressman Homer Blunt's death. The National Rifle Association has already announced their endorsement for Republican David Madison. And Madison leads the first Arizona Daily Star *tracking poll by twenty--"*

Sour palmed the radio off as he pulled them onto state route 21 heading west once again. He hadn't lied to O'Laughlin; he wasn't yet sure where the hell they were headed, but he thought he might as well start by taking Abby to visit a little Mexico border town. He was ashamed he had never introduced his daughter to the country of his birth. And there was a radiant woman there he had promised he would visit again one day. Who knew if he would feel that same connection with Resplanda, or if that had just been one of those occasions of two souls in need colliding at the perfect time? Who knew how long they would stay in Puerto Palomas?

Sour relished that nervous chill of uncertainty. Wherever they were going, they were leaving everything that had come before far behind them.

Ty's hair was still wet as he ran from the bathroom. "Bye Grandma!" he sing-songed as he sprinted for the door. He had lost track of time in his grandparents' pool, and even though his mother knew he was at her parents' house, she was relentless about him getting home at the times he had promised, without exception. He knew most kids would have gotten annoyed with her overprotectiveness months ago, but after all that had happened to his family, Ty had promised himself to cut her some slack.

"Ty!" his grandmother called out just as he pulled her front door wide, the hot inland empire sun warming up the foyer like a furnace. "I forgot to give you this." She emerged from the kitchen carrying a small manilla envelope, wrapped with several revolutions of tape and battered with shipping wear.

"What is it?" he asked as he took it between his hands, running his thumb over the blank space where there should have been a return address.

"I don't know. You weren't expecting anything?"

He shook his head, letting the door close behind him as he stepped into the living room and brought the parcel to the small side table over the arm of one of the white couches. It took him several twists and pokes and pulls to even loosen the tape, and his grandmother rushed back to the kitchen to retrieve scissors.

By the time she returned, he had gotten it open on his own, and had dumped its contents out next to the lamp. "Ty?" she asked, but he was frozen by what he had found inside, not turning or looking up at her. Not even uttering a sound.

She had to step up next to him and bring her reading glasses to her nose to make out the small golden eagle, a trident, anchor and flintlock pistol gripped in its sharp talons.

THE YOUNG &
THE DEAD

AUTHOR'S NOTE

The Young & the Dead was originally sold separately from *The Guns of Ridgewood* to introduce its characters and serve as a promotional tool. This short story takes place approximately one year before the events chronicled in the novel.

Sour Manco knew it would be a mistake to return Diane's call on his way into Maryland, but her message had been pained with that sharp edge of urgency, that spice she only gave calls that had to do with Abby. And Sour would do anything for Abby, even show up late for a meeting with his boss.

Sour knew the call with Diane would require at least twelve minutes: two minutes to relay her latest parental conundrum, another minute for Sour to offer his opinion, then seven for Diane to explain to him as only a lawyer could why his suggested solution was a terrible one. Sour would take the next minute to politely (or sometimes not so politely) ask why – if her mind on the best course of action was already made up – she had bothered to consult him at all, followed by the final minute of the call, devoted to Diane's realization that she didn't know the answer to that.

This particular call, connected right as Sour took the Chevy Chase exit off 495 and continuing until his Beast came to a rest on the curb in front of Poughkeepsie's house, was by no means more important than any of the others he had shared with Diane since he fled Texas for DC. It did concern Abby as he had suspected, something about whether she could spend the night at a friend's house on the night of the winter formal, and was it okay if her new boyfriend-slash-date also stayed there. Eddie. That was his name, Abby's boyfriend. Abby and Eddie, didn't Clayton think that was cute, like they had met in a '50s rom-com sitcom.

(For the record, Sour thought the post-formal sleepover to be a terrible idea, no matter how cute their names were together, even when

Diane explained that the friend's mother had assured her that any and all boys would be sleeping in a bedroom separate from the girls.)

No, the reason this call was notable was its final minute, a last minute so unlike all those other calls.

"It'd be a helluva lot easier discussing these things face to face," Diane said this time. "If you were here."

Sour had to pause to let that settle. "If I was there, we wouldn't be face-to-face. Unless you came to my swanky bachelor condo in Northpoint Crossing."

Diane laughed. He hadn't heard that laugh in so long. "I do miss you, you know," she whispered.

"Di, I have a meeting. Poughkeepsie--"

"Just think about it. Every application she's gotten in the mail has a New York or Massachusetts return address. She only has one more year here. And then we could go our separate ways again."

Sour knew if he returned to Texas, he would never be pried from Diane again.

"You know I lobbied to get us this gig, Clay?" Parker Poughkeepsie grunted from the corner cushion of the L-shaped leather couch dominating his family room. Sour had been standing behind him for three or four minutes before he spoke; Poughkeepsie was riveted to his flat screen, covered with Fox News images of an Iranian halfway house in Oregon, where their elite Hostage Rescue Team had gotten into a shoot-out that ended with the death of a ten-year-old girl. Sour was surprised to find himself looking away from the shots of her child-sized body bag; the violence of life never used to get to him, and it still rarely did, except when it had to do with little girls, with someone's young daughter.

Sour cleared his throat, and Poughkeepsie pushed forward to the edge of his cushions, still not moving his eyes nor ears off the looped video and rote commentary. "This could've been High Value. This could've been us." He rotated his neck to look up to his agent with a smile. "But someone spared us from this. You still believe my praying doesn't work?"

"What about the five times those Muslims prayed today?"

Poughkeepsie shook his head as he stood, coming around the couch and drifting a hand over Sour's triceps as he headed for the door to the basement. "Downstairs."

Sour followed him down the creaky steps into his musky man cave, the only place his superior liked to discuss the kind of business he was sure Parker was about to bring up. Poughkeepsie was too paranoid to do it in the office, sure that J. Edgar Hoover had left some bugs in the walls. He didn't broach these topics on the main floor of the house, for fear his wife or kids might overhear. And even when the backyard was warm enough, who knew who was lurking in the adjoining properties with prying, eavesdropping ears aimed fence-ward?

"Things are about to change, Clay," he began as he procured a Sprite from the fridge. Sour's mouth watered for a mezcal and his head for some caffeine, but he knew the FBI's highest-ranked Mormon would have neither within his walls.

"I don't follow."

"What happened tonight, Portland, that's going to be a game changing embarrassment for the Bureau. For HRT. They're going to need a new face going forward."

"And you would be the perfect little Mormon mascot for the Director."

"While he's around, yes. I can only imagine the heat the President's going to take to clean house *completely* after this."

"You think you might be next up?"

"Clay, in all the little, um, little *tasks* you've assisted me with over the last three or four years--"

"Eleven of them."

"You ever notice a common denominator with all our, what would you call them, *clients*? Ekman, Wyley, Leader Dudley…"

"They're all on the Judiciary Committee." Of course he had noticed. It was his job, his life's work, to notice patterns everywhere.

"The committee that will hold hearings whenever there's a nominee for new FBI Director. The committee that will let the President know what kind of nominee will get the friendliest reception in a hearing."

Poughkeepsie took a long sip of his Sprite. "Sister Ekman, *Senator* Ekman, we attend the same church. She introduced me to the concept of helping the Judiciary members, off the books, like we have. She planted the seed, she was the one who first whispered to me how glorious it would be to someday have a Mormon reach the top of the country's preeminent law enforcement agency. Because it was coming from another Mormon, I don't know, I guess that made it okay in my mind." He looked up into Sour's eyes with his own dampening orbs. "I commend you on never calling me on my… hypocrisy. That's what it is, I know that, hypocrisy, claiming to be such a religious, such a moral man, while all the while--"

"Or are you the one who *protects* the Bureau from hypocrisy, Park? From corruption? You don't carry out the tasks-- you give them to me. To do in my own time, for my own personal gain."

Poughkeepsie turned away, as if the longer this conversation went on, the less he could bear to keep human eye contact. "If you say so."

"You didn't call me here just for confessional, did you?"

Without turning to face him, Poughkeepsie held up a slip of paper between two fingers. Sour knew what he would find on it: an address, most likely a home one.

"Sidney Fox, Republican of Iowa," Poughkeepsie explained as Sour drew the note from his grasp. "He brought me an extortion case. But we can't pursue the case without airing his dirty laundry. I told him you're the one who does our most sensitive dry cleaning."

"Tell him I'll be there in an hour," Sour said as he mounted the stairs back up into the house.

"An hour?" Poughkeepsie asked, confused. Sour usually took three or four days to study a client, to research what he was walking into.

Sour wouldn't tell Poughkeepsie that this would be his last 'task' – not after the importance he just admitted Sour's little jobs had in the future of his ambitions – but Sour had decided he needed to complete this mission more quickly than he had ever completed one in his life.

It was time to get home to his girls.

No one answered the front door, but it was unlocked. Only the lights necessary to illuminate Sour's path were on: from the foyer, around through the kitchen, down the two steps to the carpeted living area, to the French doors leading out to the glowing azure rectangle of the pool. That didn't stop Sour from deviating from the path of light, peeking into all the other rooms, on the ground floor at least, cramming a half-assed version of the studying he typically did on any prospective client into less than five minutes. The house was impressive; many elected officials holed up in glorified frat houses (the C Street house which future President Irving had once shared with legendary Marcus Carpinello in the '90s was now a museum), but Fox was in his second six-year term, making the investment in this Virginia McMansion a worthy one.

Sour found him out there in the back by the swimming hole, lounging across a deck chair, drink in hand, glass carafe on the nearest table where you might find sunscreen and magazines during a summer day. They exchanged some pleasantries, some small talk, before the legislator segued them into the business they were both here for. "There's an intern in my office. Cheri is her name, Cheri Levinson. The first time I laid eyes on her…"

Sour raised a hand to cut him off. "With all due respect, Senator, I don't need the play-by-play, just the box score. And where I'm going for Game Seven."

"Friday night. Tomorrow is the last day of the session, everyone is heading home for the holidays. The building will be empty by Friday night. She wants me to be in my office at 10 PM. She'll meet me there.

She'll erase the video she has of us on our phone – and I'll give her a check for ten million dollars."

"Senator, that video *can't* be erased. It's probably on three different clouds. It will exist as long as Ms. Levinson knows of its existence. It will still exist when she spends that ten million and comes back for twenty more."

"Why you think I called Agent Poughkeepsie?" he whined.

"I can take care of this for you, Senator. If you explain one thing first."

"I'll try."

"There was only one car in the driveway. There are no scented candles in the bathroom, none of the downstairs bedrooms are decorated for children, only one of the bedside tables is stacked with books--"

"I'm divorced. Three years ago."

"And even if you weren't, politicians banging hot young things doesn't hold quite the shock value it once did. I know some consultants who would tell you this video might actually help your future electability, especially for national office. No publicity is bad publicity, that sort of thing."

Fox's hands shook as he picked up the second, clean, glass from his lounge-side chair. He filled it with brown liquid, then held it up in offer to Sour. Sour accepted it, not drinking it in right away but holding it to his face, savoring its warm aromas. Finally, he opened his mouth...

"Fuck me with that black cock."

The bourbon slapped down onto the asphalt between Sour's boots. "Excuse me?"

"That's what I say on the video, Agent Manco. Cheri is wearing a, a..."

"I'm familiar with the devices, Senator."

"She's fucking me from behind and I'm telling her to fuck me with that black cock. Agent Manco, I imagine you have to follow politics in your job..."

"Not regularly."

"There is a church in Iowa City, they gave me quite a bit of money for my last campaign. Quite a bit of money. And in return, I've been trying to get some funding for the therapy they specialize in onto some bills--"

"What kind of therapy?"

"Some people believe, Agent Manco, they believe with enough prayer, with enough faith and belief, that homosexuality... that you can..." Fox trailed off, digging into his pocket for a handkerchief to dab his tears.

Sour chided himself – this was the intel he should have known before he met with a client. Now he seemed amateur, unprepared, and had driven the Senator to this emotional place needlessly. But he got the point: if a champion of 'Pray Away the Gay' therapy was revealed to be himself closeted and repressed – with irrefutable, delectable video evidence, no less – he would not only become a national laughing stock, but lose some of the constituents who had sent him to Washington, not to mention one of his biggest fundraising sources.

"Stay here tomorrow night, Senator," Sour assured him as he turned back for the house. "I can take care of her for you."

"Them."

"What?"

"Take care of *them*, Agent Manco. I was getting to this: Her boyfriend, Cheri's boyfriend – I didn't know she had a boyfriend. A capitol policeman. He's her insurance, her protection so I don't just make her disappear. He knows about everything. I think he was in on it the whole time, probably. Playing me like the sucker I am. I don't know if he'll be with her tomorrow, or hiding out somewhere making sure she gets home safe. But we have to deal with him too."

Sour smiled. All these elements made the whole problem more nauseating for the Senator, but they were old hat for him. "I can take care of *them* for you, Senator."

"Shit!" Sour turned back on the rattling of glassware, just in time to see Fox use his handkerchief to try to sop up the booze he had spilled all over his checkbook.

Sour raised a hand. "I don't need that, Senator."

"You, you don't want the job…?"

"I'll take the job. That's just not how it works. I don't need a check till later." He smiled as he opened the backdoor and let the central heat of the house wash out over him again. "You'll see."

Cheri Levinson hadn't parked in her usual spot in Senate Lot 17 next to the Hart Office Building. Sour figured this was because she didn't want any record of her visiting Fox's offices on this night.

He was parked in Beast outside her Georgetown apartment when she brought two suitcases out to her Nissan Sentra, then drove the sedan to the mammoth Union Station garage. He veered off to park a row over from her so as not to be conspicuous, backing into his spot so he could see her leave her car and head for the elevators. Her Capitol Police boyfriend would let her into the Hart, Sour imagined, so she again could avoid using her own ID, and after they had waited long enough to realize that the Senator had stood them up, would flee to this car, to collect her things if not the entire vehicle. They wouldn't post the black cock video from the Hart (they probably couldn't even get on the internet without logging on with one of their identities), but instead flee to some far-off place to start a tabloid auction for the highest bidder.

If the boyfriend was smart at all, he would counsel Cheri not to come back to the Sentra, but Sour had done this enough times to know either the boyfriend or Cheri wouldn't be smart at all, and wouldn't be able to avoid coming back here. So Sour waited in Beast as he watched Cheri board the elevator, doing the math to calculate he had at least an hour until her return, probably more like two or three, depending on the mix of patience and courage she and her boyfriend possessed. He tried Diane a couple of times, but got only her voicemail, and didn't leave a message. Sure, he could just show up on their doorstep down in Bryan, but he didn't think that was fair; better to give her some warning, not to mention himself a chance to gauge in her voice if she really wanted him back or had just suffered from a moment of nostalgia in their last talk. He needed that response, and wouldn't get an honest one if he left news of his decision in a message, of course.

Ten or fifteen minutes into his wait, Frazier knocked on the passenger side window. Sour unlocked the truck so he could get in with his delivery. High Value's resident equipment and gadget expert, 'Queer' (as Sour called him in jest as a nod to James Bond's own gadgets guy) always came through with exactly what Sour needed, even with the less-than-forty-eight-hours Sour had given him when he called in his request from Fox's driveway. Queer held out the box across Beast's front seat, and Sour made sure to glove up before opening it and picking up the purse-sized Ruger LCR revolver from inside. "Christ, that's light," Sour chuckled. "Might as well just throw it."

Queer left Sour to the final ninety minutes of his wait. He was just hearing the first words of Diane's outgoing voicemail message for the third time when he saw Cheri stumble out of the elevator and head for her Sentra. She was alone, which concerned Sour. But he knew now was the time to insert himself into this drama regardless. Beast growled to life and Sour whipped her forward with her headlights dark.

Cheri was just getting her driver's door open with her quivering hands when Sour screeched Beast up right behind her, blocking any attempt to reverse. She let out a gasp and shot into the car, slamming the door behind her. Sour killed Beast's engine, stepping down out of her belly, leaving the door open behind him as he approached to knock on Cheri's window. Each tap forced another tiny little scream out of her breast. "I'm not going to hurt you," he assured her, with enough warmth behind his words to encourage her to roll the glass down about a quarter of the way. It was enough for Sour to offer the stuffed envelope through the slot.

Cheri sensed what was inside, and couldn't stop herself from accepting it, as any red-blooded American would. "What, what is this?" she stuttered as her fingers fluttered through the fresh cash inside.

"It's ten thousand dollars. Enough to start a new life somewhere."

"He sent you. Fox. This isn't what I--"

"You're going to leave Washington. I don't care where you go, as long as you don't share any videos with anyone while you're there. And you're not going to come back to this city, and I mean not even an hour-long layover at Dulles, until Sidney Fox no longer holds public office."

"Fuck you," she spit out, trying to feign toughness. "What makes you think I won't just take this and sell my video anyway? What makes you think you'll ever find me, or get this money back?"

"I don't want that money back," he grinned. "It's an investment. I'm investing in you. If I do have to come find you again, I will have to do something much more serious to you. And the Senator will owe me a lot more than that ten grand for doing it. So, please, go ahead and sell your video. The way I pay my mortgage is by occasional investments like yourself breaking their word to me."

Cheri looked down into the cash again, and Sour saw a tear splash down on top of the pages of green.

But eventually, she nodded compliance. "All right. I'll do what you say."

"Good. Now, we also have to talk about your boyf--"

The plastic rattle of a phone hitting concrete spiked into both their spines like they had heard a gunshot. Sour whipped around to Beast, his eyes peering right through the open cabin and through the passenger side window to see an African-American man standing on the other side, staring back at them.

"JEROME, NO!" Cheri cried, but the black man was already scrambling for his fallen phone, picking it up, launching into a sprint down one of the other rows of cars.

Sour smiled at Cheri's tactical error – revealing she knew this kid, giving away with the terror behind her voice that *this* was her boyfriend accomplice – then started the chase. By the time he had rounded the corner to take the next column of cars down, Jerome was already rounding the corner below him to keep descending. Jerome knew this garage, at least well enough to know which way to head for the ground level and the exits, and he was younger and faster and more athletic than Sour.

But I don't need to catch him, Sour reminded himself as he felt his back right glute vibrating. Sour ignored the call, disregarding his brief hope that it was Diane returning his earlier tries. He just ran, as fast as he could after Jerome, swiveling his head this way and that to get the geographics of this garage down enough to design a plan.

Sour pulled up to a stop. He turned to his right, looking down the small alley formed between a large van and an oversized SUV, a Navigator or Escalade, both shoved into spots labeled 'COMPACT.' He reached not into his right back pocket for his buzzing phone, but into the right pocket of his overcoat. He raised the Ruger that Queer had provided him, listening to the sounds of Jerome's footsteps building as he descended the concrete ramp just on the other side of these large cars' noses. Sour for a second wrestled with his doubts – he didn't know this gun, didn't like how much less it weighed than his Sig, didn't like how he couldn't wrap more than half his palm around its tiny handle – before stowing them into a box of silence. He knew he would have less than a second to react, not enough time to aim, barely enough to get off a shot when Jerome passed through that slot between these two behemoth vehicles.

Footsteps getting closer… closer…

Sour could feel his heartrate lowering, his breath slowing the way it always did when he was about to use a firearm – that odd reaction he always had to situations like this that would make most human beings fill their pants with excrement.

Another vibration from the back of his pants, another call, a new call. He couldn't let it throw off his concentration, his aim, not even a speck--

A flash of fabric and dark skin – Sour pulled the trigger –

Jerome's momentum shifted sideways, jarred off his running path, his jellied body tumbling to his left, rag dolling down into the asphalt.

His phone shot out from his fingers, skittering across the asphalt until it was just under the cars poking out from Sour's upper level. He lowered his gun and stepped between van and SUV, crouching to stick his arm through the rail and reach his hand down for the device. He quickly confirmed that while its last three photos were of him at Cheri's car, none had been transmitted anywhere else by text or email; and the phone didn't have a wifi connection, so it surely hadn't clouded them yet either. Sour turned it off, pocketing it for its complete dismantling which would come later.

By the time he looked back at Jerome, blood was seeping out from under the right side of the boy's head, rolling downhill in that same direction the Capitol Policeman had been running when he ran right into the path of Sour's .357 slug.

Good. Sour could get back to Cheri. He dropped the gun back in his coat as he double-timed it back up the way he came, moving his hand back around his waist to pull his own phone out as he marched.

Missed Call – Abby (2), the display read when he thumbed the screen to life. Two missed calls from Abby. She was a teenage girl, she rarely called him, unless she was returning one of his calls. And she didn't owe him a call now; he hadn't called her yet this week. Something wasn't right.

But Abby would have to wait. Cheri Levinson's Nissan Sentra was empty.

It took Sour way too long to determine Cheri's possible escape routes. If he had done his proper research, the research he usually put into an assignment when he wasn't distracted by dreams of returning home, when he didn't already have one boot on the highway, he would have known her to be the daughter of David and Hedi Levinson, the same Hedi Levinson who was serving the Salas administration as Ambassador to Lithuania. And with the Levinsons away at their Vilnius Embassy, their Spring Valley home would be vacant, a potential hiding spot for their daughter when she believed her life was in danger.

But Sour didn't know any of that. Instead, he had to get Poughkeepsie involved, enlist his help in obtaining a ping off Cheri's cell. Sour hated having to get Parker involved; he took pride in the distance from these jobs he gave his superior. But this time, it couldn't be helped. Of course Cheri was using her cell phone; of course she hadn't had the instincts to toss the SIM or even just turn the thing off.

Cheri had just gotten out of the shower and was wearing only a towel as she wrenched her suitcase onto the guest room bed to unzip it. This wasn't the house or bedroom she had grown up in, but one her parents had moved into when her mother's business and later diplomatic career exploded. Sour didn't want to do what he was going to do while she was at her most vulnerable like this; he would wait until she was dressed and had gone downstairs or plopped in front of one of the many TVs.

Unfortunately, his phone had other ideas. He should have left it in the car or turned it off, what with the level of activity it had received tonight. But he had forgotten about the damn thing, and when it buzzed with a new call while he was melted into the shadows of the upstairs Levinson hallway, the towel-clad Cheri was alerted to his presence.

With a scream she darted out of the guestroom, headed for the stairs.

Sour rushed after her, grabbing her from behind on the landing above the entrance foyer. Cheri screamed over the banister as Sour gripped her right wrist, forcing her hand open so he could lay the Ruger inside it, then close her fingerprints around its handle.

"Ssh, ssh," Sour tried to calm her, "I'm still going to let you run. This is just my insurance."

"NO! NO! NO ONE WILL BELIEVE THIS! NO ONE WILL BELIEVE I KILLED JEROME! NO ONE WILL BELIEVE THAT'S MY GUN!"

"Of course it's your gun, Cheri. You bought it just yesterday. If you ever go back into politics, you'll have to fight for a waiting period in Virginia."

"NO! NO!" Cheri turned to try to punch at Sour's chest, hammering the butt of the gun into his ribs, gyrating against him as he attempted to grab her wrists again.

He didn't get his hands around them before the bannister broke behind her. Cheri tumbled straight backwards, and Sour heard the snap of bone and flesh on the hardwood below.

He didn't even need to look to know what he was going to see when he peered down through the splintered slats. Cheri was no longer making any sounds, after all, no struggling, no whimpering, no attempting to get up. But he still stepped forward to confirm it:

And there she was, eyes staring straight up at the ceiling, towel jarred open so one breast and the complete length of her left leg were visible, hand open with the gun that took her boyfriend's life still resting in her palm.

Sour stumbled back. Why did this happen now? Why did his worst fuck-up have to happen right before he told Poughkeepsie he was never doing this again, that he was driving straight back to Diane's arms?

A single vibration burst from his phone. **Missed Call & Voicemail – Abby**. Abby for the third time in as many hours. He needed to find out what was wrong. Then he could call Poughkeepsie and tell him this was his last off-the-books assignment.

And how royally he had fucked it up.

Abby had just hung up on him. She was so full of sorrow and confusion and rage, it took the first several minutes of the call just for Sour to wrest out what had happened to her mother. As she spoke, Sour could hear all her emotions, all her sadness and grief, coalescing into white hot anger. Sour tried to plead with her not to do anything rash or dangerous, to just go to her aunt's where there was love and comfort waiting.

But Abby wasn't listening, she just wanted to rail against and hurt and kill everyone – most of all, her father. This was his fault, for leaving them, for not being there, for not being a good husband.

Sour made the mistake of trying to explain that he knew that, that he regretted all that too and was going to change it, that he had called Diane several times to say he was going to come home. But that all rang so false to Abby. She had Di's phone, and though Sour had called a few times, there were no messages from him. Abby didn't believe him. Abby didn't want to hear a thing he had to say. Abby didn't want to see him ever again.

"Wait, now, Abbs, where are you going? What are you going to--" But she was already gone, the line already dead.

Sour tried her again, but it didn't even ring, just fell right into her voicemail, her cheery, energetic, a whole-other-girl voicemail.

He leaned over his seat to pull his Toughbook laptop from the rear of the cabin, pulling it open as he slammed it down on the passenger seat next to him. His hands shook as he opened the window as Queer had taught him, cursing under his breath as it took a minute to find an internet connection and then locate that red dot that represented Abby. It was moving, but not in the right direction, not towards her aunt's house as he had asked…

What was she doing? Where was she going?

Sour had already started Beast to get the heat pumping before he had even called Abby. He didn't need to start her back up now, just put her in gear.

And drive. He would drive all the way back to Texas, all the way back down to Bryan. In one shot. He would go back to Abby, like he had promised. He knew why she didn't want to go to her aunt's. She hated her aunt, he hated her aunt. Everyone hated her aunt.

Sour was ripping through Spring Valley at over 80. He didn't even know Beast could go this fast, but the ol' truck must have known he needed it tonight. He could feel the tires slipping on fresh black ice, but he didn't give a shit, he needed to go as fast as he fucking could. He was either going to get home or he was going to die.

The phone buzzed again across the seat next to him. Sour caught the green ACCEPT button with his peripheral and fingered it without reading who was on the screen. Only one person had been calling on this night. He lit up the speakerphone button with a touch as he talked. "Abbs. Listen to me. I need you to go to your Aunt Nicole's--"

"Mr. Manco," a smooth voice crackled out of the tinny and tiny iPhone speaker.

"Who the fuck is this?"

"My name is Homer Blunt. I represent the second district, southeastern Arizona, in Congress."

"I can't talk right--"

"Mr. Manco, I'm afraid this is one phone call you have to take. You see, I'm afraid even the best eventually screw up, Mr. Manco. And that's just what you've done. You've screwed up."

Sour didn't say anything. He didn't know who the fuck this guy was or what he was talking about, he just needed to get home to Abby. Maybe he should hang up on him, hang up on a member of Congress. Who gave a fuck anymore?

"My assistant, he was in the Union Station parking garage tonight. He was in one of the cars you ran by, Mr. Manco. He saw what you did to that Afro-American young gentleman."

"I don't know what you're talking about."

"I think you do. You were there, but you were sloppy. You should have examined that young man you killed, Mr. Manco. You see, that Afro-American young gentleman, he was clearly a police officer. He was wearing one of those new body cameras, even though he was in his civilian clothes. He wanted to make sure he got you on film, evidently. But you couldn't see it on his dark clothes. After you left him there in the Union Station garage, my assistant went and got that body camera."

"He didn't give it to the Police?"

"This young man, he's only been working for me for six months, Mr. Manco. He wants so badly to get in my good graces, for me to say I'll be his mentor, and shepherd him into a successful political career of his own. But he can tell we just aren't clicking, he and I. This camera, this was like a gift from God, a chance for him to make a real impression on me. He brought it to me, to ask me if he should take it to the Police. Or if there was some other advantage *I* could get out of it.

"Now, as far as we can tell, the data that's on this camera, it's not uploaded to the police until it's returned to its charging dock at the station house. The Police haven't seen what's on this camera, Mr. Manco."

Sour took a long time before he spoke again, just listening to Beast's wheels chewing up the road. "What do you want?"

"I want you to come work for me. Exclusively. Head of Security. And some other little things. I've heard about you. I know how talented you are, what you're capable of. I have big plans, Mr. Manco. But they involve bending rules sometimes. I could use someone like you to straighten things out when I have to bend them."

"You're too late. I'm out of this game."

"Mr. Manco, have you understood a word I've said? You can't be out of this game. I hand this video over to someone, and this game will come and get you."

"Do your worst. I don't give a shit anymore."

Sour stabbed his finger into the red button to kill the call.

The first thing Sour saw was his drool filling a crevasse between floorboards. He didn't even notice the knocking until he had sat all the way up, and let his pounding head and desert-dry throat settle in for the morning.

"Clay." It was Poughkeepsie, just beyond the front screen door, knocking on the side of the door frame. Sour had left the front door open when he passed out? "I'm coming in, Clay."

Sour rotated his head to the right, then to the left, eventually locating the bottle of Cuervo he knew he had polished the evening off with.

Although it lay on its side, he could see there was just a swallow or two left, a glorious ounce or maybe two that hadn't been poured down his throat or spilled out onto the floor. Sour pawed at the bottle, struggling for the motor skills to get his fingers around it and empty it into his gullet.

"The funeral, Clay. I need to take you to pick up Abby, and then the funeral. You can't miss the funeral."

Sour thought about putting up a fight, but he knew it was one he wouldn't win. He stumbled to his feet and past Poughkeepsie and out onto the front porch. "Wait, Clay, you can't go looking like that--"

Sour was already in the shed, finding the boxes Sharpied with **CLAYTON – CLOTHES** in Jill's perfect handwriting. He ripped three open until he found a black jacket, and threw that on as he re-emerged onto the dusty drive where Parker's rental sedan waited. "Okay, that'll work," his superior admitted.

They had sat in the car for at least thirty seconds, engine humming, before Poughkeepsie had to ask, "Clay… Abby? Where…?"

"Waterford," Sour grunted. "It's called the Waterford."

Poughkeepsie typed it into the maps app on his phone, glad to see it was a twelve minute drive away in College Station, giving him some time to broach the topic he had made this trip to broach. He let the drive settle in for three or four minutes before jumping in headfirst. "I met Homer Blunt. The Congressman, from Arizona."

Sour had to squint for a moment to even remember that name. It had only been three weeks, but felt like three years. He had to sift backwards through so many memories to identify it, back through so many bottles, so many fistfights and whores.

And the mole. When he had first seen Abby in the hospital, he didn't even recognize her, with all the wires and tubes and IVs and open wounds and lifeless limbs. But the mole he recognized. He hadn't thought about it in years, hadn't even seen it in at least fifteen, since he had last dressed her himself. It was in a place no one else would ever see it, on her left hip right at pubic level. It was so tiny and light-brown, but when he used to change her diapers, he thought it was just another little adorable mark of her perfection.

A decade and a half later, the EMTs had been forced to cut her out of her clothes. She was naked when he saw her at the hospital. And there was that mole. Sour didn't want to believe it was her. But there was that mole.

And all of this, the pain and loss and seeing that mole he never should have seen again: Sour knew he deserved it all. Killing Jerome Young, Jr. without even a thought; peering down on Cheri Levinson's broken body with barely more emotion than the cold annoyance of a man suffering a professional inconvenience; and they weren't even the first, were they, just more chaff in a long career of carnage. There had been many Jeromes and Cheris, twenty-one of them, and Sour was finally paying the karmic price. The mole was his sentence; the mole was his penance; the mole was the symbol of all that Clayton Manco really deserved.

"Blunt showed me the video, Clay."

There was Poughkeepsie again, talking about Homer Blunt. Sour had forced his memories far enough back now – to that call. In Beast. From that Congressman, from Homer Blunt. About the body cam video Poughkeepsie was now talking about.

"He says he's going to go public with it, unless you go to work for him. He's going to leak to a reporter he's friendly with that I ordered you to kill this young man. And the girl too, Cheri Levinson. You didn't leave any evidence you were in the Ambassador's house, but that won't matter, not once the media and social media start running with the narrative that it was you." Parker swallowed his tongue. "That it was us."

"You need to fire me, Park. I'm not coming back. You need to cut ties with me, and let me face this on my own."

Poughkeepsie didn't answer, and didn't say another word the remaining eight minutes of their drive to the Waterford. He didn't bring it up again as they struggled to get the shadow of the girl that used to be Abigail Manco into the car, nor during their drive to the funeral. Nor did he think it appropriate over drinks at the wake, nor as they returned Abby to her care facility, nor during the twelve minute drive (that in afternoon traffic, might have been more like sixteen) from the Waterford back to Sour's remains of a ranch in Bryan.

But once Sour had gotten out of the vehicle, had stepped onto the bottom stair up to his front porch, Parker said one more thing on the topic of Jerome Young, Jr. and Cheri Levinson and now Homer Blunt. "I'm not going to fire you, Clay. I can't fire you. Not right now. I can't rob you of your benefits. Your pension, not right now. But I do have an idea."

"I told you to let me handle this, Thomas," Homer Blunt smiled as he wilted back into his desk chair, arms crossed over his chest.

"Yes, I know, Sir," his assistant whined. "But, but you didn't tell me the FBI was going to come *here*, to Bisbee. What if he's here to play hardball? To say I obstructed justice by taking that body cam--"

"*Let me handle this*, Thomas. I promised I would, and you promised you would keep your panties untangled. Now. Show this agent in and I'll handle him."

Thomas opened his mouth to say more, but thought better of it. He spun on a heel, charging down the hall back into the main part of the house where he had left the G-Man waiting.

Blunt admitted to himself he was a little nervous, just like young Thomas. But staring up at the portrait of his Daddy in his mining helmet, sledgehammer over one shoulder, reminded him he was exactly where he wanted to be. If he didn't know how to play dangerous games like this, he would be working in a mine himself, or doing some equally backbreaking form of work. Blunt wouldn't be where he was today – not just representing the second district, but according to Bradley Benedict's campaign manager, on his short list for Vice Presidential consideration should he win the nomination – if he hadn't been willing to ruffle every feather that got in his way and burn down every fucking bridge after he crossed it.

"Congressman," Parker Poughkeepsie nodded as he entered the office, Thomas stepping back out into the hallway and shutting them in for some privacy.

"I wasn't expecting you to come all the way down here to Bisbee, Agent Poughkeepsie. It's not the most convenient destination."

"I was closer than usual. And this is something I never want to discuss in Washington again."

"I hope we all maintain such control over the matter."

"I am suspending Clayton Manco from the High Value Targets team, a suspension which shall be indefinite. The reason for his suspension is not going to be listed in his record. But you make any part of the Jerome Young, Jr. matter public, and I will have a press release ready that disavows any Bureau involvement in it, and explains that Manco was suspended for his role in it."

"You would hang your man out to dry like that?"

"It was his idea. He'll hang himself out to dry-- if you make him. I'm hopeful you won't make us take all those steps."

"Agent Poughkeepsie, you've lived and worked in Washington long enough to know the most successful politicians don't achieve their stature by being merciful, kind souls."

Poughkeepsie took a deep breath, wrestling with how to handle this. He knew the most decorated men in the history of his Bureau would spit an even deeper threat back at Blunt, something about how he didn't want to make an enemy of the FBI, about how every politician who ever had gone toe-to-toe with them lived to rue those decisions.

But what he had realized during this whole unraveling was that the biggest mistake he ever made was his original sin, his first compromise, accepting the off the books 'tasks,' even if they did make his career what it was, and even if he did hand all of them off to Sour. He found himself wishing he was just a junior agent in some field office, but a *happy* junior field agent, who slept well every night knowing he was following his moral compass.

Parker Poughkeepsie promised himself that from now on, and no matter what, he would always remain true to himself -- and if that stunted his career growth, so be it.

"In my religion, Congressman, there is nothing more important than family. And I'm not going to tell you what's happened to Clayton Manco's family just in the last month, but you should trust me when I say it's double or triple what any man should have to suffer in an entire lifetime.

"I know you see in Clayton an asset you'd like to exploit. But you have to trust me that, unfortunately, you stumbled upon him just as he became a broken man. And even if you succeed in getting him to come work for you, he will never be the man you think you're getting, the man I know and love. He will always be a shell of that man, and in this line of work, placing responsibility in the hands of a shell of a man is a very, very bad idea. So I hope you take my advice, and instead of going to war over a man who is going to struggle to even get through a full day for the foreseeable future, you give him his time and his space to figure out how to make his life, and his family, whole again."

For once, Congressman Homer Blunt didn't answer. After the room had been enveloped in silence for a few seconds, Poughkeepsie nodded, and turned for the door back to the hall. "Thank you for your time."

His hand had reached the handle when Blunt finally spoke up behind him. "Tell Agent Manco – *Mr.* Manco – I will give him his time and his space."

"I will. Thank you, Congressman."

"But you also make sure he understands… when I do call on him someday, Agent Poughkeepsie – and I *will* call on him someday – it is because it is a matter of life and death, for *my* family. And I expect him to respect that when that day does come."

AARON COOLEY'S *FOUR SEATS*
IS A CONSPIRACY TOUR DE FORCE!

When a terrorist bombing kills four Supreme Court Justices, Homeland Security's prime suspect goes on the run to find the persons responsible for the attack. Back in DC, a former First Lady assists the President in nominating replacement Justices -- but is this all part of an elaborate plan she put in motion before the bombs even went off?

"A remarkable thriller ... would make a good series along the lines of *True Detective* or *The Killing.*"
- **MenReadingBooks.com**

"Copious surprises ... delightfully puzzling ... a scorching pace makes this savvy thriller a quick read."
- **Kirkus Reviews**

"The action is explosive, the plot decently paced, and the tension steadily ratchets up with each new revelation ... literally, a television show in book form."
- **IndieReader.com**

"Cooley delivers again. A riveting political thriller that is somehow educational and page-turning at the same time."
- **Dave Callaham, screenwriter, *Godzilla* and *The Expendables***

"Cooley writes with knowledge and skill about a shadowy world few truly understand... at times richly emotional, hilarious, and challenging."
- **Eric Lodal, Creator & Exec Producer, TNT's *Murder in the First***

Aaron Cooley is a producer and development executive for famed film director Joel Schumacher. His first novel *Shaken, Not Stirred* was named one of the Best Indie Books of 2013 by IndieReader.com. He has also written screenplays and teleplays for MTV, A Band Apart, Lorenzo di Bonaventura Productions, Winkler Films, and Twisted Pictures. A native of Portland, Oregon and graduate of Yale, Aaron now lives in Los Angeles with Whitney, Beatrix and Mitten.

https://www.facebook.com/fleming17f

@fleming17f

www.ingramcontent.com/pod-product-compliance
Lightning Source LLC
Chambersburg PA
CBHW051431170626
46809CB00006B/2417